SLATER'S LEVERAGE

THE OPAQUE TASK FORCE

CLAUDIA SHELTON

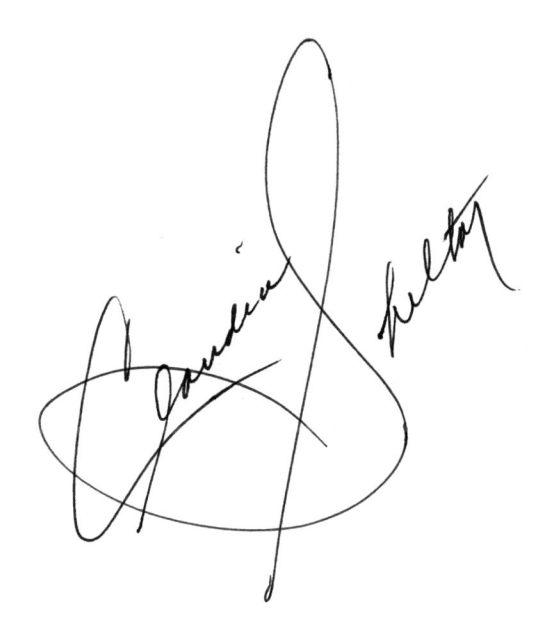

BOOKS BY CLAUDIA SHELTON

Risk Series
Risk of a Lifetime

OPAQUE Task Force Series
Slater's Leverage

Copyright © 2015 Claudia Shelton

This is a work of fiction. Names, characters, places, and incidents are either the products of the author's imagination or are used fictitiously, and any resemblance to actual persons, living or dead, business establishments, events, or locales is purely coincidental.

All rights reserved under International and Pan-American Copyright Conventions

By payment of required fees, you have been granted the *non*-exclusive, *non*-transferable right to access and read the text of this book. No part of this text may be reproduced, transmitted, downloaded, decompiled, reverse engineered, or stored in or introduced into any information storage and retrieval system, in any form or by any means, whether electronic or mechanical, now known or hereinafter invented without the express written permission of copyright owner.

Please Note
The reverse engineering, uploading, and/or distributing of this book via the internet or via any other means without the permission of the copyright owner is illegal and punishable by law. Please purchase only authorized electronic editions, and do not participate in or encourage electronic piracy of copyrighted materials. Your support of the author's rights is appreciated.

No part of this book may be reproduced or transmitted in any form or by any electronic or mechanical means, including photocopying, recording or by any information storage and retrieval system, without the written permission of the publisher, except where permitted by law.

Cover Design and Interior format by The Killion Group
http://thekilliongroupinc.com

*This is dedicated to my wonderful family
—my two sons, my 'daughter' and my grandsons—
who shower me with love, laughter and motivation!
Love ya' always.*

CHAPTER ONE

"Are we about done here?" OPAQUE Agent Josh Slater shot to his feet, knocking his chair over backward. He'd had enough of this beat-around-the-bush, quasi interrogation for one day. Loud and to the point, the chair hit the floor with a resounding thud.

The past two hours of debriefing had made him wonder what the hell he'd done wrong on his last assignment. There'd been nothing out of the ordinary, just a simple tourist kidnapping case. Go in, rescue the hostage, get home. Everything had gone as planned. In fact, except for the knife-in-his-back fiasco, he could have done it blindfolded.

Sure as hell hadn't come close to the hard-line leverage assignment Operation Protector Agent Quantum Elite (OPAQUE) was known to fight against Coercion Ten. Those jobs were adrenalin-pumping, hazardous-to-your-health rides all the way to the final bullet. That was one of the reasons he'd joined OPAQUE. The other reason was still at large.

Agent Granger shuffled papers around. "I've got only a few—"

"No. You've asked me the same damn questions again and again." Josh rolled his fingers in and out of a loose fist. The two of them might be friends most days, but right now Granger was an obstacle. "In fact, if I didn't know you better, I'd think you doubted my credibility." Josh fisted his hand tight. "That would be a mistake on your part."

"Calm down. Okay?" Granger stood, pumping his hands in front of him. "I'm just following the boss's orders."

"Which are?"

Granger braced his hands on the table between the two men. "To keep you in this room."

"You and what army?" Josh knew he hadn't done anything to get fired, reprimanded, or a thousand other unpleasant procedures. Yet everything about this scenario screamed trouble.

"Listen. I'm not in the mood for any of your macho-dude attitude." Granger's eyes narrowed. "Now stay in the damn room."

Josh leaned across the table, invading Granger's space. "And just why the hell do I need to stay in this room?"

"Why not?" Drake Lawrence's words cut through the tension as he walked up to the table.

"Son-of-a—" Josh winced. He'd missed the opening of the door as the boss had walked in. Drake might be the Director of OPAQUE now, but he still moved with the quiet stealth of an agent on the prowl. A technique Josh had mastered for his own use.

His boss quirked the side of his mouth with the cockiness that came from one-upping someone. "That is, unless you've got a hot date."

Josh straightened, figuring Drake's hot date question didn't need an answer. "How've you been, sir?"

"Never better." The boss casually stepped farther into the room.

Faster than a kid released for recess, Granger grabbed his paperwork and fled the room. Evidently he wanted no part in Josh's chewing out. Reprimand. Or whatever the hell this turned out to be. Josh couldn't say as he blamed him.

"Good to have you back, Josh. I missed your in-my-face attitude gracing the hallways." Drake reached out for a brothers-in-arms forearm grasp. "By the way, the hostage's family sent word to thank you for bringing their father home alive."

Josh clasped the offered arm. "Just doing my job, sir."

Drake walked to the window, then back to the door as a half-snarl grabbed his expression. "I meant to be down sooner. Got tied up with our decoders. They intercepted a message from Coercion Ten last night."

"Good intel?"

"Yeah, I got the message."

Josh zeroed in on his boss's harsh tone, then the fact he'd used the word *I* instead of *OPAQUE*. But the most telling sign that something was off was the snarl...angry, personal, and real. What the hell had Josh walked back into? Drake pushed a button on his phone and listened, then shook his head.

"Something wrong, sir?" Josh asked.

Ignoring the question, Drake pushed speed dial again.

"Looks like you're kind of busy, sir. Think I'll head on home," Josh said.

All he'd wanted when he'd stepped off the plane this morning had been to check into some fancy Miami beachfront hotel and sleep twenty-four hours straight. Instead, Granger had picked him up and brought him straight to OPAQUE headquarters. There'd barely been time for a quick shower and change of clothes before the question-answer routine began. Sleep still sounded good.

"Wait." Drake ended the call and took a seat, motioning Josh to the chair adjacent to his.

Sitting was not top priority on Josh's agenda at the moment. Standing and moving and getting some answers were. Brain-tired and body-tired, Josh figured the faster his boss made his point, the faster he could get some rest. He walked to the window and leaned back against the sill.

"What's going on?" Josh asked.

"OPAQUE intercepted Coercion Ten's Target List again last night. My name's still there. So's yours."

"Sounds about right." Most every OPAQUE agent had

their name on the enemy's list. If not, then Josh figured you needed to work a little harder at pissing them off.

"They've added a new column. Titled it—Leverage. There's nothing in that column next to yours. Next to mine is one name." Drake speed-dialed his phone again. "Mackenzie Baudin."

Josh's chest tightened as if a belt had been notched three sizes too small. Not only was Macki an ex-cop, a wealthy hotel owner, and the boss's niece, she was also the only woman Josh had never shook from his system. The idea she was a target in the underbelly game of life and death hit him like a brick.

The two men shared a glance, then looked away. Josh had controlled his breathing. Controlled his expression. But he'd felt the flare of his nostrils. Coercion Ten had gone too far this time. There'd already been too many deaths in Macki's family.

"Do you think it's real?" Josh asked.

"All the signs point that direction. I've been trying to reach Mackenzie all day." The corner of Drake's right eye twitched. "All I get is her damn voice mail."

"She's probably just busy. You know, running a high-class hotel isn't all glamour and glitz." Hearing the words come out of his own mouth didn't make Josh feel any better.

Drake shot him an evil-eye look. "Don't give me that bull. You and I both know this is damn serious."

Josh had to agree. When someone was targeted by Coercion Ten, every hour, every minute, every second counted. He nodded.

"They'll try to break me and OPAQUE by targeting her." Drake paused. "We can't let that happen."

"You can count on me. What's my assignment?"

His boss's expression blanked, the look he always got when he was torn on which way to turn. Torn between going with his gut or overthinking the situation. Josh knew the look. Not only from Drake, but from himself as well.

Squaring his shoulders, Drake rose to his feet. "Bottom line, I need you to go to Riverfalls, Illinois and protect Mackenzie."

"No."

"Yes."

"Get this straight, old man. There's no way in hell I'm going back to my hometown." For years, Josh had accepted every assignment. Every duty. Every dirty job out there. All for OPAQUE. All to pay back the debt he felt he owed. But the old man had stepped over the line this time. "You don't know what you're asking me to do, sir."

"Did you happen to forget I'm the one who got you out of town that day? And I've sure as hell been there every step of the way as you've dealt with the past." Drake pressed the point. "I'm not asking for anything you don't already do as a protector on every job I assign you. Only—"

Drake answered his ringing phone and pushed the speaker button. "Mackenzie, where have you been?"

"I'm tied up in very important negotiations for the hotel and a multimillion-dollar conference. But you've been calling every ten minutes for over an hour, so I called a recess." She sounded stressed, like a woman trying to handle five things at one time and hoping this call wasn't going to add one more thing to her plate. "What's wrong?"

"There's been a threat made against you."

"Another one? You know, being rich isn't all it's cracked up to be sometimes."

Josh knew she wasn't blind to danger, because he'd kept track of her. Never mind the fact that ten years ago she'd inherited her parents' estate when they'd died in the plane crash. Mackenzie Hotel, money, and grown-up responsibilities had landed on her in one fell swoop, and so had risks she'd had no idea existed.

Drake shot him a glance. "Trouble is this one's not like the others. Those were just crackpots, this one is CDS."

"Code dead serious?" Her tone barely changed with the

half-question.

Josh and all the agents knew the boss did not use that statement lightly. And when he did, they listened because the word "dead" meant your life was on the line. Right now, she was probably letting the implication tumble through her mind till it founds its place in her fear mode. From what he'd heard, when she'd worked undercover vice on D Street in Riverfalls, she'd been fearless.

"So how do we handle this?" Mackenzie asked.

"I'm sending someone from OPAQUE to protect you."

"OPAQUE?"

"Yes. They're a first-class security firm."

Drake's intense expression revealed more than he'd want anyone to know, but Josh had read him plenty of times. This was his niece. This was important.

She cleared her throat in a gotcha. "I thought your security firm only installed burglar alarms in the Miami area. This makes it sound like you do more than that." She paused.

Drake ignored the insinuation.

"Okay... Why not use one of the Riverfalls security firms like you usually do?" she asked.

"They aren't reliable for this threat. My protector agent will be on the plane in less than an hour."

Even though OPAQUE had never been exactly sure who had connections to Coercion Ten, the Riverfalls Police Department had always been the top guess for the original breeding grounds.

She sighed. "Sounds good. Can you shoot me his photo and stats, so I'll know to trust him when he arrives?"

Josh raised his eyebrows at Drake, then turned to look out the window. This should be good. Even Drake was taking longer than usual to answer a question. Maybe he'd change his mind and make it easy for all of them.

"You'll know him when you see him," Drake said. "I'm sending Josh Slater."

"No."

"Yes." Drake sounded annoyed. "And I'd appreciate it if both of you would stop saying no to this arrangement."

"There are a lot of things you don't know about the two of us. Things I never planned to tell you, but let's just say that when a woman gives—"

Josh spun around. "Macki, I'm in the room. Don't do this."

"Josh?" She spoke his name the same way she had the last time he'd seen her. The day he'd said good-bye.

He turned back to the window before his own expression could be read by his boss. "Yes."

"You should have told me he was there, Uncle Drake." She sounded confident and controlled and calm.

"Couldn't. You'd have hung up."

"Still might."

"I'll just call back."

She sighed in capitulation. "Okay, I've listened to your suggestion. Now here's mine. You can tell Josh Slater to take his hard body elsewhere. I don't need his kind of protection."

Josh continued to stare out the window at the waving fronds on the tallest queen palm tree in the parking lot. What could he say? To her, he was nothing but a no-account guy she'd given herself to—and then he'd left town. Didn't matter he'd left to save her even more pain than the loss of her parents. He couldn't tell her that. He could never tell her that. Even if his own life depended on it.

He jerked his mind back to the moment. If the boss insisted on his being the protector, then Josh would need to clear his mind of the past. He'd need to focus on this as just another assignment. Another person to keep alive. Might be damn near impossible, but if push came to shove, he could keep Macki at arm's length and his body under control.

One of Drake's attention-getting throat growls hit the silence. "The plan is for Josh to fly to St. Louis and drive the rest of the way to Riverfalls. He should be there—"

"I know you're looking out for my best interest, Uncle

Drake. But...when I turned twenty-one eight years ago, I started thinking for myself." She paused as if waiting for a rebuttal. None came. "Right now I've got a meeting to get to. I promise I'll call you afterward. And yes, you can send someone for my protection. Just not Josh. I don't want him here."

"No changes, Mackenzie. Not this time. Josh will be in Riverfalls by ten tonight." Drake's tone implied she shouldn't argue. "Don't make his job any harder than it already is."

With her disconnect, the room went quiet. Quiet enough to let the past sneak in and grab a toehold. Josh couldn't believe Drake hadn't seen all the pitfalls associated with opening doors closed and locked long ago.

"All things considered, I think that went fairly well." Drake shook his head and lowered it into his hands. He looked back up with an edged embarrassment in his expression. "Appears there are things I don't know about you two. Care to enlighten me?"

"Nope." Josh turned to face his boss. Some things were between him and Macki, no one else. Ever. "You heard her reaction. Just the idea I'm being sent to protect her has already put her on defense where I'm concerned. Think what happens when she discovers why I left in the first place."

Drake folded his hands in front of him on the table.

Josh swallowed down a lump of guilt the size of the ten years he'd been gone from Riverfalls. He didn't want to be the one standing there when her perfect world crashed. Sure, he owed his boss more than he could ever repay, but this was too much to ask. "How will she feel when she finds out my dad had something to do with the death of her parents?"

"She doesn't have to find out."

"But what if she does? She'll be devastated."

Drake fingered the edge of the table. "Sounds to me you've got your facts a little mixed up. Don't you mean you'll be devastated?"

Josh flinched with the words. The son-of-a-bitch had always known how to motivate his agents. Or goad them into doing what he wanted. Wasn't going to work this time. He wouldn't let the words get to him. "You don't know what the hell you're talking about."

"Don't I?" From the corner of his eye, Drake briefly looked in his direction. "Okay. Have it your way. I'll give the job to Granger."

Josh balked at the idea of another man doing the job. That would be a weakness he couldn't abide. Besides, he'd already faced his hell by the time he was barely twenty. How tough could going back be?

"Some days I hate you, old man."

"I'm sure you do." Drake lifted the sides of his mouth and grunted. "Some days I hate myself." He laid a plane ticket and a stack of money on the table, then held out his hand. "You take care of yourself out there. Coercion Ten already knows who you are. And if it serves their purpose, they'll try to take you out."

"Won't be the first time." He shook the man's hand. "And just for the record, I still haven't said yes."

The two each retreated to a spot in the room to focus their thoughts. Some decisions needed to be evaluated for more than their surface value. This one needed space and quiet and time. Just not so much time that the agent's edge got lost in the balancing act of yes versus no. Josh had never lost his edge yet. And he didn't intend this to be the first time.

Years ago, he'd left Riverfalls and Mackenzie to save her pain. And he'd stayed away. Far away. Not one phone call. Not one letter. Not one anything. He'd stayed away to protect her, not himself. The boss had been wrong on that front. Damn wrong.

"If I take this assignment, the past is going to come roaring back. And it won't be pretty. People's lives will never be the same." Shaking his head, Josh blew out a sigh.

"Not mine. Not Macki's. And not yours either."

Drake nodded. "Understood. That's a risk I'm willing to take. What about you? What are you willing to risk?"

That was a damn good question. One he didn't have the answer to yet. All he had lived for during the past years was the hope that one of his assignments would help him bring down Coercion Ten. Specifically the man who'd bought his father's honor with cold, hard cash. Maybe luck would be on his side this time.

"Doing what's right in this world has cost a lot of lives. I draw the line at my niece. So do whatever it takes to protect her. Because you and I both know she deserves the best." Drake opened the door to leave, then glanced back over his shoulder. "And you are the best I've got."

"Yeah, yeah, yeah. I bet you say that to all the agents." Josh grabbed the ticket and money from the table, then pushed past his boss and out the door. Then he stopped, glancing back. "Drake, I want to thank you for getting me out of Riverfalls when you did. For giving me a home and guidance all these years. Don't think I haven't appreciated everything you—"

"Get out of here, Josh. We'll talk when you get back."

Josh gave the thumbs-up gesture and walked on down the hall. He'd said what he wanted to say. Yeah, he'd be back. As long as he could get up off the floor, he'd be back. Trouble was...this was just the kind of assignment that killed an agent faster than a bullet to the brain. Personal and close to home.

* * *

Threats, texts, and now a protector. Could life get any more complicated?

Mackenzie hadn't just been in hotel negotiations today, she'd also had a lunch meeting with the Mackenzie Baudin Charity Gala board to finalize some details on the upcoming event. And to top everything off, the phone call with her Uncle Drake had only confused her mind even more. She'd called him back the moment she'd walked in her penthouse. For the last ten minutes, they had discussed the threat against her, and she'd paid close attention.

The added threat implications had her nerves revved even further than the creepy text she'd received earlier in the day. The one that had requested her appearance on D Street tonight. The message had been specific about which outfit from her days working vice she should wear.

When she'd called her uncle back again this afternoon, she'd told him about the weird text she'd received after their earlier call. She'd told him she'd already given the police a heads-up, and he'd praised her with a good-job comment. Then she'd told him she intended to keep the appointment. Drake had blown a gasket. He'd even thrown out the fact that the text and the threat from his end might all loop together. Did he think she hadn't thought about that possibility after talking to him earlier?

He might still be uber-protective of her, and with his background as chief of police in Riverfalls, she couldn't blame him. But she'd been a cop also, just like her dad had been. Making her have a security chauffeur all these years was one thing. Managing her day-to-day life was another thing.

She'd stood her ground. She was going to D Street. Tonight. In that damn pink outfit.

Her uncle had finally agreed to have Josh meet her on D Street. She'd agreed to talk to one of her sources in that neighborhood before she headed there. A win-win situation...or at least close.

Hopefully, her source wasn't entertaining at the moment.

She speed-dialed Roxy, the woman who had shown Mackenzie the ropes her first night working vice on D Street a long time ago. No one knew Roxy's last name, but she'd worked the street for years. Now she watched out for newcomers and anything out of the ordinary in the neighborhood. Plus, she still worked the street.

The phone rang and rang and—

"Hey, you've got foxy Roxy. What can I do for you?"

The woman's voice and phone tag never changed. Even the breaths she made sure you heard were always measured, almost a purr.

"Hi, Roxy. This is Mackenzie Baudin. Have you got a second?"

"Sure. Anything for you."

Mackenzie doubted the "anything" but figured Roxy would do what she could as long as nothing implicated her. What the woman didn't say was as important as what she said.

Still, Mackenzie trusted her. "Somebody sent me a text. Requested I be on D Street tonight. Seems kind of strange after all this time. Have you heard my name being passed around? Someone looking for a pink outfit? Anything?"

"I haven't heard anything, sweetie."

Mackenzie smiled at Roxy's use of the familiar endearment for people she liked. As a vice cop, Mackenzie had been saved by Roxy more times than she liked to admit. One time in particular, Mackenzie would never be able to repay.

"If I hear anything, I'll give you a call," Roxy said. "You're not coming down here, are you? I mean, you're not even with the police anymore. Maybe you should stay home. Take care of yourself."

The text hadn't sounded like one to ignore. "That's okay. I'm almost ready. I'll come on down for a while."

Mackenzie checked herself in the oversized, full-length triple dressing mirror in her master bedroom. This had come in handy, even if she had fought her security company when they'd suggested she install one to conceal the entrance to her private elevator.

After shoving the push-ups into her bra and tugging the top into place, she gave herself an approving nod. The shortie-short skirt, clingy low-cut top, and flashy vest she'd had sewn to replace the original outfit still clung in all the right places. To anyone on D Street, she'd look like a hooker, just like when she'd worked as an undercover police officer.

Of course, she'd quit the police force two years ago. Sure, she was still going out there tonight as bait, but this time it was personal. She didn't like people she didn't know sending her texts. And she didn't want to give the creep time to become even more confident about contacting her.

The phone conversation with Roxy had gone quiet. Didn't surprise Mackenzie—talking to the woman was like pulling teeth some days. "Roxy, I heard there's been some trouble for the girls lately."

No response.

"Anything I should know?" Mackenzie waited for an answer.

Still nothing.

"Roxy?"

"Nothing major, just a couple of the women got roughed up. You know how it is. Life's not easy down here." Roxy's tone had changed with her words. There'd been a stammer. "You should stay home. Take care of yourself."

Twice the woman had said the same thing about staying home. About taking care of herself. From what Mackenzie got when she'd reported the text to the police, the women who'd been assaulted had survived a lot more than being roughed up. What was going on?

"Are you all right, Roxy?"

The woman's throaty laugh passed through the phone. "Of course I'm okay. I belong on the street. But it might not be a good idea for an ex-vice cop to be on D Street right now."

Mackenzie wanted to shout *Why?* but instincts told her not to waste her breath. "Thanks for the info, but I think I'll head on down there anyway. See you later tonight."

"Whatever. No skin off my shoulders. I gotta go now." Roxy ended the call.

Strange. Roxy wasn't usually so abrupt.

Mackenzie tucked the phone in her hip pocket. Maybe the person who'd sent the text had something to do with the assaults. Maybe not. But if her being there could save a woman from getting hurt, there was no way she could stay away. She didn't want to live with that on her conscience.

Besides, she would make sure she stayed in sight of a police officer at all times. She might even be able to point out some of the finer details about the area to the cops. Maybe they'd nab the guy. Or put enough fear in him that he backed off.

Bottom line...much as she hated being back in what she had named her Pink Flurry outfit, much as she didn't want to face the street again, much as she understood her uncle's warning to reconsider...she had to go. She'd never let herself be scared off D Street again.

Almost dressed in the requested pink outfit, she walked into her master bathroom to tackle the one thing she still had to put on before her transformation was complete: the spiky blond wig. Her own auburn hair was longer now, and tucking every last strand into the too-tight wig cap was frustrating. Plus, the more hair, the tighter the wig. The tighter the wig, the more her head felt like it might explode.

"Damn it all." She'd probably have one pounding headache tomorrow morning.

She outlined her lips in bright red, then finished off with a darker pink lipstick, completing the look she'd been known for on the street.

"There. That's it." She blew out a small sigh, then walked to the French doors that led to her bedroom's balcony. When she stepped outside, the lights of the city greeted her, and she smiled. She loved this view. This town.

Sounds of the city drifted up from below. Stop-and-go traffic, bings from the crossing lights at the street crossings, and general rumble of a busy street filled the air along with the hum of chatter and music and laughter. She loved the energy of the town along with the friendly, hardworking people.

Riverfalls might not be the big city of Chicago, but it

also wasn't Springfield, the state capital. This city placed somewhere in between with all the sights, sounds, and smells of big city life but on a lesser scale.

In the distance, past the dimmer streetlights of surrounding neighborhoods, the bright lights and neon colors of D Street glowed. They always gave her the feeling of an oasis in the middle of a desert. Only this oasis offered less water and more liquor.

She turned back to her own oasis and thoughts of her conversation with her uncle. She wasn't exactly sure what line of work he was involved in since he'd retired to Miami. He said he ran a small security system installation company for homes. But past conversations had led her to believe there was more than that to his business. Way more.

She'd always figured he'd tell her when the time was right. Things he'd said during their last phone call had made her think the time was close. But she had a lot of questions right now.

First, who or what was OPAQUE? When she'd pushed for an answer, he'd said something very disconcerting. He'd promised that by this time tomorrow she'd know the truth about her life. What the hell did that mean?

A chilly shudder crossed her back. She didn't like surprises. Surprises had a way of not being good. But this one had come from nowhere and taken a firm spot in second place on her question list.

And third?

Third was a whole different matter.

The idea that Josh Slater would be back in her life didn't sit well. She'd ground him out of her mind, but there were still times he showed up in her memories. Worse, in her dreams. She could control memories, but the dreams had their own way of yanking her around.

Josh had been nothing but a first love. First time. First broken heart. Life had forced her to grow up fast, and she had.

As far as the protection went, she hadn't lost her cop

skills. She could still take care of herself when it came to criminals on the street. Yes, she was grateful Josh would be coming to add an extra layer of protection against Coercion Ten. Everything she'd ever heard on the sly from others in the police department regarding Coercion Ten had stressed their ruthless reputation. But as far as she and Josh went, she needed to keep barriers between the two of them.

Barriers like resistance, confidence...sarcasm...

"And distance," she mumbled to herself.

She walked to the bedroom mirror and tapped the rim. The center opened to her private elevator. The one with exits on three levels only—her penthouse on the fifteenth floor, her fifth-floor office, and her private garage in the lower level. She entered the code in the keypad Uncle Drake had insisted be part of the security system.

After stepping into the elevator, she pushed the Garage button and waited for the enclosure's smooth descent to where her chauffeur waited. From there, he would use her fake taxi to drive her to D Street. Then he'd wait close by for her call. Pick her up and drive her back here.

Fake taxi, black limo, or silver SUV, the routine never changed. Years ago, she'd balked at Drake's insistence that she have a driver, feeling he was trying to keep tabs on her. But once he'd explained he might not always be around and was only thinking of her safety, she'd believed him and agreed. Ultimately, the arrangements had turned out to be invaluable at times.

She leaned back and sighed as a memory tried to take shape. One of her...and Josh...a blanket and— She shoved the thought aside. The last thing she needed tonight was the past invading her emotions and dulling her instincts. Instincts could be key on D Street.

Besides, Josh had probably changed with the years just like she had. Maybe he'd changed into a buttoned-down guy who dressed in nothing but brown, hadn't been to a gym in years, drove a nondescript white compact car, wore dirty tennis shoes even with his Sunday suit and...and...

And played Friday-night bingo with his buddies.

Her phone rang, and the caller ID said OPAQUE. "Hello?"

"Macki, it's Josh Slater." His voice had matured to quiet and confident. "Drake texted I'm supposed to meet you on D Street. Any place in particular?"

Her emotions churned with recognition at the sound of his voice, and from nowhere, a lump took hold in her chest. One she'd crushed several years ago. And one she for damn sure didn't need to revive.

"Macki? You there?" He sounded like a man who expected answers when he asked questions.

"Yes, uh... The neighborhood hasn't changed much. Still the same few blocks of fun as before you left." She sucked in a breath as the last time she'd seen him flashed to the forefront of her mind. This was going to be difficult, more difficult than she'd thought.

"Okay. Drake said something about you wearing an old vice outfit?"

"Yes, it's short and tight and pink. Lots of pink and—"

"I get the picture." Josh cleared his throat. "I'll see you there. And Macki, just so you know, this wasn't my idea. But Drake sent me to protect you, and that's what I'll do."

Realizing she had no recourse at the moment but to go with the plan, she still wanted some answers. "Have you done this before?"

Josh laughed or grunted or a mixture of both. "I don't know what all Drake told you, but I'm a protector agent with OPAQUE. And I'm good at my job. If you're worried about me and you, don't be. I'm a professional at all times. Trust me, our personal past will not enter into this mission."

During her time on the force, she'd heard about the organization known as OPAQUE, but only in passing. No one had ever sat down and talked to her about what the group did exactly, and she hadn't asked. The little she had heard led her to believe they were on the right side of law enforcement. That was what mattered then. And what mattered now.

Evidently her uncle had known more about OPAQUE than she had. Known what they did. Known how to contact them. Funny, he'd never filled her in on the group.

"You're right. Our past has nothing to do with the threat at hand. Besides, I'm sure we've both moved on with our lives." The truth was that the naive girl he'd left behind had turned into a successful woman of the world, both in business and in private life. "Bottom line. I trust Uncle Drake. He trusts you. That's all that matters."

"Good to know. Makes working together all that much easier. By the way, Drake told me about that crazy text you received," Josh said. "Coincidence? Maybe. Maybe not. But either way, I don't like coincidences, and there seem to be a lot of them at the moment."

"Don't try to talk me out of going." Mackenzie used her best I'll-do-what-I-want tone. "Uncle Drake tried that and it didn't work. And it triple-damn well won't work coming from you.

I'll see you later on D Street."

She ended the call and straightened the fringe on her vest as she swallowed down her unease. Who was she kidding? Handling the whole bodyguard protector setup would be a breeze compared to handling her emotions.

No problem. She'd give him a room on the opposite side of the hotel and five floors below hers. He'd be by her side for protection when they left Hotel MacKenzie, but once they returned, they'd go separate ways. Sounded like a plan that would solve everyone's problems, and she couldn't believe she'd let his coming back to Riverfalls upset her for most of the day.

After all, she was a grown woman who could handle Joshua Slater. All that would take was...distance. Lots and lots of distance.

CHAPTER TWO

After two commercial flights, a charter to St. Louis, and three hours of driving, Josh was within sight of his goal. Riverfalls, Illinois. D Street. Mackenzie Baudin.

He didn't look forward to being close to her again, but this was his assignment, and he'd do everything in his power to protect her. Besides, the phone conversation he and Macki had just had seemed to go well. He'd been professional, to the point, and emotionless. So had she.

Might have been ten years, but memories were like switches to be turned back on at a moment's notice. His switch had been on most of the way here. But he couldn't afford for this to be any more than a job. In and out fast.

Hell. At least he didn't still fantasize about her anymore. He blew out a cheek-puffing sigh. Not much.

He pulled off the interstate and followed old paths with shiny new halogen lights, bike lanes at the edge of the streets, and people braving the heat in upscale outdoor cafes. After he took a left turn, the next few blocks dimmed. Except for a couple of dimly lit decorative streetlamps by the sidewalk, the only light came from lamps glowing in modern row-house windows. A couple of vacant lots led him to believe this was an area in transition. Good or bad, only time would tell.

Turning right on D Street, he saw the glow of neon about six blocks away. A beat of music and life grew louder and louder with each passing needs-some-updating apartment building and Craftsman house, some with a/c units hanging in the windows, some with fans blowing the warm air around, and some with nothing more than an open window, curtains hanging still at the side of the frame.

"Yep, not much change in this area." He pulled into a parking spot in the main part of the D Street drag. Same fun district, too.

He glanced at a crowd gathered at the intersection. Crime scene tape blocked onlookers while policemen and plainclothes detectives besieged the area. After yanking the keys from the ignition, he jumped from the truck. Playing the cameraman game, he began walking toward the scene, snapping photos of the surroundings on his cell phone. He'd like to know what had happened, but he'd also like to stay out of law enforcement's eye a bit longer.

He edged closer to a group of teenage boys that reeked of marijuana. "Hey, guys, you know what's going on over there?"

A kid probably still in high school held out a joint in his direction. "Want a drag?"

"No, I'm good." Josh shook his head, then made eye contact with one of the others. "What happened over there?"

"One of them working ladies got hit by a car."

"Accident?"

"Buddy, all I know is she looked dead." He swooped his arm out in front of him. "All sprawled out there like a rag doll. You know what I mean? Dead." The kid took the joint from his friend and inhaled deeply before the group headed down the street.

Josh wondered if the kids would even remember what the woman lying in the street looked like by tomorrow. Part of him actually hoped they didn't.

He rolled his shoulders as a trickle of sweat etched a path down his spine. This humidity-fueled heat wave felt like initiation to hell tonight. Scary thought, since he knew for damn sure he was no saint. Without thinking, he raked his fingers through his damp hair.

An unexpected sting from salty perspiration against the wound in his back made him flinch. No big deal. He'd had worse. But, why did every place he got assigned lately have to be so blue-blazes hot?

The scent of cheap perfume stepped up beside Josh.

"Looking for anything tonight?" A soft-spoken twentysomething woman with clear eyes, short sleeves, and fresh breath brushed his arm. "Maybe I can help you find what you need."

Josh took a step back. No drugs, no tracks, no booze. The woman looked fresh on the street. He forced a smile and raised his hands, palms facing her. "Not tonight, honey. I'm completely out of money and need."

Before he had even finished his statement, the woman had moved toward a passing guy in a button-down shirt, black horn-rimmed glasses, and a gaudy toupee. Evidently the heavy gold-link bracelet and shiny-shiny black shoes the new customer wore made him think he was cool.

The man put his arm around her shoulders as they walked on down the street, whispering in her ear. In return the woman wound her arm around his waist and lightly giggled. Newfound friends to be sure.

Josh shook his head. Nothing he could do but hope she stayed safe.

In his peripheral vision, he caught sight of a woman pushing the far side of forty, red hair, painted lips, and three-inch heels. She was perched on a bar stool at one lone high-top table situated in front of a small cafe called Mama's Kitchen.

Seemingly at ease in her surroundings, she leaned back as if she owned the world, but her eyes looked tired as they glanced from one end of the street to the other. She didn't look like a pimp, but he'd bet money she took care of the women working this street.

That was who he needed to talk to.

On the next pass of her up-and-down-the-street glance,

he locked gazes with her. She paused for a moment, then glanced over him as if he didn't exist.

He walked to her table, braced his hand on the top. "Can I buy you a drink, ma'am?"

"You need to get off this street, mister."

"Josh. My name's Josh."

She zeroed her look in on him. "Well, Josh, you're bad for business. So get off the street."

"Last time I looked, this was a public sidewalk." He straightened up and took one step back from the table. "Listen, I'm not a cop, if that's what you think, ma'am."

She never took her eyes off him. "Then you're something worse. And I've got enough of them around here already. Now if you know what's good for you, you'll get out of this area."

The woman had guts. She also had a keen sense for reading people. He bet she also had a temper. Temper could sometimes lead to a dropped clue in the heat of word exchange. He'd push his luck and see what shook out.

"Well, ma'am—"

She slammed her palm on the table. "You call me ma'am one more time, you're going to be in serious pain."

Her stare flowed down to his crotch as she angled her foot in a upward position.

He stepped back a little more, gave her a slight laugh. "I sure don't want that. Uh... I didn't get your name."

"Roxy," she stated proudly with a slight throaty sound at the beginning, then started her up-down-the-street glancing once again. He'd been dismissed.

His phone vibrated with Drake's personal signal, and for privacy, Josh walked up the sidewalk away from the intersection.

"Did you do a follow-up phone call with Macki?" Drake asked.

"Yeah, we talked."

Drake paused as if waiting for a more in-depth report on the conversation. Too bad. That was all he was getting out of Josh at this point. The silence dragged for a bit.

"You need something?" Josh asked.

"I followed up with one of my reliable police sources there in Riverfalls. Found out there've been some assaults in the D Street neighborhood."

"Macki didn't mention any of that to me." That information made this stakeout take on a whole different flavor. Josh scanned the street with new perspective. "Call her back and tell her not to come."

"She won't listen. I told you before how close she got to the prostitutes when she worked D Street." Drake paused. "Hey, one thing I forgot to mention. Be very careful who you trust in the police department there."

Josh already knew to be on guard when it came to the police in the area. Most were okay, but somewhere there had to be at least one thorn. Maybe more, from what OPAQUE had been told previously by the FBI.

"Will do."

Another lull in the conversation. Silence that played in sharp contrast to the sharp beat on the street. Drake was usually on and off the phone in a flash. Why was he dragging out the call this time? Macki...that was why. Drake had been responsible for her welfare for so long, he didn't know how to do otherwise.

"Anything else?" Josh asked.

"No, just... Keep your eyes out for her."

"Don't worry, I got this. No sign of her yet."

Drake sighed heavily. "Stay sharp. You may not recognize her in that lady-of-the-evening outfit and wig." The call ended.

Josh stopped cold. Yellow tape. EMT van. Cops. Detectives.

What was it the kid had said happened across the street? Something about a lady...a lady...

Accident? Crime? Macki? Josh pulsed with adrenalin as he focused toward the intersection. Cold fear flashed through his body as the scene shot to his brain. Then he jerked with reaction and slammed the phone in his pocket as he strained to move. To run. My god, what had he missed? Why hadn't he checked? Checked? He should have checked.

"Please, God. Not Macki." He mumbled. Caught his senses. Knees pumping. Arms pumping. Heart pumping. He raced toward the crime scene. Toward a finish line he wanted to be wrong.

"Get out of my way!" People stepped aside and when they didn't, he pushed them out of his path. "Move."

Police at the scene looked in his direction. Some of them moved their hands to the hilt of their guns, others unsnapped their holsters. He didn't care if they thought he was crazy. Didn't care if they shot him. All he cared about was getting to her.

"Macki!" The yellow tape was within a few steps. "Macki?"

"Josh. Josh! Stop."

He stopped. Turned to his left. And stared. Where had the voice come from?

"Josh. It's not me."

A woman in pink with spiky blond hair stood with her arm straight up in the air, pumping a stop-wave to get his attention. His mind tried to focus and failed. Because she for damn sure looked out of place in his thoughts.

He jerked his attention back to the crime scene. Then back to the woman in pink as she stepped in his direction. Smiling—

Recognition shot to his core and grabbed hold like a vise, twisting and turning till his brain caught up with his body. "Macki?"

CHAPTER THREE

Mackenzie's insides vibrated with sparks of excitement and hints of too little, too late, all because moments ago she'd watched Josh charge down the street like a crazy man. A crazy man chasing the last train out of town before the typhoon hit. He'd been screaming her name, shoving people out of his way, and from the look on his face, he'd thought she might be the victim behind the crime scene tape. Once he'd finally heard her shout, he'd stopped.

Maybe he still cared after all. Cared about her and him and... She felt a smile spread across her face, but she wasn't so sure she wanted the spark to ignite.

Instead of coming toward her, he turned around and walked across the intersection as if nothing had happened. Turning back to face the crime scene, he stared as if making sure of what he saw, then leaned against a lamppost on the corner. He quirked the corner of his mouth and did that quick head-jerk sideways nod he used to do.

Figuring he didn't want to be part of any police questioning, she walked in his direction. The closer she got, the more she realized she'd gotten part of her wish from back at her penthouse—Josh had changed. Just not how she'd hoped.

Josh the man looked tired, tanned, and tough. He was more than broad shoulders and muscles beneath the black shirt he wore like skin. He also walked hard, stood hard, and gave off one damn hard aura to people walking past.

His hair was still the same, though. Dark and thick and sleek. She brushed her fingers against her side to still the remembered feel of his hand holding hers years ago.

So much for her vision of a nerd who wore brown. Josh's shoes were black. Jeans were dark. And if it were daylight, she bet he'd be wearing one sexy pair of sunglasses. She couldn't keep herself from glancing at the way the jeans snugged around his calf muscles, across his rear. Damn, he was tempting.

"You okay?" She reached out and touched his jaw line. Even that was hard to the touch.

He pulled back, giving her a back-off look from the corner of his eye. "Hell no, I'm not okay."

Sliding her palm down his arm, she hoped for a response. A hug. A how-are-you. Maybe a peck on the cheek.

Instead, he nudged her arm away. His forearms with taut muscles and bulging veins caught her eye. A scar across the top of the forearm looked like the wound had been long, deep, and fierce.

"I'm sorry. I thought maybe you were worried about me." Mackenzie stumbled over her own words, fighting to hold onto her emotions. She longed to reach out and run her fingers in his slightly long, dark-as-sin hair like she used to.

"You got that right." Josh stared at her as if he'd never seen her before. His remembered blue eyes were almost gray at the moment. Penetrating. Intense. Vigilant. "Drake would have my hide if I lost a client before I'd even laid eyes on them. And you. Who knows what he'd do if I don't keep you safe?"

"Well, you've got nothing to worry about because I'm still here." She backpedaled a few steps. Calmed her thoughts. The glow from the streetlight allowed her to see more clearly now. His words had made everything ten times clearer. Clear as an empty glass. Holding out her hand, she lifted her chin. "It's good to see you, Josh."

He grasped her hand like a businessman intent on

networking at a conference. "Good to see you, too."

"Got a problem over here, Macki."

Just when she didn't need the police, here they were. Not one of the cops on the block, but the one detective who made her feel uncomfortable. Not in a creepy, intrusive way. Not in a sexual, tingly way either. He was none of those things in her thinking. Still, he made her uncomfortable.

"No, Detective Cummings." Macki moved out of the man's space. "No problem except you blowing my cover again."

The man pushed closer, leaning into her personal space. "Come off it, Macki. You aren't part of the force anymore. So give me a break before I haul your... Before you find yourself downtown making bail."

Nobody on the force would dare lay a hand on her. They all still respected her uncle. If Drake found out one of them ever disrespected her, she shuddered to think what would happen to the man's, or woman's, career. That was why she kept a lot of static she received from the police to herself. No need to make a fuss when she could handle the insults herself.

Much as other people's words and thoughts hurt, she still gave them benefit of the doubt. She knew being rich made some people hate her. Others hated her for being the ex-chief's niece. Thought she got special treatment. She didn't. She hadn't. And she never would.

Still others hated her for so-called reasons dating back to when her father was the captain at Riverfalls Police Department. Times before the crash. Before he died. Those hurt the most. Then again, they were the ones it was easiest to give the benefit to, also.

One thing she'd learned, though, was that she had to stand up for herself and give just as deep as she took. She stepped forward, staking her own claim in the man's space. "Bring it on, detective. Bring it on."

Cummings ignored her sass. Instead he flicked his hand

toward his cuffs, then glanced at Josh. "Who are you, buddy? You the guy who likes to text? The one Macki called the station about?" The detective took a step in Josh's direction. Laced his words with intimidation. "The one getting his jollies off her outfit?"

Josh didn't answer. Didn't move. Didn't react to the goading. His expression blanked, jaw jutted a bit to the right, eyes narrowed. "You should be careful who you're accusing, officer."

Her mind shouted this situation could deteriorate faster than melting ice cream in this heat. Faster than she might be able to defuse. Being stuck as mediator between two alphas was not her idea of how to end the day.

She edged her side between the two men. "If you must know, he's a friend. Now I've got some questions for you, detective." Macki changed the focus back to herself. "Two weeks ago a different girl was assaulted. Why didn't anyone call me?"

Cummings loosened his attention from Josh and refocused on her. "Funny. Since when does the Riverfalls Police Department have to report every occurrence on D Street to you?"

"Don't give me that." She ignored the insinuation she'd heard for years. At least he hadn't tacked on "your highness" like he did most times. "I heard about this assault on the way down here. My chauffeur did a quick check with some people we know in the force."

"So?"

"So evidently the police received a phone call after the last woman was beat up. One that said if I didn't make a showing on D Street, the next woman wouldn't be so lucky."

Cummings didn't back away from her or her words. "This isn't something we need to discuss in front of your..." The man nodded in Josh's direction. "... Friend."

"Why not? I want to speak to whoever was in charge that night."

"That would be me. Lieutenant Grey was out of town and left me in charge." Cummings made the statement without an ounce of regret.

Josh glanced away, blew out a sigh, rolled his shoulders. She knew he was listening. Trying to pick up on any clues to his assignment. But this wasn't his problem. This was local neighborhood trouble. Trouble she planned to get to the bottom of.

"Why didn't anyone call me, Detective Cummings? I want to know." Macki set her tone on confidence. "Or maybe you didn't let Grey know. Should we give him a call? See what he thinks about sheer neglect."

Cummings jaw edged again. "Grey might have been out of town, but he still made the call on that one. Said not to bother you about some guy who'd probably never show up again. So don't go roaring on me."

"Don't you think I should have been allowed to make that choice? Look what happened because I hadn't come down here sooner." She felt the pinch of the tiny lines between her eyebrows as she watched the woman's body being taken away. "How am I supposed to live with this on my conscience?"

The detective narrowed his eyes, swallowed big, then cleared his throat. "You want to know how, Macki? Do you really want to know? You damn well suck up it up. Get out of bed each morning. Do your job. And go home to a beer and television every night. One fucking day at a time. Like we all do."

She'd pushed too far, but she hadn't meant it as a slam at the detective. No way would she ever bring up a situation involving the death of another officer. Cummings had taken her question that way though. She reached out to touch Cummings's arm. "I didn't mean—"

He shook off her hand, then palmed his hand across his close-cropped hair. "Don't worry about me. Now what's really going on here?" He turned back to Josh. "What's your story, buddy?"

"First off, I'm not your buddy. Second, do you always use those words around a lady?"

"It's okay, Josh. Don't make a big deal out of it." She tried to form a triangle between the three of them. "I...uh..."

"Yeah, buddy, back off." Cummings rested his hand on the badge clipped at his waist. "Don't think I didn't see you running down the street. Yelling her name like the world was gonna end. And no matter what you think, I keep an eye out for Macki. So what's your story?"

"We were in the same photography class years ago. I just wanted to show her some pictures I'd shot with my phone." Josh deflected the detective's question.

"Then give her the phone." Cummings narrowed his eyes.

"Here you go, Macki."

"Mackenzie. You can call me Mackenzie." She thumbed through the recent photos on the camera roll, then looked up as she handed the phone back. "These are shots of the buildings on the street."

"Don't forget the neon lights." Josh shoved the phone in his pocket. "I make extra money freelancing photos on the web. There's some great architecture on D Street so I—"

"Yeah, yeah, yeah," Detective Cummings grumbled. "If you and your photo friend are finished, Macki, I'd like to talk to you." He motioned to the crime scene, then walked back across the street.

"I'll be right there." She shot Josh a look and tensed.

Pretending she didn't still have feelings for him would be a lie, one her body would betray to her again and again.

The thing she hated most about the whole situation was feeling out of control. She'd gone years managing her life. Now in less than three hours, everybody else owned a piece of her. First, Uncle Drake. Then Detective Cummings. Now, Josh. Of course she'd already picked up that to Josh she was nothing but an assignment. Fine. She'd play their game. Sooner or later assignments ended.

In fact...what was to stop her from requesting a different

protector one more time...say she couldn't work with someone she knew personally...point out that she'd feel responsible, would try to protect the protector, would be a liability...might get them both killed? The plan formed in her mind.

Assignments could always be changed, right? At least it was worth a try.

* * *

Josh ignored the whole ongoing conversation between Macki and Cummings because he had more important things to work out in his mind. Like what the hell happened to him a few minutes ago when he acted like a deranged man?

Sure, he'd surmised the woman lying in the street might be Macki, but he'd out-and-out lost it back there. His mind had processed she was dead. Processed his loss. Processed his pain. While his body had charged to stop the clock and turn it back. He'd made a fool of himself. Might have blown his cover if anyone on the street had any inkling of his profession.

That for damn sure couldn't happen again. This was an assignment. As an OPAQUE agent, his job was to keep the client safe at all costs, and that was exactly what he intended to do. He didn't care what lengths he had to go to in order to convince Macki he didn't care about their past, he had to approach her as nothing but another client.

No emotions. No personal feelings. No explanations.

Starting now.

Once the detective was well out of earshot, she turned to face Josh. Her body was so close he could trail his finger across her arm like a whisper of wind. But he didn't.

Instead he looked into the same clear hazel-green eyes that had captured his soul years ago, the night his senior year when he'd stumbled out-of-bounds during a high school football game. She'd been reading and hadn't seen him cross to make a catch. He'd knocked her flat. She'd glanced up, laughing, and when he'd grabbed her hand to pull her up, the heat between them had boiled. From then on, everyone knew they were exclusive.

Now, she tilted her head, challenging him with the stare of a woman set on revenge. So much for wondering how long till the past reared its ugly head between them. At least this way his tough-guy, no-emotions role would be easier to handle. He clenched his jaw against her onslaught as she motioned him to follow her to a less congested area.

She punched one button on her phone, pushed the speaker on, and lowered the volume.

"Yes, Mackenzie." Her uncle answered with stark bluntness.

Josh figured that should have signaled her Drake was in no mood for a showdown. Agents and adversaries knew to tread lightly when he used that tone. Not that Josh had ever treaded lightly with anyone.

Macki shot an insufferable glance in Josh's direction. "I want him out of here."

A door slammed on the boss's end, echoing through the speaker phone. Josh knew everything about this case was confidential. Since the boss had personally assigned him to this case, Josh knew only a need-to-know would get another OPAQUE agent any information.

"Agent Slater, you got a problem with this assignment?" Drake asked.

"No, sir. Just doing my job." Josh sucked up any qualms he had. Every mission came with a white-hot danger zone. Dealing with her couldn't be any tougher than outrunning a Columbian drug lord with a Jeep-mounted AK-47 zeroed in on you.

"Good. You know what I expect. Make it happen. Got that?" Drake cleared his throat. "Or maybe I should send Granger instead."

Josh didn't take kindly to orders. Less to being reminded of his job. And no way in hell would he let Granger within ten feet of Macki. "Let's get on with this, sir."

"Now, Mackenzie..." The boss huffed a loud sigh.

She rolled her eyes upward and sucked in a deep breath. "Yes, Uncle Drake?"

"Agent Slater leaving is not an option. It's not on the table no matter how much you want him gone. So play nice. You know I don't intrude in your life, but this is different. Damn different." Another door slam echoed through. "For the record, Josh is one hell of an agent. And nice isn't always in his job description. So don't get in his way."

The head of OPAQUE hung up.

Macki shifted slightly, and again the fringe fluttered. "Exactly what the hell is going on here? I want some answers."

Surveying the surroundings, Josh shook his head. "Not here. We'll talk later."

"Fine. Stay." Macki tapped her finger on his chest for emphasis. "But I don't want you anywhere close to me. Got that?"

Josh stifled his response. This had been a long day, and maybe his patience level was narrowing, but if he heard one more *got that*...somebody was getting one back.

"Afraid not. Think of me as your shadow until the bastards targeting you are put out of commission." He nodded to the crime scene tape. "Finish up your business here and let's head back to your place. We need a plan."

"My place? Why?"

"First, I need to set up equipment. Second, I need to keep you close." Trying to appear nonconfrontational, Josh walked over to the closest building and leaned back. She followed at a distance. "I'm sure you've got some guest rooms in that penthouse. I only need one."

Catching up with him, she poked his chest hard this time. "No way in—"

He jerked away from the wall and nabbed her finger before she had a chance to react. She yanked. He held. This was going nowhere fast, and they couldn't keep having this conversation standing on a street corner. Finally, her lashes fluttered with the slow blink of her eyes as he released his hold.

"Macki, this is serious. These men who've targeted you are ruthless. They'll use you to get at your uncle. To take down his...business." Being vague for now would be enough to get the point across. Hard details on OPAQUE would come later. Josh raked his fingers through his hair, shook his head slightly. "You and I have got to work this out. I know you'll never forgive me for taking—"

"Stop right there, mister." She raised her hand in protest. "You didn't take anything from me, Joshua Slater. I gave you my virginity. That I never regretted."

He cringed at how matter-of-fact she made their one afternoon of love sound. Her resilience surprised him. In hindsight, he should have realized she'd move on with her life.

Josh's core gripped in sickening pain. Sure, he'd had needs. Had had women. But he'd never let himself consider that Macki might have the same needs. Now, like it or not, the thought shot through him like a hollow-point bullet.

Maybe Cummings. Maybe they were lovers.

Psychology sometimes said a person would always be attracted to the same look in the opposite sex. Judging the detective, Josh calculated he was about the same height, build, and age as himself. Demeanor on face value said he was probably one tough lawman, from the edge of his jaw line to the edge in his flat-brown eyes. Of course, edges could lie on both sides of the law. Either way, the tone of his voice had hinted at an assumed influence over Macki.

"Someday, hopefully you'll be man enough to tell me what I did to drive you away." Anger edged her voice, along with sadness. "I forgave you for leaving years ago. But making me feel like nothing more than a one-night stand, that I'll never forgive. You don't deserve that forgiveness."

Josh felt like he'd been gutted.

Yeah, he had walked away. Fast and far. He'd been so

caught in his own web of pain and anger at the time that anyone else's had taken a backseat. It had never dawned on him she might think he'd used her for nothing but pleasure. How could she not have known how much he cared? How long he'd waited for that day? How—

Didn't matter. He'd learned a long time ago that no one could change what happened in the past. Not even a second ago. But he was back now. Nobody was going to hurt the woman giving him what-for. Nobody. Not even himself.

"Macki!" Detective Cummings yelled from across the street, motioning for her to come over to the crime scene.

She turned to go, then glared back at Josh. "This conversation isn't over. Got. That?"

Took restraint not to laugh out loud. She actually thought she was in charge. True, he was sure the conversations weren't over, but they were for now. Time she learned who commanded this team.

Josh jerked back to protector mode. "Mackenzie Baudin. Stop right there."

She stopped.

"You've got ten minutes tops to wrap things up. Then we're getting off this street." He heard the way his voice had dropped to a don't-mess-with-me tone. He didn't want to be the bad guy, but her life was that important. "The point man. That's me. Keeps eyes on the target. That's you." He pointed from himself to her, then leaned forward. "I will. Stay at your place. I will. Set up my surveillance. And I will be in charge. Got. That?"

Her back tensed, but she nodded. "Of course, Agent Slater. You're in charge." Sarcasm dripped thick and sweet like honey from each word she spoke. "Whatever you say...Josh."

He was so screwed. In fact, he'd bet his next paycheck that she was already contriving her next ploy to get Drake to pull him from the job. No chance. He and her uncle could both be tougher than cheap steak when they dug their heels in. And they were both dug in for the long haul on protecting her.

Heading on across the street, she snapped the heels of her boots hard and loud against the pavement with each step she took. Halfway across the street, she altered her determined march into a slow, hip-swaying walk. She glanced back over her shoulder and shot him a bright-eyed, playful look complete with a sultry smile.

Evidently she'd remembered to play the part for whoever might be watching who had sent her the text earlier in the day. Good idea, because until they ruled out one episode's connection to the other, he'd take every clue he could get.

He zeroed in on the sway of her hips, the tease of her skirt just inches below her bottom. And her legs, those damn long, sexy legs. She worked her assets with finesse. He bet many a man had gotten hauled off to jail by that vice routine years ago. Then again, maybe she'd deliberately used the moment to show Josh what he'd missed.

Hell. He'd be screwed if not for one thing. Sure, meeting her had been tougher than he'd imagined, but he'd gotten past his reaction and moved forward. Now his mind and body were on the same track. She was his assignment and nothing else. No matter how much she pushed to get him out of her way, he'd push that much harder to keep her safe. She had no idea the lengths he'd go to when protecting his assignment.

Rolling his right hand in and out of a loose fist, he slid the phone from his jacket into the palm of his other hand. A few people seemed a little too interested in her. And him. He clicked more inconspicuous photos to run through the computer later. Probably nothing, but couldn't hurt.

He could do a ten-minute countdown in his head, but glanced at his watch to make sure this time. Minutes gone. Seconds ticking. From across the street, she'd noticed his glance and peeked at the street corner clock. Why, he didn't know, because he'd bet money she planned to defy his order. Fine with him. Might as well get the first major showdown between him and Macki done.

Ten minutes, he'd said. Ten minutes, he'd meant. Ten minutes till the tone of the assignment would be set.

He leaned back against the side of the building again. He could wait.

CHAPTER FOUR

Mackenzie waited outside the crime scene tape as Detective Cummings motioned he'd be there in a second. Just what she needed, another go-round with the overprotective detective.

To occupy her time, she tried to get some perspective on her uncle's phone call earlier. Once Drake had retired as the chief of police for Riverfalls a few years back, he'd kept his new venture close to the vest. Told her he'd bought an established security firm that installed burglar alarms for the rich and not-so-rich in the Sunshine State. Told her that way he could keep his hand in the law enforcement field while he sat back safe and sound in his office. Told her his crew did the work.

His explanation had made sense at the time. Now, not so much. She needed to get home to her computer and research this OPAQUE organization, Josh Slater, and her uncle, too. Her woman's instinct said her uncle was into something more than burglar alarms.

From across the street, Josh flashed nine fingers in her direction. She snapped her hand in the air with a half-round jerk. How long she stayed on D Street was none of his business. He grinned and tapped his watch. Flashed her eight fingers. That had been one heck of a fast minute. Evidently he planned to do a minute-by-minute countdown from the ten he'd given her.

Detective Cummings walked up, nodding toward Josh.

"Who is that guy?"

"Some jerk I used to know in high school." She wasn't about to flip on Josh no matter what. If her uncle wanted her to have a bodyguard, she'd have one. At least until they had time to talk.

"Looked like more than that." The detective stepped in front of her. "Looked like you were cozying up to the guy."

"Get out of my way." She stepped to move around Cummings.

"Don't try to pull high and mighty with me, Macki." He blocked her path. "You may have already forgot Blake, but I haven't. What do you think he'd say about you throwing yourself at some guy on a street corner?"

Mackenzie sucked in air. Cummings had crossed a line. "Seeing as how it's been three years since Blake died, I'm sure he'd be the first to say, 'Enjoy life before it's too late.'"

The detective leaned closer. "Blake told me how much he cared about you. Said he'd do anything in the world for you. Anything."

"Would he? Would he really? Maybe you didn't know him as well as you thought." Her so-called engagement to Blake had been all for show on both parts. Evidently they'd deserved an Oscar for acting, because everyone who knew them treated her like a grieving fiancée. She pushed past the detective. "Now what is it you called me over to talk about?"

She knew Cummings blamed himself for Blake's death. They'd been partners for years, but when Cummings's annual physical ran late that day, Blake had charged into the crack house by himself. Hadn't waited for backup to arrive. The place and everybody inside had blown into a million pieces. From what Lieutenant Grey said, there was barely enough found to identify the victims. There'd been no funeral, only a memorial service a week later.

Cummings chewed the corner of his mouth as his shoulders relaxed. "You know I'd never do anything to hurt you. But when I saw you with that guy, all I could think of was you and Blake. "

Late to the crime scene, Lieutenant Grey joined in their conversation. "What's going on?"

She inched closer to the lieutenant's side. Anything to get away from the detective and the vibe of ownership he was giving off. Not much need. Grey had been almost as much of a dad to her as Drake for the past ten years. "Beats me. Cummings evidently thinks I can help with this case."

Lt. Grey wrapped his arm around her shoulders. "Well, I'm sure we'd all appreciate your assistance. But you should be careful wandering around this neighborhood."

This had been one of the reasons she'd quit the force a few years back. Too many people trying to protect her. Trying to tell her what to do. Who to know. What to wear and on and on and on. In the end, none of them had truly protected her.

"I'll be fine, Lieutenant." She figured he acted like a father figure to her because he missed his daughter Peggy, who'd overdosed in college. Mackenzie still missed her friend, too. "Besides, I worked vice in this neighborhood, or did you forget?"

"I remember." Grey glanced down the street. "I remember a lot of things."

"Cummings said you made the decision not to call me after the last assault. The one that had a message for me." She wouldn't back down, even if she and the lieutenant had known each other since she was two years old. "Why is that?"

"I don't have time to discuss this right now." Grey excused himself and walked toward a gaggle of reporters with news cameras.

Brushing back his gray hair, he smiled and patted people on the back. He always had liked the spotlight. Trouble was, his jowls and late-fifties age belied the tall, lanky runner's frame he carried from jogging three miles a day.

"I do think you could be of help to the police on this case." Cummings took out his notepad and pen.

"Such as?"

"Look around. Anything seem out of place?"

Did he really want her help, or was this just a ploy to see what she might already know? Which wasn't much this time. There hadn't been the usual calls from friends and snitches she'd kept in touch with on the street. No tips. No *help us* conversations. That in itself seemed odd.

Then again, it had been well over three years since she'd left D Street. She hadn't come back since the night—

"Anything?" Cummings interrupted her thoughts.

"Uh..." Mackenzie scanned the surroundings, then narrowed her gaze to the only thing that remained of the victim—the chalked outline. Small cones marked any spots the police determined significant. For some reason, the outline drew her back.

"Could she have been pushed?" She glanced at the detective.

"Maybe. Witnesses were all over the place on what they saw." Cummings scanned the dwindling group of people hugging the edge of the crime scene tape, the ones still mesmerized by the scene. He looked back at the outline for a minute. "Then again, maybe she stumbled forward and fell. Worst case scenario, it's another D Street serial victim."

"Another? How many have there been?"

Grey cleared his throat as he walked back from his interview. "Do we know the victim's name? Who to call with the bad news?"

"We're still working on that," Cummings said.

"I'm sure Roxy can fill you in on her real name." Mackenzie nodded across the street. Most of the working women floated from name to name. They were always happy to be whoever the john wanted them to be. Roxie knew the particulars of who belonged on the street, though. And everyone who didn't.

Lieutenant Grey turned to look. "Who's Roxy?"

Cummings's brow furrowed as he pointed to the woman

sipping a cup of coffee at a table across the street. "That's her. Most of the girls call her Mama Roxy. Others call her Mama Business."

Mackenzie nudged the lieutenant's arm and laughed. "I figured you knew everyone on D Street after all the years you spent patrolling the area."

"Guess I'm getting forgetful in my old age." He laughed, then pointed to the redhead in the revealing business pantsuit. "Oh, you mean Roxanne the Dancer. That's what she called herself years ago when she kept her hair some kind of platinum color instead of that firebrand red today."

She noticed Josh stepping off the curb across the street and heading in their direction. Grey seemed to notice, too. He suddenly pulled his phone from his pocket, pushed a button, and walked the other direction.

In Mackenzie's years on the force, she'd never heard Mama Roxy go by that dancer name. Had never known her to be platinum, either. Talk on the street said the woman had been around since she was twenty, even had a kid she'd given up for adoption way back when. There'd been a couple of times she'd even read everybody a letter from her daughter who'd tracked her down once she was grown.

Roxy'd been proud that night. Had cried. Too bad life had deprived her of that part of being a real mama. The way she took care of the women on D Street said she'd have made a good mother.

Quietly, the last couple of police cruisers drove away, probably headed to the next crime. Pretty soon the street would return to its loud, salacious entertainment. Gambling, girls, and—if a guy had a fifty and knew the right contact—drugs. Mackenzie remembered it only took $20 to buy a bag back when she'd first started working vice. Inflation had hit everything.

"If we're done here, I need to get going." She planned to say a few words of condolence to the women before she headed home. There'd been no sign of the creep who'd sent her the text telling her to dress in the pink outfit. At least none that she'd seen. Of course, he could have been watching from a distance. Might have just wanted to see if she'd come. Or the accident might have scared him off. In fact, she hadn't really known what to expect.

Hopefully the police would follow up on any leads they'd got. Maybe track down whoever kept targeting the women. She'd do her own legwork on the case with the street contacts she'd stayed in touch with over the years. Besides, she didn't hold out a lot of hope the police would solve the case, especially considering that in the past ten years, the police still hadn't solved her dad's death. And he had been one of their own.

Cummings mumbled something as he glanced over her shoulder.

A hand lightly brushed across her back as Josh's still-the-same male and musk scent enveloped her. There was a time she'd have leaned into his touch. Tonight she stiffened her stance.

"Time to go." Josh tugged her closer.

She wiggled free. What the hell did he think he was doing?

He held out his hand toward the detective. "We didn't have a chance to officially meet a while ago. Seemed like everyone was more interested in my phone. I'm Josh Slater. And you are?"

"Detective Cummings." The men shook hands like a couple of lions circling their territory.

"I didn't get the first name, Cummings."

"I didn't give it...Slater." The detective glared, then walked away.

She bit her lip to keep from laughing. Her evening had just perked up. The two men she liked least in the world had slammed each other. Damn, this bodyguard arrangement might turn out okay after all if it meant these two were in each other's faces all the time. Might keep them out of her way.

* * *

Josh twined his fingers with Macki's, using just enough pressure to let her know they were heading back across the street. She didn't resist. Wouldn't do any good if she did. "I meant what I said. Ten minutes, then off the street."

"You think you're one smug son-of-a gun, don't you? Well, you're not." She caught up with his stride, struggling to keep pace.

"I don't know what you mean." He didn't slow down.

"That whole 'I'm Josh' bit with Cummings. You did that to embarrass me."

Josh shook his head. "Nope. Did that to get a handle on your friends and the cops in town. By the way, what do you know about the woman with red hair? The one all the girls are grouped around."

"That's Roxy. She watches out for the others." Macki tugged to go toward them. He didn't let go. "Hey, I know these women. At least give me a minute to tell them I'm sorry about their loss."

A chill crept across the sweat on the back of his neck. He and Macki had been out in the open too long. Only half a block and they'd be to his truck with the bulletproof glass. "Should have used some of that time I gave you when you went across the street."

"Well, I didn't, so get over it. To most people around here, that woman's death is nothing but a few bucks out of their cash receipts for the night. But..." She pointed to the prostitutes gathered on the sidewalk. "Look at them, Josh. They're scared."

He'd felt the vibe as he'd waited. Somehow fear always came with a walk, a murmur, even a smell. For the past ten minutes, he'd watched the street from one end to the other of a two-block length.

The woman's so-called accident had seemed a little too coincidental. Whether it was aimed at Macki by some local-yokel jerk or came from Coercion Ten, he'd lay money the woman hadn't stepped in front of the car on purpose. Or on accident.

From past experience, Josh's instincts said somewhere on this street or in a storefront or in one of the upstairs apartments, one, if not more, assailants stood watching the excitement play out.

"I know this death isn't why you're here. But it matters to me. They matter to me." Macki's voice cracked with hidden emotion. "Please. Give me a minute. Please."

He stopped. The heartfelt plea seemed out of line for the situation even if she did have a soft spot for the women. Still...he knew that for Macki to say "please" to him was like begging. To say it twice was desperation.

"Make it quick." Josh's hold tightened on her hand. "And you stay right by my side."

He'd noticed Roxy watching him with a cross between disgust and nervous apprehension. She'd also watched Macki. Difference was, her face had held an almost protective expression as she kept an eye on Macki.

The group of prostitutes crowded around Macki the moment she stepped on the sidewalk. He released her hand from his hold and placed his palm against her lower back, gripping the waistband of her skirt with his fingers. One after another of the women came to lean on her shoulder, shed tears, give hugs. All but Roxy.

Roxy stayed where she sat. Challenged him with a dare in her look. Josh had seen this type of attitude in enemies before. Chest out, shoulders back, chin up, eyelids half closed. A good way to wield intimidation or seduction. She faced him with the guts of a person used to getting her way.

He fought back a laugh. She might coerce the girls working the neighborhood, but she was a damn amateur when it came to bullying him.

Josh narrowed his eyes, settling into his take-your-best-shot stance. "You got a problem with me?"

"What makes you think I've got a problem?" The woman adjusted her top, tossing him a wink. "Maybe you're the one with a problem."

Macki stepped in front of Josh, leaning to give Roxy a

hug. The redhead accepted the gesture and for a split second looked like she needed the sentiment. Just as quickly, she pulled her fifty-buck attitude back in place, nudging Macki away with her shoulder.

Shooting Roxy one last glance, Josh slipped his hand back around Macki's. "Time to go. Now."

He used his authoritative tone not to be mean, but to let everyone within hearing distance know he was in charge. Not only tonight, but also if he ever came back to D Street. Steering Macki toward his truck, he let the pressure of his fingers guide her. The sooner they were out of this neighborhood, the better he'd feel.

Years ago the strip had offered amusement mixed with sexual undertones, maybe a little pot. Now the vibe teemed with gritty businesses working to make a buck or a connection. From all indications, that included Roxy. Once he'd seen her up close, he'd remembered her from the night he and his friends had ventured to the strip club when they were barely seventeen. The bouncer had told them that if they were game for more excitement to ask for Roxanne the Dancer. He and his friends had barely had enough money for the bouncer's bribe and the show, which was all any of them wanted anyhow.

He glanced back over his shoulder for one final look. Yep. Roxy had been around a long time. She was showing her age.

Macki kept pace with him. "See, that wasn't so bad. Nothing happened."

Josh didn't bother to tell her she was wrong.

CHAPTER FIVE

Josh scanned D Street from the perspective of a pickpocket, a burglar, a hired assailant. Because whether Macki had noticed or not, the street had changed in those few minutes she'd taken to talk to the women.

He casually pulled his shirt from his jeans, being sure to not dislodge his gun tucked in the back waistband of his jeans. Preparation was half the battle.

Police had cleared out for the most part. The all-night crowd had come out from hiding. And business now churned with one-AM boozers, sellers, and clients. A haze from skyrocketing humidity hung in the glow of the streetlights. Or was that a cloud from anything and everything being smoked? Anyone with a lick of sense had headed out at least an hour ago.

The one remaining patrolman had eased his cruiser to the curb a couple of minutes ago. His orders were probably not to interfere unless a riot broke out or there were gunshots.

As they neared his truck, Josh clicked the key fob to unlock the doors. "Get in."

"I have my own transportation."

"I'm not going to argue about this. Get in."

"No." Her hazel-green eyes flashed with annoyance as she straightened to her full five-nine including the three-inch boots. Heart-shaped, pouty lips and long lashes made it hard to take her seriously in her pink hooker getup, but serious she was.

"Who are you, Joshua? I mean, what is it you do for Drake?"

Now? She wanted to get into that now? "You want my job description?"

"No, I just need a little more information. Such as what does OPAQUE stand for?"

"Operation Protector Agent Quantum Elite."

"And?"

Talking to the intelligent adult Macki while the mini-skirted version pushed the spiked hair behind her hooped earrings was a little disconcerting. Also kind of sexy.

"Anything else you want to know can wait till we call Drake in the morning." Josh needed to set up the secure OPAQUE communication system prior to that conversation.

"Why not tonight? I need answers, and you need his approval on what we do next."

"Approval?" Josh squared his shoulders, tamping back his temper from the edge of boiling. "Let's get one thing straight right now. I don't need Drake's step-by-step feedback. Besides, it's late. Let your uncle get some rest."

He glanced at what little he could see of the real Macki beneath the damn wig. Her eyes were puffy, shoulders slumped, and, from the way she rolled first one foot then the other, the boots were working her last nerve.

"From the looks of it, you could use some sleep, too," he said.

"You don't seem to have much respect for my uncle." Disappointment laced her expression.

His insides cringed with the idea that someone might think he disrespected Drake Lawrence. He was one of very few people Josh would stand by no matter what. Drake had taken him in, set him on a good path, and never even hinted that Josh was anything but one hell of a man with nothing to be ashamed about. Josh was the one who couldn't let go of his family's past.

Respect? Respect wouldn't begin to describe how Josh felt about the man who trusted him without reservations. But approval? Josh didn't need that from anyone.

Macki hadn't taken her eyes off of him. "Well, do you?"

"There's a difference between respect and needing him to tell me how to do my job." Josh damn well knew his duties. Actions required to keep a target safe weren't always pretty, but extreme measures were his forte. Also his load to carry in the light of day. "No one tells me what I can and can't do once I'm on a job. No one."

"If my uncle heard you say that, he'd smash you like a bug." A mischievous smile etched her lips.

Josh leaned into her space. "He already tried and lost." He leaned closer. "You see, there's very few things in this world I won't do. But the main one? I don't stay down." He brushed the tickle of her fake hair from his nose, then gently pulled the wig from her head. Her own hair tumbled free. Silky and soft and inviting.

Another dose of jasmine and vanilla filled his senses as her auburn hair rushed to frame her face. The space between them grew muggy. Heated. A racy bass beat from the strip club down the street vibrated the air as he struggled to keep his mind focused. And his breath under control. From the look of the rise and fall of Macki's top, the rounding of her breasts, her own emotions were compromised too. Would be so easy to reach out and touch her arm. Her cheek. Her lips.

"Oh, Macki..." He groaned, swallowing the words another whisper away. She was more beautiful than he had dreamed. More enticing than he had steeled himself to ignore.

He took a step back. Then another.

"Mackenzie." Slow and deliberate, she took the spiked-hair wig from his grasp, then clutched it to her stomach. "You. Call me Mackenzie."

Backfire from a car down the street along with the squeal of tires broke the tension. His hand whipped to the gun in the back of his jeans waistband. Her hand rammed into the bottom of her purse. The car sped past with too-young-to-drink kids, their shouts filling the air.

"Guess we're both a little edgy." She blew out a long sigh, pulling her cell phone out of her purse.

"What are you doing?" He reached for the door handle. "My truck's right here. I'd rather have you behind bulletproof glass driving through town."

"Thank you, but I have my own taxi with bulletproof glass. Drake had it installed a couple years ago." She pressed a number on her phone, then huffed when it evidently went to voice mail. She hung up and rang again. "Darn."

He'd heard about her fleet of cars. Heard about the authentic-looking taxi complete with lights, ticker, and always-needing-a-wash look. "Problem?"

A tiny beep on her phone caught her attention. After reading the text message, she smiled. "Nope. My driver's on the way. I'll see you at my place."

"Meaning I'm not welcome in your taxi?"

"That's right. Of course, I'm sure you know where I live." Smooth and nonchalant, she eased the oversized hoops from her ears and deposited them in her bag. She let her eyes do a quick once-over of his jeans before she looked back in his eyes.

What the hell? Macki had checked him out. He wasn't sure how he felt about that.

Not wanting her out of his sight, he spread his arms in front of him, palms up, in a pleading gesture. "Ah, give a guy a break. We're both headed to the same location."

She shook her head and smiled. "What about your truck? You wouldn't want to leave it in this neighborhood overnight. Besides, I don't give breaks to people who try to con me."

"What do you mean?"

"From what you've said, I think you're more than a guy who installs burglar alarms for my uncle." She paused.

"You've got a lot of explaining to do before I trust you again."

Were they talking about now or a lifetime ago? Either way, she had a point. Yet, he didn't recall Drake saying he installed burglar alarms. No need to make a point of that though.

Josh dropped his arms. "Fair enough."

"Tomorrow morning, you, me, and Drake are going to have a nice long talk." Her brow pinched with seriousness. "I expect answers from both of you."

He grinned. Mackenzie had turned out to be a strong-willed woman used to getting her way. This time, she deserved to get her answers. She wouldn't like them, but she'd learn to live with them. "That's fair, too."

She waved at a taxi as it angled to the curb twenty feet away, right under the streetlight. Good. Tinted windows all the way around were telltale signs this wasn't a true taxi. Number 256 emblazoned on the trunk was the number he'd gotten from her OPAQUE file. Everything looked right. According to Drake, the driver was A-1 security certified. He'd been her chauffeur for years.

Josh could argue the point of different vehicles, but it would be a small victory. He'd save his battles with her for another time. Once she got in the taxi, he'd jump in his truck and stick to her bumper like glue. With two secure vehicles, one behind the other, everything should be okay for the short ride across town.

"Gotta go. That's my ride." Macki speed-walked toward the waiting cab, shedding her pink vest as she went.

"Macki." He stood by the driver's side door of his truck, watching her walk toward her cab less than half a block away.

She glanced back over her shoulder. "Yes?"

"I know you've got that personal garage beneath Hotel MacKenzie, so don't try to lock me out." Her uncle had also told him about the private elevator that led from the garage to her penthouse.

She nodded and kept walking.

Josh tensed. Why was she still walking? Something was off. The cab had inched a good ten feet past the streetlight. He'd have never have let her walk that far without him. His peripheral vision targeted a movement in the shadows.

"Down, Macki!" Already drawing his weapon and running, Josh vaulted the fender of a red car coming out of an alley. "Step away."

Already opening the rear passenger door of the taxi, she looked inside and screamed. Stumbling backward over the uneven concrete, she fell, slamming her head into the sidewalk as she landed. A ski-masked man darted from the shadow of a building. He picked her up. Shoved her toward the rear seat of the taxi.

She braced her hands against the doorframe of the taxi and kicked backward at the man. She missed his knee, and the thug shoved harder. A flash of light ricocheted off a knife in his other hand.

Josh checked his urge to shoot. There was no clear shot without hitting Macki. Tucking the gun behind his back, he lunged forward. The assailant cried out in pain as Josh jerked him away from her and slammed his fist into the thug's jaw. The guy sagged, then jabbed a hit to Josh's ribs. His next blow already in play, Josh crushed his right fist into the man's nose. He heard the crackle. Saw the blood spurt. The man fell to the sidewalk, then got up and ran into the darkness beside the building.

A stopping screech of tires echoed on the other side of the taxi. Crouching low behind the taxi, Josh pushed Macki in back of him. Cautiously, he peered over the trunk. One car. Red. The one that'd pulled out of the alley. The passenger window powered down a couple inches, revealing another masked man at the steering wheel.

"Job's blown. Get out of here." The masked man gunned the car down the street. The taxi roared away from the curb and kept pace behind the red car. Josh rapid-fired at the retreating cab, aiming for the tires. Too late. Both cars sped off into the darkness.

"That wasn't my driver in the taxi," Macki shouted. "What's happened to him?"

Josh gripped Mackenzie against his left side and raced farther into the shadows of the street. First priority—save Mackenzie. Whatever had happened to her driver was in the past. Josh shoved her back into a recessed entryway to a shop. Keeping her behind him, he inched his head around the corner, surveying the perimeter.

Bullets had been fired. Why hadn't the cop down the street reacted? Why didn't Josh hear sirens headed to D Street? He glanced down the street. Roxy hadn't moved. Her street-wide glances continued, though. She made eye contact with him. Paused. Paused. Stretched her neck as if trying to see behind him. Suddenly, she jerked her head in the other direction.

Gut instincts grabbed Josh. Something had changed in the past few seconds. Something more than an attempted kidnapping. As if on a switch, the street had turned on them. Turned to an ominous vibe. The neighborhood threatened. They were no longer welcome. Not him. Not Macki.

Drake had been right. Josh couldn't trust the cops. Couldn't even count on them when shots were fired. He was on his own in this town. And right now he needed to get them the hell out of Dodge.

"Come on, Macki. We're nothing but sitting ducks." He tugged her close and headed to the truck.

Continually he scanned the street with his gun as he shielded her behind him. A quick glance in a storefront window showed him she had her gun drawn also. Facing backward, she was doing follow duty.

He clicked his key fob to disengage the security. "Get in."

She reached to pull herself into the cab of the truck. Couldn't. "Ahhhh...damn."

Joss lifted her inside. "Stay on the floorboard."

Running to the driver's side, he pushed Drake's number. "Coercion Ten struck. Failed. We're okay."

Josh hung up and jumped behind the steering wheel. Blowing his horn, he eased his way through the crowd still partying the night away. After a block, he maneuvered his truck onto a side street that ran through a residential neighborhood.

"I called the police." Macki's voice cracked with a couple of breaths. Slowly, she climbed into the front seat. "They're on their way."

"You shouldn't have done that." Now people he wasn't sure of would ask questions. Reports would be filed. Until he talked to Drake again, he didn't plan to trust anyone on the Riverfalls police force. "Don't ever call the police again unless I tell you to."

"Why?"

"Do what I tell you. Don't ask why." He flipped on the overhead light, glanced at his left palm. Blood? He looked in Macki's direction. Damn it! Bright red stained the side of her blouse. "You're hurt."

She raked her palm across the material. Flinched. Grunted. "Feels like he cut me."

Bright red trickled from the edge of her hairline also, leaving a trail down the side of her cheek. She must have also hit the sidewalk harder than he'd thought.

"Hospital still at the same place?" He flipped the cab light off and sped down the middle- of-the-night empty street.

She grunted. "Yeah. Same place."

Josh took every corner on two wheels as he sped toward the medical center. Blew through every red light. He should have never let her out of arm's reach.

Son of a bitch. What the hell was wrong with him? Where was the agent who let nothing and no one get in his way? Drake would have his hide. Josh slammed his fist into the side panel of the door. He'd let the damn jasmine and vanilla get to his thinking. Wouldn't happen again.

Josh calmed his insides. Got control of his emotions. Never let the victim see your thoughts. Feel your frustration. Always keep them believing in you. He blew out a long sigh. "We're almost there. A few stitches and you'll be good as new."

A police car with lights flashing chased up behind them. Another pulled out at the intersection. Another from an alleyway. Sure, he was speeding. Not enough to require three cars. Not all of them out of the blue.

"They look like they're chasing us." Listening to the police scanner coming through his radio system, she frowned. "Why are they making it sound like we're the bad guys?" She stared out the rear window.

"Good question."

She glanced back again. "Josh, you've got to stop before someone gets hurt."

"No way in hell." Even if he trusted every damn cop in town—which he didn't—he still wouldn't pull over. Not when it came to keeping her safe. Two blocks later, he veered into the hospital entrance and circled to the emergency doors. He stopped. Killed the engine.

Quick and to the point, he clasped his hands behind his head and interlocked his fingers.

Police surrounded the truck, their guns trained on him. He knew the Glock lying on the truck seat would not make them happy. His hide-away would definitely piss them off. And the knife concealed on his leg would be the tipping point.

Josh figured he and the pavement were about to come face-to-face. No big deal. He'd been there before.

"Why?" she whispered, raising her hands in front of her. "Why didn't you stop when you had a chance?"

He stared straight ahead. "I'm your protector, Macki. Let me do my job."

CHAPTER SIX

Twelve hours later, after numerous police questions, a few stitches, and restless hours of sleep, the words still rang in Mackenzie's mind. *I'm your protector.* She'd heard her father say the same words to her mother years ago.

Groggy, Mackenzie glanced at the clock on the nightstand—three PM. Had she really slept that long? The pain meds had probably fuzzed her mind. Zonked her out.

She stretched. Winced. "Well, that wasn't good."

Padding to the bathroom, she brushed her fingers across the bandage at the edge of her hairline, and a moment of nausea charged her stomach. A splash of water to her face helped the queasiness. But the quarter-plus-sized lump would take a few days to go away. She eased a few strokes of the brush through her hair, then flicked a coat of lip gloss on.

She leaned closer to the mirror over her sink. Face it. She looked like hell.

Her favorite baseball team's sleep shirt barely covered the shorty bottoms she'd wiggled into early this morning. And somewhere outside her bedroom door, Josh would be waiting. Should she put on more clothes? No, that would require more oomph than she had at the moment. Last night's fight to survive—and the pavement—had tested her resilience. All she needed at the moment was coffee. Coffee and sunshine.

A vague memory of Josh helping her to bed after she

changed clothes floated in her mind. He'd insisted on her getting some sleep, then he'd stepped back into the living room and closed the door behind him. Fine, she'd slept. Now what?

She made her way to the living room and opened the drapes. Last night, early this morning...whatever she wanted to call it had caught her off-guard. First, the woman's death on D Street. Then her own near-kidnapping. Plus, her driver had been found unconscious in the trunk of her personal taxi when the police had found the car hours later.

Question after question, report after report at the police station. Josh had been right—calling the police had opened up a can of worms. From the scrape on his cheekbone when they finally let him join her, his meeting of the minds with the police had been eventful. When she'd brushed her fingers against the welt, he'd jerked away with a look that said "Keep your distance."

The smell of brewed caffeine grazed her senses, so she pulled her favorite mug from the cabinet and poured. Savoring the warmth of the cup through her palms, she sipped. Gagged. Bitter...bitter and strong. Tasted as if the pot was freshly made, but the maker seemed to be in stimulus-needed mode.

"How are you feeling, Macki?"

She jerked in the direction of Josh's voice. Had he been watching her? She tugged at the bottom of the shirt. "I've been better."

He nodded, and she noticed the scrape on his cheekbone had darkened.

A distant ding from the guest room caught her attention.

Josh motioned toward the sound from down the hall. "I have Drake on the system. If you feel up to it, we'd like to hash some things out. Get you some answers."

He sounded so bright and chipper...so damn in control.

"What system?" She vaguely remembered pointing Josh to one of the guest rooms once they'd gotten home. And she knew for a fact there wasn't a computer in that room, so where had the ding come from?

"You'll see."

Sure, he'd lugged three oversized and heavy-looking totes from his truck and slung them on a luggage cart when they got to the hotel. Had shook his head at the bellboy's offer of help. And when the valet had tried to hand him a parking receipt, Josh had told him the truck would stay right where it was till he came back down to move it to her personal garage. Period. She'd agreed.

Crossing the lobby, his left hand had stayed at the small of her back. His right pushed the cart but stayed low, near the gun clipped at his belt. The Hotel MacKenzie staff had given them a wide birth. Probably best, considering Josh looked like a man not taking any more questions right then. At one point, a plainclothes hotel security guard had started in their direction, but she'd waved him off with a smile and their coded signal that everything was okay.

That was then. This was now. Now she wanted answers.

"Guess we might as well get this over with." She followed him to the guest bedroom.

"How's my niece?" Her uncle's voice met her before she made it through the doorway. "Ask her yourself." Josh stepped to the side.

Mackenzie set the cup on the chest by the door and walked the rest of the way in. The room had gone from a classy retreat for guests to a covert-op setting. One wall of the room was filled with a mini-computer, scanner, printer, and contraptions she didn't have a clue about. They sure as heck weren't part of her usual decor. Neither were the small video cameras that clung to each corner of the ceiling.

A couple of high-powered rifles stood in the corner, their cases scattered on the bed along with scopes and boxes of cartridges. She'd stepped into a different world. One she didn't travel.

Drake's image watched her from an ultra-thin trifold monitor, his expression serious. "How you doing, sweetie?

Heard you had to have some stitches."

She swiped her hair down to hide the bump. "It's nothing. How are you?"

"Fine." He nodded with that jerk she'd learned long ago meant he was anything but fine.

A touch of gray at the temples gave her uncle's already honed masculine appearance an edgier look. Fierce. No-nonsense. And his eyes held the same intense look as Josh's. His stare zeroed into your soul and never gave away an iota of what went on in his own. Through the years, she'd seen people intimidated by his powerful expression alone.

Today, her uncle looked tired. Or stressed. Hard to tell. But she'd bet money he was still on top of his game. She'd expected nothing else.

Josh hovered by the door, outwardly nonchalant, inwardly anybody's guess. Drake glanced back and forth between the two of them as the silence loomed loud and clear. If either one of the men thought she'd ask for an explanation, they had another think coming.

Drake cleared his throat. "You know, you might want to wear a few more clothes around the house."

"Did you forget I'm twenty-nine years old and this is my place? I'll wear what I want." She knew she should have gotten dressed.

"I just meant since Josh is staying there—"

"Get one thing straight, just because I let him bring me home from the hospital doesn't mean he's staying." That idea zinged her with a thousand tiny *no way in hell* twinges—followed by a sensible *maybe*. "In fact, if I don't get some answers, he's out the door the minute this conversation ends."

Her uncle sighed in exasperation. "Josh will be staying. And damn it to hell. Wear more clothes."

That was the final straw. She'd held her temper. Held her control. And would even admit having Josh there last night had been the only thing that had saved her. Even with all her training, the attackers had been one step ahead.

"Clothes?" Mackenzie didn't want to talk about clothes, she wanted to understand what had suddenly happened to her under-control life.

She slammed herself into the desk chair, leaning within a few inches of the monitor. "You're concerned about how many clothes I've got on? Do you know I was almost kidnapped last night?" Of course he knew. That was probably why he looked so drained. "I could have been held for ransom. Or killed, from what you guys have insinuated so far."

Josh grabbed a smaller individual panel of what appeared to be another viewing screen. Instantly his image popped into the upper corner of the main monitor.

"How did you do that?" she asked.

He pointed to the video cameras, then motioned to another panel for her. "If you use that, you won't be tied to the chair to be seen. Try it. You'll catch on quick."

She raised another screen. Now all three of them appeared.

"Time to talk, Mackenzie." Her uncle's set-in-stone expression sharpened his words. "You won't like what you hear, but you'll face it because you're a strong woman. Face the facts. Face your fear. Face the future."

Heaven help her, she was surrounded by alphas. Alphas who talked in circles and gave pep talks like they were charging into battle.

"Good. Last night needs to be straightened out." She had accepted the fact that the attack on her hadn't been random.

"I'm afraid it's about more than last night. In fact, we're going to start over ten years ago."

Heat flushed her face. That long ago would mean before her parents died. She glanced at Josh. Back at Drake. "I'd rather not go back that far."

"Like it or not, the story starts there, Macki." Josh walked to the window. Turned his back and braced his arm against the frame. "I've faced the storyline and survived. So can you."

Survived what?

Focusing on the screen in her hand, she stared into the image of Josh's steel-blue eyes. He seemed distant. Expressionless. In fact, his flat expression flashed way more ominous than the keep-your-distance clench of his jaw she'd been privy to before.

From the recesses of her mind, she realized she'd seen that expressionless look once before. Ten years ago. The day he'd said goodbye and walked away. That outer shell of a look had haunted her all these years. Right now, it appeared he had mastered the trait.

He raked his hands through his hair, and she noticed the veins in his neck, pulsing fast and hard. He might be able to hide his emotions from the world, but not from her. She knew his tells, and right now he was working hard to control whatever his Achilles' heel might be.

"Sweetie, I haven't been completely honest with you." Drake's tone was somewhere between fact, compassion, and unknown territory. "I guess I should start at the beginning...but there are a lot of beginnings and—"

"First tell me about OPAQUE." Mackenzie crossed her arms in front of her chest.

"It's an acronym for Operation Protector Agent Quantum Elite."

She waited for more. Nothing else was said. "Okay, you guys want to be that way. I'll ask the questions and I want the answers. What does OPAQUE do?"

"They protect people." Josh spoke with the assurance he was right.

"Who?"

"Innocent people. They keep them out of the hands of very, very bad guys known as Coercion Ten." The corner of Josh's eye twitched. "And if the group has captured a victim, we go in and get them out."

"You mean kidnapped?"

He tilted his head to give her his full listen-to-me

expression, one that said *been there, done that*. "Kidnapped. Taken. Captured. Different words. Same meaning. Bottom line. I do what's necessary to keep the innocent alive."

His looked dared her to ask if he'd ever failed. A good interrogator would ask. She wouldn't. Because like it or not, somewhere deep inside, she didn't want to know. And didn't want to hurt him if he had.

Her uncle cleared his throat to break the tension climbing the walls. "What Josh means is—"

"Okay, I get that the good guys are you all." Mackenzie gave a throaty laugh as she focused back on the screen. "So exactly who are these...what did you call them, Coercion Ten? And why do they want me? And don't give me that because-I'm-rich story."

"You're right, money isn't what they're after in this case." Drake nodded at her. "But anyone can be a target. You. Me. The guy at the bus stop. The waitress at the corner diner. The CEO on vacation in the Bahamas. Most everybody on this planet has something or someone that can be used as leverage against them."

She couldn't wrap her mind around what her uncle was getting at. Sure, leverage could be a means to an end. She'd used it on the force to gain information, broker a deal, get a reduced sentence. This sounded more ominous. "Meaning?"

"Some people in this world control others by blackmail. But blackmail doesn't always work, and Coercion Ten resorts to some very unpleasant tactics. The OPAQUE group levels the playing field. Decimates the odds."

She frowned. "You make it sound like a commercial for a new interactive game."

"Not hardly." Josh gulped the dredge of his coffee. "OPAQUE agents put their lives on the line to save another life. Being someone's protector is not a game you switch on when you're bored and off when you're tired."

"I didn't ask you to protect me." Mackenzie's defiant

look glared into his own.

"No, but your uncle did."

Drake cleared his throat. "Hey! You two need to settle your differences. Or put them on the back burner for now. We've got to work this out. Together. Got that?"

"I want Josh out of Riverfalls on the next plane." She'd already faced the fact that part of her could still be moved by merely the sight of him. Being in the same place might prove more than she could handle. "Send someone else."

Josh leaned toward her. "Not possible."

"Why?"

"Because you need me."

"Didn't stop you from leaving the last time." Her voice trembled with anger for a second. "I needed you then too."

CHAPTER SEVEN

The room stilled. What could Josh say? Macki was right.

Last time he'd run. Erased his feelings for her along with the life he'd had before. This time, he couldn't afford to take the easy way out. Too much was at stake—her life...his future... Hopefully, even the end to a nightmare that never eased for him.

He raised the screen. "I've got this, Drake. You can disconnect."

"You sure? There's a lot to talk about." The boss steeled his expression. "I can—"

"I said I've got this. I'll tell her everything she needs to know." Josh pushed the disconnect button, and the screens went blank.

She swiveled the seat around as Josh sat down in the corner chair.

Elbows on his knees, hands clasped in front of him, he stared at the floor. "Do you think I want to be here any more than you want me here? I could have turned Drake down when he gave me the assignment, but I didn't. I came back to protect you, Macki. I owe you that much."

"You don't owe me anything. I can always call Grey or Cummings or a zillion other Riverfalls police if there's a problem."

His head shot up to face her. "You can't call anybody. You can't trust anybody. You can't believe anything others tell you." His tone was ominous. "Like it or not, I'm who you call. I'm who you trust."

"That doesn't make sense." She eyed him with distrust, but at least she didn't turn away.

He raised his hand, motioning for her to hear him out. "Mackenzie, your name has showed up on the target list that Coercion Ten puts out. Rumor is they'll pay good money to see you dead, but luck may be on our side."

"Me? Dead? Why?"

"I'll get to that in a minute."

She sighed in exasperation. "Then tell me about this so-called luck."

"If they kill you, they have no more hold on your uncle. My instincts tell me Coercion Ten would much rather take you alive, so I did a little checking this morning. Nothing. But about an hour ago, I intercepted an update on your name. Coercion Ten tripled the payment if you are taken alive."

Her laughter gurgled deep in her throat. "Well, I hope I'm a six-figure target. Not some two-bit—"

"This is not a joke!" Josh invaded her space as images of past leverage scenes he'd broken up snapped to the forefront of his mind. He'd die before he let Macki face that kind of end. "These men are ruthless. If they can't convince someone to do what they want for money, they use people they care about as leverage. Coercion Ten started out small. Now it's international."

Her eyes widening was his first clue that she might be starting to grasp the danger. "So leverage is..."

"Leverage is a person's weakness. The one thing in their life that means more than anything else." He had always tried like hell to not care about anyone or anything that might be used against him.

His brain might know his leverage, but his brain also knew that giving in to save that person just meant they'd keep being used. Sooner or later, the leverage would be killed. He swallowed back the truth that his weakness stood in front of him. All he could hope was that no one else ever figured that out. Because Josh could never afford to give in. Never.

She took a few steps, sighed. "So the leverage can be an addiction, your reputation, a debt?"

"Could be. But the most effective leverage is what pulls at the heart of the target."

"In other words, a person."

"Usually." He wouldn't lie to her. Sure, there had been a few times when an inanimate object's emotional value far outweighed the monetary. But that was unusual.

From what he'd been able to find out, Macki was a strong woman, but everyone had their weakness. What was hers? Maybe she didn't even know she had one. To save her, he'd have to figure that out. For now, he needed to drive home the point at hand.

He clenched his fist, then released it. "When people are involved, Coercion Ten will sometimes kidnap them. Sometimes torture. Most times, the real target will break. They'll do anything to save their loved one. If they don't, then Coercion Ten will kill the family member before they finish off the target."

With each step he took toward her, she backed away. Finally, her back hit the wall. Josh closed the distance and bracketed her with his arms.

He'd said enough, should probably back off and shut up. His heart pounded with each beat. Emotion smothered him in a gut-wrenching grip. His temples pulsed in recognition as the realization he shouldn't have taken this assignment hit him like a flash of lightning. Right now...this instant...he should break away. Run and never look back before he got them all killed.

Because the one thing he couldn't allow on any mission had happened—he cared. For her. This arrangement was dangerous if Coercion Ten found out. A cold chill raced through his body. Not for himself, but for Macki.

He leaned his forehead against hers. "I'm not going to let

any of that happen to you, I promise. No matter what it takes. No matter what I have to do. You will survive."

Her essence charged its way to his core. Her hair invited his fingers. Her skin rested against his, soft and smooth and silky. How could she still have that effect on him? If he wasn't damn careful, Coercion Ten would not only take Drake down, they'd skewer him also.

She sidestepped from his touch and straightened away from the wall. "Maybe you misread the name. Or...or it's one of the other people in the world with the same name. I'm simply a hotel owner. Why would they want me?"

Josh nodded toward the monitor. "Maybe we should get Drake back on the system."

"No. You answer my question. Why would they want me?"

"There are only two people left in the family of the man who formed OPAQUE. Drake was his brother-in-law. You are the daughter."

Disbelief. Shock. Questions filled her expression. She rubbed the bump on her forehead, pinching her eyebrows together. From the change in her expression, realization had begun to take hold. "My dad?"

"That's right. Your father formed OPAQUE a few years before his death. He got tired of turning a blind eye to corrupt politicians and lawmen, so when the Feds contacted him with the idea of a covert, off-the-record organization to do things they couldn't...he agreed."

She paced back and forth across the room as her breathing intensified. Josh had been gone too long to know if this meant she was about to disagree with him or was opening up to the idea. At least she was still in the room.

"You're wrong." She stopped pacing. "My dad was a captain with Riverfalls Police when he died."

"True." Josh had to lay it all out for her. Hard as it might be, this had to be done. Now. "At first no one knew who was in charge. Then OPAQUE grew in stature. Speculation on the leader grew. Your dad must have been closing in on

Coercion Ten's leader, otherwise they wouldn't have killed him."

"Killed him?"

Josh nodded, staying quiet, giving her time.

"That means they killed my mother too."

Josh nodded again.

"You have proof?"

"OPAQUE has proof."

She walked to the window and swiped her fingers under her eyes. "You can't imagine how hard this is to fathom."

He knew how she felt. His own world had come tumbling down quick and to the point the day after the plane crash when Drake had showed up at his door. In less than an hour, Josh's world had shattered. If it hadn't been for Drake's guidance and kindness that first year, Josh had no idea where he might have ended up.

By getting him out of town, Drake had allowed Macki to still see the goodness in life as she grew into the smart, charitable businesswoman she was today. This revelation wouldn't take her to her knees, but nothing would ever be the same for her after today.

That he knew for a fact. A hard, gut-wrenching fact.

"You know, it was Uncle Drake who came to Lieutenant Grey's house the evening of the crash. I remember how you and I had gone to the ballgame that afternoon. In fact, if it hadn't been for the tickets Lieutenant Grey got for the game, I'd have been on the same flight as my parents. Instead, my dad let me stay for the game And I went back to the Grey's house with Peggy for the night." Her voice was melancholy. "Remember?"

The best Josh could do was nod as he bit the inside of his cheek. Yeah, he remembered the day, the game, their walk, their kiss, until finally—

"Josh, Josh." She nudged his arm. "Where are you?"

"Just thinking about something I need to make sure to do." Another lie. He was good at covering what needed to be covered. "Go on with what you were saying."

"Uncle Drake sat right there in Lieutenant Grey's house and said...said there'd been an accident. That the Cessna carrying my parents had crashed. An accident." She gasped on a sob she fought to control, then raised her eyes to face him. "He lied? All these years, Drake has lied to me?"

"Sometimes a lie is better than the truth," Josh replied, unrepentant. "Safer."

"For who? Him? Me?" She staggered to her feet as if she'd been sucker-punched.

Stepping in front of her, Josh looked directly into her eyes. He needed to get this finished. "Bottom line. Your dad formed OPAQUE. Eventually, your mother joined him in the work. And together they died for OPAQUE."

She didn't move except to narrow her eyes as if she could make him take back the words. "No. You're wrong. You're...you're..." Pausing, she slowly shook her head. "Uncle Drake said the plane crash was an accident. You make it sound deliberate. Murder. Murder isn't an accident, Josh. Murder is a crime with a victim. Two victims, in this case."

He nodded.

Mackenzie glanced around the room, focusing on nothing. Back into her chin-up control mode, she shook her head. "You're lying. My dad wasn't some hero type who tried to save the world. And my mother ran this hotel after my grandpa passed away. Baked cookies for the women's shelter."

He leaned against the windowsill, letting her doubts fuel her anger until it burned itself out. She'd been a cop and knew the secret lives some of them lived to get the dirt on sleaze and dishonesty. Sooner or later, the realization that her undercover work for vice, and her father's for OPAQUE, weren't so different in the ideology, Hopefully, that would ease her into acceptance.

"My mother would never have approved of that danger to the family." Mackenzie set her jaw as she narrowed her eyes. "She'd have never—"

"Your mother more than approved." Josh leaned forward. "She helped with some of the behind-the-scenes investigating work and—"

"Stop. Please stop." Macki covered her chin with her hand. "I need a little time...to...to come to grips with this. Understand?"

He longed to take her in his arms and tell her how much he understood what she was going through, but that wasn't going to happen. Because when she learned of his father's involvement, there'd be nothing good left between them. "You're right. We need to take a break."

Feet shuffling, she walked calmly out the guest room door, picking up the cold cup of coffee on the way. He'd give her time before he added anything else to the mix, so he pulled Drake up on the system.

"How'd it go?" his boss asked.

Blowing out a long sigh, Josh shrugged his shoulders. "She'll be okay."

"And you? How are you?" Drake pushed forth with his all-business tone. "I was thinking, you may not have to tell her everything."

Nice thought, but since life never seemed to give him anything easy, Josh doubted this situation would prove any different. Nothing had gone exactly as he'd planned on this assignment so far.

Of course, things could have been worse. The police could have thrown him in jail—would have if it hadn't been for Detective Cummings making a phone call to Lieutenant Grey. That would have meant Drake or the Feds would have had to be called to get him out. So staying out of jail had been one good thing.

Other things had worked in his favor too. The tech stuff had synced on the first try. Macki had gotten off with a few stitches. His barely healed ribs hadn't broken from a more-than-rough slam to the pavement. Plus, the layout of the penthouse was an open-floor plan straight from the kitchen to the living room to the balcony. The formal dining room off to the side was open to the great room. Made for a good line of sight to see intruders. Even better for setting up a perimeter if the situation deteriorated.

He needed to start thinking of this mission like any other assignment. What was working. What wasn't. How to fix what was needed.

"Make sure you get me the equipment we talked about." He flipped the usual requests through his mind's-eye view of the case. "Send me your files on the chauffeur. Plus what you've got on cops, city officials, anyone who's still around from the time of the plane crash."

"You got it."

"And Cummings. I want to know about him, too."

Drake cleared his throat. "Cummings? Why? Him and Blake didn't come into Mackenzie's life till years later."

"Just covering my bases."

"If you say so."

Josh glanced in the direction Macki had gone, sighed, and looked back at his boss's image on the screen. "I hope you know what you're doing sending me here."

"Like I said, you are the only man I trust for this assignment. Don't let yourself get sidetracked with personal feeling."

Josh laughed. "You know me. Nothing's personal."

He ended the connection. Feelings? That was a joke if he'd ever heard one. His emotions died a few days after the plane crash. The day of his dad's supposed suicide. The day Drake Lawrence told him to never blame himself. None of what had happened had been Josh's fault.

The next day he'd pushed Mackenzie away, left Riverfalls far behind, and learned to live without her. Now the past had caught up with him. Maybe this would provide the final clue in the plane crash. If this led to the son of a bitch who sat at the top of the ladder, then whatever he had to do would be worth it in the end.

He glanced at the doorway. Yeah, he'd tell her everything she needed to know to stay alive. No matter how much the past might rip him apart, saving her was priority number one. Period. If the truth hadn't come out by the time he was ready to leave town, he'd at least tell her why he was leaving this time.

Would he also tell her why he left last time? Maybe. Maybe not. He'd know for sure when he heard the words come out of his mouth. Or when he closed the door behind him on the way out of her life forever.

* * *

Mackenzie retreated to the comfort of her kitchen. She never ate much. Cooked even less. Didn't need to when all she had to do was call down to the hotel kitchen for anything she wanted prepared. Still, there was something about the kitchen that always made life's pitfalls seem less threatening.

Josh walked to the wall of windows in the living room and pulled the drawstring. "I closed the curtains for a reason."

"It's my place and I like the drapes open."

"Well, your safety is my assignment. Keep them shut."

She felt Josh's stare from across the room. "Fine."

If she didn't look up, maybe he'd leave her alone. That way she could hold onto a few more precious minutes of denial, of not losing the past she'd so carefully held onto. She glanced at her watch. Josh had given her almost thirty minutes to compose herself. Time to think. Time to accept. She had. He and her uncle would never joke about something so personal. That left only one option. Her parents had been killed and she'd lived a lie for the past ten years.

But why target her now, after all these years?

"We need to talk," Josh said.

"Maybe later. Right now, I'm hungry." She opened the refrigerator, then methodically retrieved every vegetable in the salad drawer, stacking them on the counter one item at a time. Her way of confronting the worst was to be precise, concentrate on the details of another task.

"Now, Mackenzie." His voice was no-nonsense stern. Strong with authority like the expression on his face. Evidently, refusal was not an option.

He reached to grab the cutting board stacked behind the canisters, but she jerked it from his hands. That was all she needed. If he saw the scene baked into the plexiglass board, he'd make assumptions. Ask questions. This wasn't the time to drag up their personal past. She laid the cutting board next to the mini-sink on the kitchen island, then covered the scene with the vegetables.

"Okay. You talk. I'll make dinner," she said.

Josh walked to the kitchen island, then leaned against the dark granite top. "We've laid a heavy load on you. Is there anything you need clarified? Anything you want to ask?"

Her insides twisted. One part of her wanted to make a flip remark about blue cheese or ranch dressing. Her other side held her back. This was serious. Josh had come back to Riverfalls to protect her. The least she could do was give him the respect that went with laying your life on the line.

"Let's say I believe you and my uncle." She diced the celery with precision into tiny chewable pieces, making sure not to cut too heavily into the board for fear of scratches. After all, she hadn't had the board made to actually use, but rather as a bit more comfort in her kitchen. Comfort she didn't want to explain to Josh.

He picked up a stalk of celery and crunched into the crispness, then a bit of onion and tomato. Pushing the vegetables on the board aside, he started to turn the plexiglass. She nudged his hands away and re-covered the board.

"My being a target still doesn't make sense to me. I mean, it just seems strange that Coercion Ten would even care about me after all these years." She rinsed the head of lettuce and set it on the cutting board. "I'm certainly not a covert agent like you. So why now?"

He held her gaze with his. "They want to use you."

"Against someone?"

"Yes."

"You?"

Why had she bothered to ask that question? He certainly had no interest in her. He'd proved that years ago...she popped the cutting knife against the onion...and every year since that he'd stayed away.

He laid his hand over hers. "Calm down, Macki. The onion isn't fighting back."

"Okay...okay." She laid it down, motioning that she was done. "Who could possibly care about me enough that I'd be their leverage?"

"Your uncle. Drake Lawrence."

She tilted her head in puzzlement.

Josh scooped the vegetables into the salad bowl. "After the crash, Drake kept the secrets to himself. Don't hate him for keeping you in the dark. We all thought...I mean, he thought that was best. Times have changed. Powerful people have grabbed hold of even more powerful people in the world. He couldn't live with himself any longer without acting on the secrets. That's why he finally retired from the Riverfalls Police Department."

She quietly nodded, slipping the cutting board into the dishwasher. The conversation headed toward an end she wasn't sure she wanted to hear. But if everything the two men said was true, then she came from a line of strength she had never imagined. Strength that would help her face this conversation all the way to the end. She rolled her hand at Josh for him to continue.

"Your uncle's closing in on Coercion Ten's head guy. The mastermind. The man who controls who lives. Who dies."

Josh exhaled long and longer, then inhaled deep and deeper. "Mackenzie, I wasn't hired by your uncle for this job. He's my boss. Drake's head of OPAQUE now."

She braced her hands against the counter and lowered her head. A cloud of nausea made her lightheaded. First her dad. Now her uncle. "Why isn't he the one with the price on his head?"

"Control. He's worth a lot more to them if they have him under their thumb." Josh gently took the knife from her hands and dropped it in the sink. "Ultimately, you're the one person in this world Drake would give his life to protect. You're the leverage. They plan to turn you both."

"Well, they've got another think coming. There's no way in hell I'll ever help the scum-sucking bastards who killed my parents." Two years ago, in the alley on D Street, she'd let the taste of evil trap her in its hold. Not this time. She ripped the head of lettuce in half with her hands. "And why haven't the police ever solved their murders?"

* * *

The slippery path had opened up and Josh had to respond. "From the files I've seen, there was only one lead on the case. The man who rigged the plane to crash."

"Probably made a boatload of money jimmying the Cessna. What did he tell them?" Macki asked.

"Nothing. By the time they found him the next day, he'd took his own life."

She became quiet, too quiet. "What's his name?"

Was this finally the moment to tell her the truth? To open himself to her wrath? To see the look in her eyes when she realized she'd kissed the son of the man who killed her parents? Was he ready? Was he?

No. Not yet...not yet.

As he refilled his cup, hot coffee sloshed over the rim, over his fingers and down his hand, but he kept pouring and pouring until the pot was empty. Maybe the hot pain could numb his senses, because he didn't like this line of questioning.

She snatched the empty pot from him and grabbed an ice cube from the refrigerator, then rubbed the ice on his reddened hand. "What are you doing? Didn't you feel the hot coffee?"

Sure he'd felt it, but he'd been focused on what his

answer should be.

"I was thinking about the men who attacked you last night. Trying to figure out if I'd ever seen them on any of my other cases." He swallowed the lie with a gulp of coffee, then pushed the dish towel into the coffee liquid spreading across the counter. If he was lucky, this case would end before she found out the truth.

"And?"

"And what?"

"Have you ever seen them before?" she asked.

"No. Never. How about you?" Maybe he could distract her from her previous question.

"Not that I remember." Leaning against the counter, she scrunched her brows together. "Now what were we— Oh, I remember. What was the name of the man who killed my parents?"

So much for distractions. "I don't know."

She slammed her fist on the granite. "Well, I'm sure the jerk's family knew something that could have helped. If I ever find out his name, I'll make sure they don't have a moment's peace spending the money."

"From what I know, he only had one son." Heat from the hot cup warmed his hands, but little more. "Don't you think he's probably suffered enough already?"

"Not in my book." She hand-swept the remainder of the salad makings into the bowl. "I doubt the son ever gives a second thought to what put the money in his bank account. Besides, you know that old saying—like father, like son."

CHAPTER EIGHT

Hours later, Josh's eyelids popped open and instinctively he closed his hand around the Glock laying at his side. What had he heard? He lay perfectly still, hoping to hear the sound again.

A couple hours ago he had tossed a blanket and pillow on the way-too-short sofa and spread out to catch some shuteye. The closer to Mackenzie's bedroom he slept, the faster he could protect her. He'd trained himself to sleep light when on assignment, so whatever woke him might have been nothing more than the wind against the windows. Or, it might have been the click of a lock, the slide of a door, a footstep on the kitchen's ceramic tile.

Wide awake now, he scanned as much as he could with his eyes as they adjusted to the darkness. Every window in the penthouse was covered in expensive room-darkening shades. She'd gotten her money's worth, because only a faint glow trickled in from outside.

Ka-bing. Whoosh...ka-bing.

Grabbing his night goggles from the coffee table where he'd put them before lying down, he vaulted the side chair, landing just outside her room. The muffled sound had definitely come from inside. He clicked the goggles in place, then dropped to his belly as he inched the door open. Someone inside the room would fire high the first time, giving him time to react.

Ka-bing. Whoosh...thud.

Hydraulics?

His instincts flashed—she wasn't in the room. He jumped to his feet, fumbling for the light switch as he slammed the goggles to the floor.

"Mackenzie?" He raced to the master bath. To the walk-in room of a closet. He retraced his steps to the bedroom and checked the balcony doors. Locked. "Mackenzie?"

No one could have made it past him. He scanned the room for signs of a struggle. None. Her barely tousled sheets had been turned back as if she was going for a glass of water. This didn't make sense...unless she wasn't gone. Maybe she had a safe room. Why would she have gone there instead of calling out for him?

Starting at the edge of the oversized, floor-length mirror, he walked the perimeter of the room, slapping the walls for any variation in sound. None. Where the hell was she? Every second counted.

Only other place connected to the penthouse was Macki's private garage. The one he'd moved his truck into after getting all his supplies upstairs last night. Had someone been hiding in the garage, waiting till they would be asleep to make their move?

He popped the rim of the mirror—it moved, then suctioned back in place. Hell, he didn't have time to search for the button. He grabbed the side of the mirror and yanked. With the ease of liquid, the mirror opened to the side, revealing the small elevator door.

Drake had been smart to install an escape route for her. But evidently someone on the installation team had sold out the place and the code. Or maybe she'd forgot something and gone to the garage to get it. Or... Or, he could be over reacting. If so, someone could yell at him tomorrow.

He pried the elevator doors apart with his fingers and sheer strength. The shaft before him was empty except for the long steel cables. He'd heard more of a hydraulic sound, but evidently the cables had been installed for added safety. Looking down, he saw what appeared to be a four-person elevator car stopped at the bottom.

The kidnappers had probably come in through her private garage, made their way up the elevator, and taken Macki while she slept. Maybe they were still in the garage?

He braced his feet against the sides of the elevator doors to keep them open, then ripped his t-shirt over his head and wrapped it around his hand. Timing his movements to coincide, he leaped toward the elevator cable. Grabbing the metal, he wrapped his legs around and rappelled down, hoping she'd put an escape hatch in the top of the car. If not, he'd be hand-over-hand climbing back up until he reached the one out-take place he'd seen on his way down.

Gliding to the elevator roof with a silent landing, he tugged slowly on the handle attached to the escape hatch. Distant, muffled voices caught his attention...one man...one woman...and Mackenzie. They weren't in the elevator car, so he drew his gun and slipped inside the enclosure like beer down the side of a frozen mug.

From his angle, the reflection in the round security mirror outside the open elevator door gave him a murky position of the three people. He tucked his gun in the back of his jeans waistband, knowing he had only one chance to surprise and take out the man. Macki's cop instincts would kick in and she'd follow his lead, floor the woman.

Josh charged out the doorway, his hunched position making for a slight target. Macki turned just enough. He aimed his shoulder ramrod straight at the male target's midsection and the man dropped with a thud. Josh rolled him on to his belly and straddled him, gun point-blank against the man's back.

Instead of moving to take down the woman standing by the SUV, Macki yanked on Josh's arm. "Stop. Stop, you're hurting him."

The man beneath him growled in pain, but still fought to get his hand free. From what Josh could feel against the inner side of his thigh gripped against the man's chest, the man had a gun stashed in a holster strapped under his arm.

Now both women were beating against Josh's back as Macki pleaded with him to stop.

Josh jumped to his feet, pulling his gun as he settled into his shoot-to-kill stance. What the hell was wrong with this scenario? "Macki, get behind me. Now!"

Instead she eased herself across the man on the concrete. Stretching her arm out at Josh, she flattened her palm toward him. "Stop. Don't shoot. This is my chauffeur. You can trust him. This is Ed Rodgers."

The situation settled in Josh's brain. Sure, Drake had mentioned Ed by name, said he could trust him, but that was before last night's attack. There was still the question of how they'd gotten the drop on the chauffeur. "Doesn't matter who he is. He may have lured you down here on some pretense, so him and his partner can kidnap you." He nodded at the woman stroking the man's forehead. "Give me the gun from his holster. Now!"

Mackenzie retrieved the gun and stood, handing it off to Josh. "No one lured me down here. Drake assigned Ed to me not long after my parents died. He's been with me forever. Earlier, he texted he needed to leave town. I told him to stop by, that I wanted to see for myself he was okay." She pointed to the woman. "This is his wife, Darla."

Just because someone had been okay when Drake had put them in place years ago didn't mean they were okay now. Something felt off about a middle-of-the-night meeting in a private garage. For all Josh knew, the chauffeur could have been in on the kidnapping all along.

"Get up. Nice and easy." He motioned to the man and woman still on the floor.

Darla reached to help her husband, but he pushed her away and rolled onto his side with a grunt. He struggled to bend his leg as he reached downward.

"Don't even think about it, man." Josh zeroed his Glock in on the chauffeur. "Pull the back-up nice and slow or you're a dead man. Understand?"

The man nodded as he rolled to a sitting position,

keeping his hands in his lap.

Josh motioned the two women to stand at the side wall, all the while still focused on the man on the ground. "Now pull the gun from the leg holster and shove it across the room."

"Leave Ed alone." Macki reached toward Josh's arm.

"Shut up and get back against the wall."

She stepped back. "You're crazy. What possible reason could my driver have to carry a back-up?"

"I don't know. Why don't we ask him?" Josh flicked his hand at the man's pant leg. "Pull it nice and slow."

The man complied, sliding the gun a few yards away.

Mackenzie sucked in a gasp of surprise before kicking the piece of steel farther down the aisle. She turned her focus to the woman against the wall.

Something in the way the man handled the weapon's holster release triggered a familiar skill set in Josh. One Drake taught him years ago. "Where's the knife?"

"Take it easy, fella. I'm on your side. I'm OPAQUE." Ed held his hands up in front of him, palms facing outward, then slowly reached to his pants leg and pulled apart the seam midway down the thigh. He eased his hand in, keeping the other in plain view, and came out with a knife.

Not as big as the one Josh kept strapped to his thigh in the same location, but big enough to do damage. Every agent Drake had trained knew the easy hideaway that could be quick-released with the Velcro seam. "Back-up blade?"

"No. I swear. Okay if I get up?"

The chauffeur might have only one knife, but Josh carried two. His theory, any pat-down would stop once either blade was found. Josh lowered his gun a notch and nodded for the man to stand. The guy might be who he said he was, but Josh never let his guard down. The two women walked back into the group.

Clutching his left arm tight against his ribs, the man rose and held out his right hand. "You must be Josh Slater. Drake said you were coming."

"I guess you're the guy he said should be able to help me. Did I hurt you?" Josh tucked the gun behind his back again, but kept his palm on the grip. "I forgot, what was the code name the boss gave you after your first assignment?"

"Nice try. You know there aren't agent code names." The chauffeur grinned and glanced at the two women. "At least none that could be repeated in front of the ladies."

Josh relaxed enough to shake the man's hand.

Stepping in front of Ed, Mackenzie set her jaw along with the tilt of her head in question. "Drake set you up as my driver to keep an eye on me?"

He nodded. "Yes, ma'am."

"My whole damn life has been one lie after another?" She glanced at Josh, then back to Ed. "I'm sure you've had more important work than babysitting me for the past ten years."

"I could have turned down the long-term assignment." The man straightened his shirt. "Don't think I took the job because I couldn't hold my own in the world of crime. I wasn't always a gray-haired man on the late side of my forties. There was a time I could have taken Josh and three others like him at the same time."

For a moment, Josh wondered if he was hearing himself twenty years from now. Would some young muscle call him to task? Challenge his speed? His trust? Worst of all, would an agent disbelieve him like he'd just done with Ed Rodgers?

Mackenzie touched the chauffeur's arm. "Thank you."

The man quick-nodded in response. "You're wrong about one thing, though. Keeping an eye on the daughter of the man who built OPAQUE into a group feared by Coercion Ten is more than important in my book."

She hugged the driver, who accepted the affection no matter how embarrassed his expression showed. "When I think of the times you were there for me. All the times you let me cry on your shoulder or grump at you when my day was bad. I'll never be able to repay you for your service."

"Now hold on one minute. You don't owe me anything." Ed stepped back out of her hold. "I've done my job and always will. I'll admit there may have been times you tested my will, but I didn't have to stay. One call to Drake and he'd have found someone else to take my place."

Josh grinned. He knew Mackenzie's ability to test the waters, to see how far she could push. He might have to consider giving this man a medal for staying so long. At least someone had stayed for her.

Darla, petite with a cherub face that looked old for its years, walked into her husband's hold. "Tell her what you told me."

Ed shook his head.

"Go ahead and tell her. She needs to know."

The man took Macki's hands in his. "I stayed because you're a good woman. You carried on your mother's charity work. Turned this hotel into a place to be proud of." He cleared his throat. "Most of all, every time life knocks you down, you stand back up and give it hell. For that, I'll drive you anyplace you want to go."

Ed walked back to Darla and kissed her cheek. "There now, it's said and done. You happy?"

His wife smiled, then stood on tiptoes and kissed his lips. Within moments, she and Mackenzie were huddled together in conversation.

The aging OPAQUE agent retrieved his weapons, checked them, and secured them in place, pressing his pant seam back together as the final bit of transformation. Nonchalant, the chauffeur walked past him, motioning him to follow. "Coercion Ten knows you're here."

Josh straightened, rolling his shoulders backward. "Doesn't surprise me after last night. I probably slammed to the top of their list fast."

He followed the lead as Ed walked well out of hearing of the women. When the man leaned against the hood of the SUV, Josh mirrored the stance. "What's wrong?"

"About ten minutes ago, Darla's phone rang. She didn't

recognize the number, so I answered." Ed glanced in his wife's direction. "It was Coercion Ten. They had a message for me. Either play along with them or Darla would disappear. They spelled out in real clear terms how they'd keep her alive until our child was born, then sell the baby to the highest bidder." He clenched his fist and ground it into the hood till the metal popped. "That's when we jumped in the truck with nothing more than the clothes on our back and made a beeline over here."

Josh swallowed hard, stretching his neck to loosen the knot closing in on his throat. The sons of bitches were into their game of leverage already. Leverage was hard to ignore, even for an OPAQUE agent.

Ed tucked a piece of crumpled paper into Josh's hand. "Now we've only known a couple of days that Darla's pregnant. This is a list of everyone we've told. Those names should give you a start on your clues."

Shoving the paper into his pocket, Josh realized how close he was to finding the head man. "Top priority right now is to get you and your wife into hiding."

"I already contacted Drake. We'll be ghosts in less than an hour."

"Good."

The garage door creaked and the two men each jerked in its direction, hands on their guns. Even Macki and Darla turned to the sound. Wind...nothing there but the wind snaking through the panels.

"Ed?" Darla called out.

"It's nothing, honey. You and Mackenzie finish your conversation."

Darla smiled as the two women leaned their heads close in conversation again.

Josh noticed Ed's expression. Shoulders and breathing had inched into protector mode for his wife. Rightly so.

"Sorry to leave you this way, but right now my family comes first." Ed's voice was strong and sure. "You understand, don't you?"

"I understand."

"That means you'll be on your own here in Riverfalls."

Nodding, Josh knew exactly what that meant. No room for mistakes. He'd hoped for a couple of days to get equipment set up, but Coercion Ten had been faster and were already in place. The key to the past was in this town—he just had to find it. Every hour, every minute, every second counted. There were only so many in a man's lifetime.

The chauffeur leaned closer. "One more thing. They gave me a message for you. Doesn't make sense to me, but this is verbatim what they said. 'We know Macki's weakness. Her cutting board doesn't lie. What's yours, Josh Slater? What's yours?'"

CHAPTER NINE

Twenty minutes later, Mackenzie watched as Ed and Darla disappeared out the side door of her Hotel MacKenzie personal garage. Would she ever see them again? Forty-eight hours ago, the answer would have been clear. Now everything was a cloud with one big question mark. The only thing she knew for sure was that the current danger was real.

"Let's go." Josh motioned her into the elevator, then stepped in behind her, pushing "P" for penthouse.

A loud hum echoed from above, catching her attention. Automatically, she glanced up to see the open access ceiling of the elevator. He'd come down the cable, and from the look of the bloodied t-shirt in the corner, he'd hurt his hand on the steel cord.

She'd been wrong and needed to admit it. "I'm sorry. I should have told you where I was going."

"Don't let it happen again." He punctuated the words with an overhand jab of his finger in her direction. "This isn't a game. This is our lives, Macki. Yours and mine."

She could almost feel the heat from his glare, the fire from his tone. "I said I was sorry. It won't happen again."

"Make damn sure it doesn't." He tightened his jaw, spitting the words out between clenched teeth. "I know you think you're invincible. The police officer who graduated top in her academy. Then took on the D Street johns. But Coercion Ten is different. Death is nothing but collateral damage."

Pinching her lips together, she didn't ask how he knew about things she'd done years ago. Instead she nodded, feeling her insides heat with a soothing warmth. Had Drake told him? Had Josh asked about her? Had all these years been a blur and he'd been there all along? Watching over her just like her chauffeur? From a distance?

No, Josh hadn't been there. She would have felt his presence. Seen his walk. Melted in his powerful musky, taste-of-honey scent that still clung to him after all these years.

Knowing he had thought about her through the years was nice, though.

Sure, he'd come when she'd called him late that night years ago, sobbing and hysterical that her parents had been killed in a plane crash. But somewhere between that night and the funeral, something had happened. Instead of staying beside her, he'd sat at the back of the church looking like the shell of the guy she'd walked in the park with a few days before.

After the funeral, he'd shown up at her front door, said he was leaving town. To forget about him. She'd asked what was wrong. Had she done something to upset him? He'd glanced past her, then focused on her face again and said something about her being young...naive...too naive. She remembered thinking they were barely two years apart in age. Then he'd walked down the sidewalk, gotten into a taxi, and disappeared from her life.

She shivered with the memory of how it had felt to shut the door that day. When she'd turned around, her uncle had been standing in the living room doorway, and when she'd started to cry, he'd held her in his arms, telling her to let it out, then move forward.

Josh...Uncle Drake...a taxi—all wrapped up together then. Back in her life now. Déjà vu?

"If they want to control Drake, why?" Her insides chilled to even consider being without her uncle in her life.

He was the only family she had left.

"Your uncle knows a lot of people, a lot about their pasts. Good, bad, embarrassing." Josh never turned away from the elevator door. "That means a lot to Coercion Ten. They need ways to manipulate people to make their organization stronger."

"Seems like there'd be a lot of people in the world better informed than my uncle."

Josh nodded. "True. But Drake has ramped up the takedown of cases since he took over OPAQUE. He's making a dent in their game. Costing them power. And power means money to them. A lot of money, which in the end buys them more power."

"It's a circle." Her tone said she had finally zeroed in on the depth of the battle between the organizations. "A circle of mean."

He nodded again. "Bull's-eye."

Upward movement stopped, and she keyed in her passcode to open the elevator doors. Without waiting for her to move, he charged across the bedroom, then disappeared out the doorway as she watched. She considered going back to bed. The clock showed almost four o'clock. Might be time for at least an hour or two of sleep before his security equipment arrived.

The slam of cabinet doors in the kitchen broke the peaceful silence.

"Where's the cutting board, Macki?" Josh shouted.

The cutting board?

She rushed to join him as the slam of doors and drawers continued. "What?"

"The cutting board you used last night. Where is it?" Bracing his hands on the granite, he never looked up. "Ed gave me a clue. I need the cutting board to make sense of the message." He raised his face to hers. "Now."

* * *

Josh watched Mackenzie open the dishwasher, then slide the cutting board in front of him on the granite top of the island. All the while, her eyes stayed riveted on the piece of plexiglass. Reading people was one of his specialties, and right now she was afraid. Afraid of what he was about to see. Why? Didn't matter what was in the scene.

Only the clue mattered. He had to know her weakness in order to protect her.

"I don't know what's so important about this." She raised her eyes to him. "It's just a photo I had embedded into the board." She bit her lip and blinked.

He looked down at the picture in the hard plexiglass. Sucked in a breath.

Granger Park. Summer. A light mist from the lake. Roses and hydrangeas shimmering in the glow from the boat lights reflecting off the water. His insides jerked as he gripped the board between his hands. Tighter and tighter. Memories bombarded him with the strength of iron.

Him. Macki. A blue plaid blanket in the cover of junipers and holly bushes just past dusk. She smelled of peaches. Her hair was soft against his chest. Gentle kisses mingled with her soft sounds. Sounds that still came to him in the middle of the night sometimes. Love...one brief evening of love.

A groan escaped from his mouth. God help them both.

Her weakness was him—Joshua Slater.

"See, I told you it's just a scene." Her fingers trembled at the opposite edge of the board. "It's Granger Park...over by the marina. You wouldn't recognize the place anymore...why, they've..."

He looked up into the same trusting eyes he'd seen that night so many years ago.

"They've put in a seawall and built a—"

"I remember, Macki. I remember a beautiful girl with auburn hair. A yellow dress that slipped from her shoulders." He closed his hand over hers. "I couldn't believe someone so special would give herself to me."

She walked around the end of the island and into his arms. Without thinking, he lowered his lips to hers. Their kiss—the same, yet somehow different—pulsed with life. The intensity deepened, strengthened. Her lips parted to take him in as his hands pressed against her back, pulling her closer.

As he nuzzled her neck, his palm slid lower and pressed her belly against the hardness behind his jeans. He could have her after all. This could be their new beginning. Their new life. They could go away. Find a place. Just the two of them. No more past. No more danger. No more loneliness.

His mouth devoured her as she wrapped her hand behind his head, her fingers stroking his neck in a rhythm meant to drive him crazy. She wasn't a girl any more. Macki was a woman. His woman. All his for the taking.

Her breath warmed his collarbone, then slid up to his ear as she clutched him to her. "Oh, Josh. Why did you go? Why did you ever leave me?"

Knee-jerk reaction pulled him back from the passion. Swallowing the choking lump in his throat, he regained his control. "We can't do this, Macki."

"We? Or you?" She held tight as he loosened his hold.

He raised his arms and gently pried her fingers from behind his neck. Walking out of her hold, he turned back to the cutting board and protector mode. He had a job to complete before he escaped back into his secret, solitary world again. And finish he would...without any further complications.

Once the danger was gone, he'd leave so she could find a good man to hold her every night. A good man to marry. He glanced into her eyes, then turned aside. A good man to father her children.

Before this was over, Mackenzie Baudin would spit on him and his family.

CHAPTER TEN

Mackenzie wouldn't push to see what made him run. But she also wouldn't keep living in the past. If this was the way Josh wanted their relationship to be, then distant was what she'd be.

"Who knows what this picture means to us?" His get-the-facts tone jerked her back to why he was here.

"No one."

"Someone must know, because the clue was that Coercion Ten knew your weakness. That the cutting board didn't lie." His finger popped against the plexiglass. "Someone must know."

She never told anyone about the photo she'd taken the day after Josh left Riverfalls. With her life falling apart from the plane crash that killed her mom and dad, plus a broken heart from Josh's leaving, she'd needed to go for a walk. When she found herself at Granger Park, she slipped through the bushes and cried herself to sleep. Hours later she woke, snapped a photo with her cell phone, and walked home. Since her uncle thought she'd be safer in the penthouse, she'd packed up what she wanted to take with her and moved. That was when Ed the chauffeur had been initiated into her life.

"I swear no one knows about the photo or what the cutting board means to me." She winced. Might be harder to stop caring about him than she'd thought...but she would.

Josh tapped his fingers on the plexiglass. "Okay, let's

come at this from a different angle. Who's been in the penthouse since you've had the board?"

She plopped her hands on her hips. "You've got to be kidding. I've had this for the past five years." She jabbed her finger right alongside Josh's. "That's a lot of people who've come and gone through my front door."

His brow furrowed. "You had this while Blake was still alive?"

She nodded.

"Did he know why you had this?"

She nodded again.

Josh shook his head. "He had to be livid."

"Blake couldn't care less about you. All Blake cared about was Blake." She slapped her palm on the granite and braced. "You want to know what I've done the past ten years? I waited for you to come back. Five years ago, I decided enough was enough.

"Blake offered a pretend engagement to help me get people off my back about dating. All he asked in return was for me to stand by his side as he climbed the ranks. I accepted. After all, he was eight years older. We were both mature enough to handle the so-called relationship."

Josh raised his hand. "I don't need to know all of this."

"Too bad. You opened the door. Now you're gonna listen." She filled the coffee pot with water, loaded a reasonable amount of coffee in the filter, and pushed Brew. "Blake never loved me. Probably didn't even care. To the world, he was the attentive fiancé. Out of the public view, he went his way, I went mine. We never shared the same bed. And only one kiss during the whole pretend engagement."

She held her cup under the stream of brewed coffee. "Funny thing is there were times we actually enjoyed each other's company. Times we laughed. But marriage never would have happened. We were convenient partners in a scenario that would have lasted forever if he hadn't died."

Hungry, she pulled eggs and bacon from the refrigerator.

Bread from the pantry. Josh followed her example and held a cup under the stream of coffee before replacing the pot once again. Content with a moment of silence, he leaned back against the counter, watching her cook.

"Now that you know my secrets, let's talk about yours." Mackenzie turned her attention to the bacon sizzling in the skillet. "What are your secrets, Josh Slater, or don't you have any?"

"Any secrets I have are on a very short, need-to-know list." He cracked the eggs and poured them into the skillet. "And you are not on the list. Let's get back to who's been here in the past five years."

Her mind raced between the two things she'd just bared to Josh. Which had been the worse? That she'd waited for him for the past ten years or that she'd agreed to an engagement in name only? Neither seemed to matter to him.

Ed Rodgers had been right when he said she got back up every time life knocked her down. Sometimes she might have taken unusual routes to stand the pain, but she'd kept her eye on the horizon. Always moved forward.

Being a vice cop had kept her busy. Once she'd gotten to know the women on D Street, she'd actually enjoyed her job. Just like she enjoyed running Hotel MacKenzie. Loved hosting the annual charity ball her mother had started. The gala not only kept her in the know of where the money flowed in Riverfalls, but put food on the table for a lot of less fortunate people.

She forked the bacon onto the platter as Josh scooped the eggs on their plates. For some reason, she felt free. Freer than she had in ten years. She intended to stay that way. No more secrets and no more pleasing people she didn't want to please.

Josh sipped his coffee, grimaced, and poured it in the sink. "Whew, that stuff tastes awful. Did you even put coffee in there?"

"Let's get something straight." She waggled her fork in

front of him. "This is my hotel. My penthouse. My coffee pot. I will make the coffee any damn way I like. Got it?"

He nodded.

She carried her plate to the table and took a seat. "If you don't like my coffee, then go buy your own pot. Your own damn coffee, too."

Again he nodded, walked to his bedroom, then returned seconds later with a pen and pad of paper plus his I'm-in-charge expression. She'd see about that. Just as she forked eggs into her mouth along with a bite of bacon, he crouched beside her, bracing his arms on the tabletop as he pushed the paper and pen next to her plate.

"Make a list of everyone who's been in this penthouse in the past five years. Everyone!" He leaned farther into her space, then tapped her nose. "Now. Have you got that?"

She tried to chew...fast...faster. She couldn't swallow. Couldn't talk. He'd planned it that way. Gulping her orange juice, she struggled to tell him what a jerk he was, but came up coughing instead.

He took his plate of food from the counter and walked to the sliding door to the balcony. Glancing back, he laughed. "You always were a spitfire if someone made you mad." He winked, along with a tiny jerk of his head and a half grin. "Cute. But still one hell of a spitfire."

Tossing her napkin in his direction, she shoved the pad of paper across the table. If he thought she planned to jump at his requests, he had another think coming. "Thank you for the 'cute' compliment. Too bad the same can't be said about you." She tossed the pen on top of the paper. "I'll get you the list tomorrow."

"I need the list within an hour." Josh stepped out on the balcony.

"Surely you don't expect me to come up with everyone who's ever visited."

"Then give me the ones that pop in your head right off the bat." He turned to close the door behind him, then paused. "By the way, Drake said the security items I asked for should be here by ten."

She took another bite of food before pulling the pad and pen in front of her. There weren't all that many people she'd ever allowed into her home. From the beginning, Drake had warned her against letting people get too close.

Josh paced back and forth on the balcony, shoveling food into his mouth as if fueling a car for a long drive. Glancing down at the blank sheet, her will to defy him was outweighed by the knowledge that her life, Drake's...and Josh's were on the line. For the next hour, she scribbled every name she could remember. Made a note by some as to who they were.

A breeze from the balcony was the first clue Josh had opened the door to come back inside. "You got that list?"

"Yes." She waved the pad in his direction.

He took the paper from her as he walked to the sink. After depositing the dirty dishware, he grabbed a cup of coffee. Grimaced with the first gulp, but downed the entire liquid in three swallows. He reached to pour more.

Patience thin, she jerked the pot from his hand. "Look at the list. I'll make you a pot of coffee."

"Thanks." He settled in at the table. "Did you write these as they came to you?"

"Yes. Why?" She added three extra scoops of coffee to the filter just for him.

"And this is everyone?" He ran his finger up and down the list again and again.

"Everyone that I thought of in the past hour. Why?"

"Cummings isn't on this list. Why?" He stared into her eyes. "You don't have to hide anything from me, Macki. If you two are having an affair, just say so."

She heard her own laughter before she realized she'd laughed. Grabbing the pen from the table, she leaned in and wrote Cummings's name at the bottom of the list. "There, are you happy? He didn't cross my mind because he only came around when Blake was alive. For the record, Cummings isn't my type."

Ask me. Ask me what my type is. Her emotions shouted to be heard. Her brain cautioned.

Josh didn't ask.

She blew out a sigh. "Now you answer my question. Why is it important how I put the names down?"

With one swift, sure stroke, Josh tore the list in half, wrote "Cummings" at the top of the section he kept. "From my experience, the perpetrator is in the top group of people."

"Impossible." Easing into the chair, the gravity of the situation set in. "These are my friends. My associates. People I trust."

"Well, one of them doesn't deserve your loyalty." He rammed his fist on the sheet of paper. "One of them is trying to kill you."

CHAPTER ELEVEN

Josh had spent the past few hours installing the security toys OPAQUE had sent by fake-UPS. He'd stopped only long enough to scan in the list of visitor names Mackenzie had compiled, then punched a few buttons on the scrambler to start the deep background check for each individual. If a red flag tagged one of the names, this case would be a lot easier. Not likely.

After breakfast, Macki had insisted she needed to go to work in her office. He'd said no. She'd finally convinced him that death threat or not, she still had a hotel, a gala, and charities to run. Together they had taken her personal elevator down to her office, loaded a few file boxes with work, and returned to the penthouse. She wasn't happy with the arrangement, but had at least settled in at her writing desk to go over paperwork.

All he had left to do was finish setting up security tools in the guest hallway just outside her penthouse door. Hers was the only penthouse currently occupied on the floor, so she would —should—know everyone who stepped off the guest elevator. He still needed to be vigilant. As for him, he could rig an elevator to bypass its system in his sleep. So could Coercion Ten.

She followed him into the hallway. "What are you doing?"

"Installing a laser beam that will send the system inside your place a signal that someone is in the hall."

"No one should be up here unless I buzz them up."

"Exactly. In fact, I want you to shut down this guest elevator." He took in every detail of the hall as he worked. In the center was the elevator, and directly across from there were two double doors. He grabbed the handle to open the doors. They didn't budge. "What's behind here?"

"A private freight elevator for moving furniture and such. I have the only keys to the doors and the run mechanism." She answered strong and sure. "It only serves this floor, so I keep it locked in place up here."

"Good."

They headed back inside at the same time, bumping against each other, squeezing through the doorway shoulder to shoulder till he stepped back and motioned her inside. Macki headed to the kitchen island where she'd set up her laptop. He scanned the outside through the drawn shades as he walked past the wall of windows onto the balcony. Could anyone see inside? With a long-range scope? He wasn't about to take that chance.

Shoving aside the tool chest Drake had shipped, Josh picked up the writing desk and carried it to the other side of the room.

"What are you doing? I like to look outside while I work."

"Sorry, this is safer."

Rolling her eyes, she flicked him a sarcastic salute. "Fine, Mr. I'm-in-charge."

He crossed his arms in disbelief. "Could you at least try to help me? Stop thinking like this is just another day in your life. You used to be a cop. Think like one. What if you were trying to keep someone alive?" Josh shot her a serious look. "Someone like you."

She glanced around the living room. Tilted her head to get a view from one place and then the other. "You're right. The desk is better where you moved it. But do we really need all the surveillance equipment?"

"Yes. Plus, there's more being shipped tomorrow for the

elevator and garage." He started toward his ladder. Only this sensor and the one for the balcony, and everything he had so far would be set up for sound and video. Then he'd do another thorough once-over search for any previously planted devices.

"Don't forget to move my boxes over."

Hoisting the remaining box on his shoulder, he cringed. "This thing weighs a ton. How'd you ever get this on the elevator?"

She sheepishly grinned. "I put the empty box on the elevator, then filled it."

"Unbelievable." He settled the box alongside the desk.

"Hey, I wasn't born yesterday."

Josh considered hooking onto the friendly banter, but reconsidered. No matter what he said, he could get himself in trouble.

She slowly turned to face him as he slipped between her and the desk. Her hands steadied against him. His hands slid along her body with the rotation before he dropped them to his side. She lifted her face toward his, lips parted, her gaze darting between his eyes and his mouth. How had he gotten himself in this position?

"What say we agree to be friends?" she said. "I mean, we aren't exactly protector and client. We have history. If we agree to be friends, I think both of us will feel more at ease."

For him, he'd always be in protector mode. But if this would make her feel better, then he'd agree. Didn't matter to him what they called their current situation—he called it risky as hell. They were walking dangerous ground—business and personal.

"Friends? Okay, we'll be friends. Nothing more." Her draw on him was undeniable. And he leaned toward her.

"Agreed. Nothing more." Her neck stretched upward, her lips straining to reach his. "Oh, come on...it's one friendly little kiss to seal our pact. Friendship forever."

"Friendship forever." What the hell was he doing?

She closed her eyes and waited. Grasping her face between his hands, he lowered his mouth to hers and took in the girl, the woman, he'd missed. One slow...escalating... forgiveness-kiss of more than passion settled the past ten years that hung between them. Together they ended the kiss.

She smiled. "We should get back to work."

He swallowed. "Yeah. We should get back to work."

The next couple of hours, the two of them mastered the art of being in their own world and leaving the other alone. At least she was in her own world of management, and Josh was busy keeping an eye out for anything he might have missed in his security setup. He was almost done—almost.

"There's one thing I still need to do, but I want your permission." He glanced in the direction of her bedroom, then pointed at the sensor wire dangling by the living room light. "I'd like to—"

"No. Absolutely not!" She raced to the doorway and flung her arms across the opening. Determined resistance etched her expression as she faced him. "Under no circumstances will I allow you to put surveillance doodads in my bedroom. No. No. No!"

He let her stand there losing steam for about a minute. "I would never do that to you, Macki."

She lowered her arms, but didn't budge. "What do you need my permission for?"

"I'd like to look around your bedroom. Plus the master bath and your closet."

"Why?"

"I need to be familiar with the layout of the place. Know the obstacles. The hiding places. Need to check for surveillance devices."

She blinked, paled. "You think someone might bug my room?"

He nodded. "Happens."

"Okay. Do what you gotta do. Just none of your spy stuff in there." She headed back to her laptop.

Walking into her master bath, his senses sucked in the hint of her bath scents and perfume. Without thinking, he brushed his hand across the velvety-soft blue towels stacked on floating shelves. His still-bare feet sunk into plush scattered rugs, then stepped on cool, creamy marble. Whoa—sensory overload. One glance at the Grecian tub and the oversized shower with multiple spray heads told him hours could be spent in this room...just him and Macki.

He jerked his head to the side. What had he heard? Imagined? A quiet sound that wasn't there, yet was. He headed for the bathroom door.

"Josh! Hurry."

He had his gun drawn before he reached the living room. Across the open expanse, her wide-eyed, mouth-parted pale expression as she stared at the laptop frightened him. Beside her in a flash, he angled the computer screen to his view.

—How you doing, Macki? That was a nice little kiss you gave your boyfriend for moving your desk. BTW, I like your outfit. Green looks good on you.—

"Son of a bitch." Josh didn't need to look. She had on a pale green, front-button blouse with three-quarter sleeves. In every assignment, he made a mental note of how the person he protected looked at all times. Easier to give a description. Easier to find in an emergency. Easier to identify in the worst-case scenario.

There was no time to lose. The cat-and-mouse game had changed. Somebody had eyes on both of them right now.

He reached for her in protector mode, putting his back to the windows as he stepped in front of her. "I wish you had a safe room so I could stash you there."

"You're not stashing me anywhere, buster." She pulled away and ran to her closet. A moment later, she returned with her own gun. "I'm with you all the way."

"Then grab your laptop and get in my bedroom. Now. And you do everything I tell you. The second I tell you. Got it?"

"Got it. But I—"

"No buts. Trust me. A second can mean the difference between life and death."

Josh motioned her down the hall to his bedroom security center. She set the laptop on the side table just as an incoming message binged. He stepped up behind her, staring at the screen.

—Macki, Macki, Macki...Now where did you and Mr. Slater get to? Oh, I bet you two wanted to spend some quality time together. Don't let me scare you.—

"Move over." Josh nudged her aside and typed a Reply message.

*Thanks for the clues, maggot. One leads to another and another and another. Finally, there I am, your worst nightmare. Come to life and standing on your doorstep. Don't try to figure out your mistake. I doubt you've got the brains to know a clue when you see one. JS*OPAQUE*

Grinning, he pushed Send. "Stupid bastard."

She noticed Josh's open expression had etched into a chiseled line of concentration. His footsteps had changed into forceful plods of determination. The hardened muscles in his arms and neck now supported corded veins pulsing with adrenalin and power.

Stakes had changed. Ante had upped. He knew it. She knew it. Staying ahead of the perpetrator was more important than ever, and Josh's signature laid him out there for Coercion Ten. Said bring it on...I'm not afraid of you.

Facing down all her fears, she forced a smile. "Great bluff."

He shoved past her, heading to the door. "No bluff. Fact. Cold. Hard. Fact."

CHAPTER TWELVE

Macki had watched the last ten minutes tick past on the laptop in Josh's bedroom. There'd been no more e-mails, so his thanks-for-the-clue message must have hit a nerve. He'd contacted OPAQUE with an update, letting her listen to everything being said. Then he'd rummaged in a box and come up with a scrambler device which he said should take out anything within the perimeter of the penthouse, balcony, and guest hallway.

Assured that they would be safe and unnoticed for the time being, Josh had searched room by room, culling each one out of what he referred to as camera potential.

Judging from his demeanor, this assignment had fallen into place like pieces on a chess board. She was the target. He the protector. To win the game meant keeping the target alive at all costs. Costs that included the protector's life. She didn't like the implication.

He stepped back inside from the balcony, holding the rifle scope in his fist. Already, he'd searched and security-scanned every room in the penthouse. The guest hallway. The skyline and surrounding buildings from every window and balcony. Nothing. Nothing. Nothing.

While pulling the drapes back in place he shook his head, his expression tense with frustration. "Where the hell is it?"

"Maybe if you tell me what clues you got from the e-mail, I can help." She ventured toward him with a glass of ice water.

"The first e-mail told us he could see you." Josh gulped down the liquid and shoved the glass back in her direction. "He knew you had on a green top."

She rolled the cool glass across her forehead. "And he knew we kissed."

"Right. Plus that I'd moved the desk."

Josh picked up the security scanner and programmed in a different setting, then started around the room again. "The e-mail back in the bedroom filled in that he had no idea where we had gone. Tells me his camera is in this area." Josh spread his arms as if taking in the living room, kitchen, balcony.

"So why did you search the other rooms and outside before this area?"

"Never hurts to cover the long shots." Josh appeared to zero his focus in on where he'd moved the desk from and to, plus where the two of them had kissed.

She followed his movements from afar. This search was different than the one thirty minutes ago. This one was defined. Almost like he had gridded a map in his mind. Step by step, he was working backward from the desk and sofa.

"Do you think he can hear us?" she asked.

"No. He'd have said something in the e-mail to flaunt his power." Josh walked the zone bit by bit and back again, then stepped out her front door into the hallway he'd secured earlier.

She stood at the open doorway, watching him stare at the painting hung on the wall opposite the bookcases in her penthouse. Slow and steady, he lifted the Monet-type landscape picture from the hanger, letting it slide through his palms to the floor. He swiped the scanner around the edges, then stopped, motioning her to his side. She glanced down to where he pointed. A long slender strip lay along the edge of the gold frame. Barely visible if you weren't looking for something.

"Transmitter?" A cold shiver trickled across Mackenzie's shoulders.

"High-tech one from what I can tell." Josh shoved the scanner back in his pocket. "That means Coercion Ten paid you a visit before I installed my own equipment."

She felt lightheaded. Clammy. Bright lights blurred her vision. Striving to push off the panic that came with knowing how close someone from Coercion Ten had been to her, she stared at the boats floating on the serene print of smudgy pastels. What would have happened if they'd come inside while she slept? If they could override her elevator system, what was to stop them from coming through her door? Would she have disappeared, never to be seen again?

"You okay?" Josh pulled her into a shoulder hold, easing her close to his side. "You don't look so good."

Grabbing hold of his hand, she sucked in air and widened her eyes. What was wrong with her? She was an ex-cop. She'd been involved in a hell of a lot worse. Heard stories that would put this to shame. Still, she couldn't get over the fact that this was aimed at her. This was different. Scary and sickening.

Finding her center once again, Mackenzie exhaled, willing the chill on her cheeks aside. She straightened out of his arm ready to face the moment. "I'm okay. What have we got?"

Lifting the transmitter strip from the frame, he shrugged as they went back into the penthouse. "For now, it's scrambled. Once I deactivate it, I'll ship it off to OPAQUE. See what they can get from—"

She jumped at the ring of her own cell phone.

He stood still as stone. "Who is it?"

"Blocked." Heart racing, she deeply inhaled as she pressed the speaker button. "Hello."

"Hey Macki, it's Lieutenant Grey. How you doing?"

She exhaled with relief and turned to walk to the kitchen. Josh kept pace with her, leaning to hear the conversation. Finally he stopped her, and pulled the phone between them, rolling his other hand for her to continue the conversation.

"I'm fine," she said.

"That's good." Grey cleared his throat. "I know you were pretty shook up at the police station the other night."

Josh grimaced as his brow furrowed and his expression hardened even more.

She understood his reaction. "I didn't think you were there."

"I wasn't. Didn't know anything about it till I saw the report later that day. Even Cummings didn't mention you, when he contacted me about Mr. Slater being detained. Boy, did I give the guys on duty what-for at not having called me." Grey chuckled. "Seriously, are you sure you're okay?"

"No need to worry. It was only a bump on my forehead." She touched the still-swollen spot. "Is there something you needed?"

"Sounds like you've got one of those ritzy events to get to."

Cringing at the same words he'd used for years, Mackenzie realized that though her world might be falling apart, at least a few things could be counted on to stay the same.

"...Or maybe the guy with you at the station is still around and—"

Josh straightened, pulling the phone out of her hand. "Hello. Lieutenant Grey. Josh Slater here. Remember me from high school years ago?"

"I remember." Grey went from considerate to cold. "You were the kid hanging around after football games. Trying to get Macki and my daughter to stay out past curfew."

"That was me. Guess I owe you an apology for being such a young punk."

The sound of a door slamming on Grey's end echoed through the phone. "The only person you owe an apology is Macki. You walked out on her when she needed you most."

Josh stopped his pacing, glanced in her direction. "Well, we've decided to let bygones be bygones. She offered me a place to stay while I'm in town. Looks like I'll be around for a while."

Quiet enveloped the three of them. A long quiet.

Ready for this conversation to end, Mackenzie took her phone back. "Was there something you needed, Lieutenant Grey?"

"There's a terrible echo with your speaker phone. Shut it off." Grey spoke like someone giving orders.

Josh nodded and stepped up close to her side.

"Sorry." She pushed the speaker off, then tilted the phone between their ears. "Is this okay?"

"Sure. The reason I called is to invite you to my annual barbeque tomorrow. Starts about two. Lasts till the beer runs out."

Josh shook his head no.

She nodded yes.

Josh shook his head along with a quick jerk of his hand this time.

"Maybe I can sweeten the pot." Grey cleared his throat. "Cummings said he might stop by."

"You call that sweetening the pot? How many times do I have to tell you that Cummings and I have nothing in common?" She struggled to leave Josh's side, but he tugged her back.

"Blake Ransom." Grey's somber tone accentuated the word. "You've got Blake in common."

"A dead man is not something to base a relationship on." She jerked away from Josh and crossed the room. "I'm sorry, but I'll need to turn down your barbeque offer. Maybe another time. Tell the family—"

"Barbeque!" Josh shouted from his side of the great room. "You can't turn down barbeque, Macki."

What the hell? Why would Josh change his mind? He'd barely let her leave his sight since he'd gotten to town. After what had happened with the e-mails today, she figured lock and key scrutiny would be next on his list. Why the sudden change?

Grey's laughter resounded through the phone. "The man's right. Nobody in their right mind turns down barbeque."

Josh pointed to his chest and to her, made the walking sign with his fingers and then pointed to the phone. She should have known.

Mackenzie clicked the speaker back on. "Okay. I guess I'll come...on one condition."

"Anything." The lieutenant smoothed his tone.

"I bring Josh."

"Sure. Nothing I'd like better than to be part of the return of the prodigal...punk. See you tomorrow."

Josh's expression flattened before the line went dead.

"I don't think Lieutenant Grey likes you." Mackenzie ventured a comment.

"Most people don't." Josh shrugged. "He's just one more."

They stared into each other's eyes as if they could penetrate a barrier to the other's soul. She might have a few secrets, but none worth hiding forever. But Josh? The blockade in his look said his secrets were deep. Very deep and very dark.

She blinked. "Doesn't it bother you?"

"I like it that way. Means I've got the edge."

Inside, her cop instincts smiled. "You've never, in your entire career, let a case become emotional?"

"Nope."

"What about your personal life? Got any emotions there?"

* * *

Josh had to admit Macki played the questioning just right. Lured him in...let him think he'd got away...then went for the kill-question. She did good. He did better. What was her simple question compared to being interrogated by bastards who didn't care if he lived or died? The best way to counter her interest was to ignore the question.

"Time to zero in on the camera."

He pointed his attention back to the corner where the desk had sat. To the bookcase between the balcony windows and the front door. Starting at the bottom, he checked each item on each shelf. One by one he ruled each knickknack and book out, laid them to the side.

Moving up to the next shelf, he picked up a pinkish-colored hunk of crystal. Strange color for the room's decor. He ran his scanner over it. Nothing. He tumbled the stone in his hand, weighed the piece in his palm. Seemed off for the size of the piece, so he stepped onto the balcony to get a better look at the consistency in sunlight.

Macki stepped up behind him, and he bumped into her as he turned around. The crystal tumbled from his hand and hit the concrete with a crackling sound. A tiny, barely audible whine pierced the air, then stopped. He knelt by the still-intact stone and scanned. Click...click...click, click, click...the screen flashed to bright green.

"Bingo." Josh picked up the piece and walked back inside. "What is this?"

"I was told it's a good luck stone for healing. For the powers to work, it has to stay in the same location as the first time you put it in your house." Her brow pinched a bit as she sucked in a breath.

"Don't think so." He pulled the knife from his leg holster. Scraped it around the edges, but didn't find a knick for the blade to slide into. He bet his next paycheck that the stone wasn't a solid crystal. "Where'd you buy this?"

"It was a gift." She twined her fingers together, then twisted.

He was picking up on each little tell from Macki. She was nervous or confused or afraid of something. "From who?"

"Roxy."

"You mean Mama Roxy down on D Street?" He'd done a little investigating of his own the first night he got to town. The lady had been there longer than most anyone else. She seemed to wield the most power besides the pimps. Sometimes more. Plus she had a rap sheet varied enough to get her some time, but no time showed up.

Macki nodded.

"Roxy wasn't on your list of people who've been here. How many other people have you forgotten?" He slipped his knife back in its holster, then grabbed a ball-peen hammer from the tool chest.

Holding up her hand as if to stop his questions, she followed him to the kitchen island. "Roxy wasn't on the list because she's never been in my home."

He spread a towel on the granite counter, then set the piece on top. Motioning for her to be quiet, he tapped the rock with the head of the hammer. He tapped again. Listened. Again. Listened. Nothing indicated it was anything more than a solid rock.

"I'm gonna owe you a new whatever you want to replace this thing." He wrapped the towel around the rock and hit the piece with a good blow of the hammer. Nothing.

He angled the piece tighter into his hold and pulled the towel taut. Times like this, his black belt in karate came in handy for focus and power. He narrowed himself into the head of the hammer. Stilled his breathing, slow and measured. Moving only his wrist, he popped the hammer up and down in the blink of an eye. He felt the give of the stone.

Peeling back the cloth, a small, square section came loose from the back of the piece. He peered inside the crystal, then slapped the piece with his palm to loosen what he saw. A miniscule camera fell onto the granite countertop.

Another piece of the puzzle had just fallen into place. Hard to believe Roxy was involved, but this, along with the fact her name had been on the list Ed had given him of people who knew Della was pregnant, sealed the lead. But if Roxy was involved with Coercion Ten, no telling who else might be. He'd learned a long time ago that a case had a lot of tips and trails to follow. No matter where they led. None of this measured up to where he thought this case would go, but he'd follow the clue.

"How long have you had this piece?" Josh kept his voice calm and noncommittal though his insides were already ten steps ahead.

Her complexion paled as she picked up the crystal. Turning it one way and the other, she appeared to be trying to wrap her brain around what she was seeing.

He touched her arm. "How long, Macki?"

"About two years." Chin quivering, she clutched the object to her heart.

Most cases were centered around recent upheavals in the everyday world. More and more, this one appeared to have been building for quite a while. Something was off with this scene, though. She should have been screaming mad. Furious at the thought someone had set her up. She wasn't. Why?

Turning to face him, she bit her lip and laid the piece back on the counter. She tipped her chin upward and looked him in the eye. "I know the routine, Agent Slater. You know what you have to do. Go ahead, ask." She sucked in a body of air. "Ask me the next question."

He steeled for the answer. "Why did Roxy give you the so-called healing stone?"

"Because she's the one who found me bruised and bleeding in an alley off D Street. She carried me to her place. Cleaned me up and held me as I cried." She paused, her hands trembling against each other.

What the hell was she talking about? Drake had conveniently left this part of her life out.

"Don't you see, Josh? Roxy can't be behind this. She's the one who saved my life that night."

CHAPTER THIRTEEN

Mackenzie poured a shot of bourbon and then lightly touched her lips to the smooth liquid fire. Josh had gone to store the crystal, camera, and transmitter in his room. Said he'd ship it to OPAQUE for analysis tomorrow.

Walking back to the counter, he gave her a stonewall stare. She ignored the expression and poured him one, too. At least he had the courtesy to roll the glass between his hands before setting it to the side. He didn't need any courage or release. Downing a gulp of her drink, she felt the sting all the way to her core. She came up spitting and coughing. Eyes watering, she sucked in a deep breath, then exhaled.

"Drink a lot, do you?" Josh reached over to the mini-sink and added a good dose of water to her glass. After setting the drink back in front of her, he climbed on the high-top chair across the counter from her. "I know this won't be easy for you, Macki. But the bottom line is that we've got to fit the puzzle together. Can you help me?"

"You mean tell you what happened that night."

He nodded. "Plus anything else that seemed off around that time."

She climbed on her own stool. This might be the hardest thing she'd ever had to do, but there was no one she'd rather have in front of her right now. "Guess you think I'm too close to the situation to know what...who to trust."

His silent, noncommittal answer said everything.

"Okay. I'll make it short and to the point." That she could do. Details could wait until he asked for them. And the agent inside of him would ask. She trailed her fingertips across the almost clear drink, then placed them against her tongue. Much better. She smiled. Maybe having that night out in the open would dilute the pain she kept hidden from the world.

"Whenever you're ready." Josh settled back on the chair.

"I'd been working vice on D Street for a couple of years. Sure, a few people didn't like me being there. Nothing major." She inhaled. "If there wasn't a big sting going down, then I made my own rules most times. Get the perverts off the street. Book the dealers. Make sure the runaways don't get pushed into a stable. Plus, I made friends with Roxy and some of the girls."

She stared off in the distance for a bit before returning her gaze to him, smiling. "You know, I collared a lot of men I know from my charitable endeavors. To this day, they don't know it was me who got them taken downtown."

Josh grinned along with her, but she was smart enough to know that was the agent following the routine. And he was right to be making things easy for her to remember. She wondered what the man inside him thought of her. What he would think of her in a few minutes?

"Nothing unusual that night," she said. "It was about one AM. Raining. Not many people on the sidewalks. I tagged a guy cozying up to one girl and then another. Never saw him before, but something about him had everyone grouping together. Not making eye contact.

"I eased over to him. No...wait. He gave me one of those hand waves to come and talk. From there I latched on to him...waited for the hook to set. Then he took me by the elbow. You know, real gentleman-like. He smelled of expensive men's cologne and beer. I remember thinking that didn't match up. Then we walked a ways down the street, discussing arrangements."

She gulped down a slug of diluted bourbon. Her hand

started to tremble, and she clutched it into a fist, covering it with the other hand. "I reached to call my backup, and the man slapped his hand over my mouth. Then someone yanked me into an alley. There had to be two, maybe three of them." She caught herself gasping for a breath. "They didn't just rough me up, they hit me. Hard. At first I fought. Finally, I just tried to protect myself from the next blow."

"Did they—"

"No. But they let me know they could do whatever they wanted. Then...then..." She couldn't get the words out. Why? It wasn't the worst part, only the scariest. But not saying it out loud meant admitting the threat still frightened her. She clasped her hands beneath her chin, tension building in her mind, her muscles, her emotions.

Josh broke eye contact. Walked into the living room as if looking for something. She knew different. He was letting her calm down before he questioned. The man was good at what he did. Watching him move eased her back to herself. She grabbed a bag of chips and poured them into a bowl, setting them on the counter between the two of them as he walked back and sat down. He rolled his hand for her to continue.

"At some point, they yanked my wig off. Barely able to breathe, I curled against the wall until a man brushed the side of my face with his fingers. And then he said something strange. He said I looked like my mother." She heard the tremble in her voice, but shoved it aside. Only a few more sentences. Another minute. Then she'd be free of the secret. "Told me to consider that night my one and only warning. To take my pink-fringed vest and get the hell off D Street. Go back to my world at Hotel MacKenzie before I had an accident like my mother."

Hearing the words come out of her mouth seemed surreal. This was the first time she'd let herself relive the entire scene. Why hadn't she told Drake? Told the police? Told somebody who could have helped her find justice? She felt the wetness rolling down her face, but she wasn't sad, wasn't scared at having shared this with Josh. Her breaths came ragged as she fought to gain control of lost emotions.

Memories flew apart, angling to the forefront of her mind. "Oh my gosh, I just remembered. He said something about Drake getting the message. I...I thought he meant my uncle would be the one notified of my death. I couldn't let that happen. Not again. The next day I left town. Never told him any of this. Once the bruises healed, I came back to Riverfalls. My part of Riverfalls."

She felt Josh fold her into his arms. Felt good. Felt needed. Felt right. His gentle hold, his cheek against the top of her head, combined to give her strength enough to let the sobs come, and once the crying was finished, she felt lighter. The tears hadn't made her weak, instead they'd released her enough to shatter the fear inside.

"Everything'll be okay, Macki. I won't let anyone hurt you ever again. I promise." Josh kissed her forehead. "Okay?"

She shook her head, crushing against him to absorb all the courage he had to give. They both knew he couldn't always protect her, but the promise was all she needed. Whether he knew it or not, she'd do the same for him. After a while, they leaned their separate ways. The pull of smile wrinkles tugged at her face. His returned the expression. The worst was past.

Walking around to his side of the counter, he looked perplexed. "Even if you didn't push your call button, backup should have seen you weren't on the street. Why didn't they come?"

"About ten minutes before, an all-night diner was robbed four blocks over. Customer and waitress shot. I told the squad car to go."

"Convenient, don't you think?"

She ran the coincidence through her mind. "The squad was only a couple minutes away. Besides, I was good at keeping the collar around long enough to pass him off to another undercover cop."

"What happened at the diner? Did it turn out to be a major case?" Josh asked. "Were the victims killed?"

"Minor flesh wounds. In fact, the jerk forgot to empty the register." Her cop instincts kicked in. "You're right. Too convenient. I was set up."

Josh nodded. "Seems like Coercion Ten's been in your life for quite a while."

A hard fact to wrap her brain around, but as Josh said... Cold. Hard. Fact.

"By the way, the guy who threatened me...he dislocated my finger and told me it would be worse next time. Then I heard a car drive off. Wasn't long after that Roxy found me." How? The alley was dark. "I must have called out for help and she heard me."

Shaking his head, Josh grinned. "That's something we're going to ask her. Along with a few questions on the crystal with the camera in it. Did she tell you where she got the rock when she gave it to you?"

"Roxy didn't directly hand it to me. You see, a few years back, Darla worked on D Street. She cleaned for me to make extra money. Then Ed took her in and they got married."

Mackenzie walked toward her bedroom. She couldn't wrap her head around much more today. Too many names. Too many coincidences. "Anyhow, Darla said Roxy called, wanting to send me a gift. Asked her to bring it to me. Even told her where to place it on the shelf. Said to tell me to never move it from the spot or the healing power would be lost."

Josh straightened, grabbing his cell phone. "Who put the crystal on the shelf?"

"Darla."

"And what did Roxy say when you thanked her for the gift?"

At the moment, Mackenzie felt like a failure for letting fear steel her in its grip all this time. She should have evaluated what happened that night. Made a report. Solved the crime. Instead, she'd let others control her movements.

"I never thanked her. In fact, the other night was the first time I'd seen Mama Roxy since the night she saved me." Mad...at this point she was mad as hell at a lot of people, but mostly herself. "Don't you see, I was so damn scared I ran from who I was and never went back. You have no idea what it's like to run from the past. It's hell, Josh. Pure hell."

He grabbed a glass of water and gulped it down, again and again. Then turned the glass upside down on the granite. "So you don't know for sure that the crystal came from Roxy?"

"No...I guess I really don't know who gave me the crystal." She narrowed her thinking to keep from going crazy with all the what-ifs flooding her mind. "What's been happening all these years?"

"Plain and simple, someone's been setting you up. Like money in a bank, they've had you in their sights for a rainy day."

"Then why send the email? Why open themselves up to you finding the device? How can that be leverage?"

He leaned heavy on his hands braced against the counter. "They're trying to mess with my mind. To throw me off balance."

She eased her hand next to his. "And have they succeeded? Have they messed with your mind?"

He cocked the corner of his mouth and winked. "What do you think?"

CHAPTER FOURTEEN

Josh's insides rumbled with trepidation the next day. The small get-together barbeque scenario had turned out to be anything but small.

Car after car lined both sides of the street in front of Lieutenant Grey's house, then stretched a good long ways in both directions. How many people were invited to this barbeque anyhow? Around the corner and halfway down the block, Josh angled his truck into a slot between a white minivan and a red roadster. Evidently everyone from family guys to men of influence had shown up.

"I don't like this." He glanced around, then pulled the key from the ignition.

Macki checked her reflection in the visor mirror. "Since you got to town, you don't seem to like a hell of lot. So get over it. I'm not a fool, I paid attention to what my uncle said on the phone this morning." She flipped the visor up. "I promise I'll be careful. Now let's go enjoy the party."

Last night on the system, he and Drake had agreed that holing up in the penthouse wasn't going to draw Coercion Ten out. They'd devised some outings where Josh felt he could be in control of Macki's whereabouts with minimum public spaces. The barbeque, her charity gala meetings, dinner at a restaurant that lived by reservations and had a side entrance, and on and on. That way Coercion Ten would need to make a direct move, which would be easier to spot and deflect.

When the three of them had shared a conference call on the secure line this morning, there had been no sugarcoating the risks of leaving the penthouse. Drake had laid down some guidelines. Macki had jumped at the chance. Against his gut instincts, Josh had agreed.

"Oh, I forgot to show you something before we get out of the truck." He reached into the front pocket of his jeans and came out with a small key fob. Round, it looked like a cheap embellishment with an O-ring attached.

"That? You need to show me that right now? Right this instant, that is more important than anything else in the world? You are a piece of work, Joshua...a piece of work."

He grabbed her hand and dropped the piece in her palm. "Yes, Macki. That is the most important thing in the world you will ever hold. Look at it and make sure you understand what I'm saying."

She listened, turning the fob over and over, rubbing her finger across the letters. "What is it?"

"An emergency call for backup. Not just for OPAQUE. If that initial is crushed into the backing, a signal goes out to OPAQUE, the FBI, and any local police department that an agent is in trouble." The piece had saved his life a couple of times and to him, that was the only lifeline he had on an assignment. His only trust was in that fob, nothing and no one else.

"Why show me the piece?"

"Because you need to know what to do if I ever go down."

She narrowed her eyes, but kept her mouth shut. He realized she wouldn't like the cold hard facts, but he also knew she'd understand the need to know.

"What do I do?"

Josh's gut cringed at the thought the instructions would ever be put in play by her. He didn't like the idea of the end being near for himself, even more so for her. "Grab the fob from my watch pocket and smash it good. If you plan to run, take it with you and smash the fob when you get to a safer location. Then wait there. Can you promise you'll do that for me? That if I tell you to go, you'll save yourself and call for help?"

"Yes. I can do that."

"Promise me, Macki." That would be the only way he'd know for sure she'd follow his instructions. She kept her promises.

The quick tremble of her chin before she bit her lower lip told him she fully understood what was being asked of her. He knew he'd made her more than a little angry last night. Knew she'd needed him to carry her to bed and love her till she cried out his name. But he couldn't do that. Wouldn't be fair to lead her on to what would be sheer disaster down the road.

At least, he gave her credit for not going ballistic on him today. Of course, the day was still young. And if she did, he'd stand there and take it like a man. He couldn't have her, but he could damn well help her even if it meant his insides were shredded and raw by the time this assignment was over.

"I promise." She handed him the key fob, and he tucked it back in his pocket. "Now don't you think we should get out of this truck before we're overcome with heatstroke? Besides which, we need to mingle with the people on your they-could-be-the-bad-guys list."

"Might as well." He hated barbeque...hated all the play-nice conversations that interlaced every get-together he'd ever been to. Glancing around one more time, he jumped from the driver's-side door. "Stay there and I'll come around."

She met him by the passenger back bumper. A blush of lip gloss accentuated her tan, and sun-bleached hair framed her face. For a moment he had to force himself back from believing they were simply a couple on their way to a barbeque with friends.

Of course her no-eye-contact gaze told him something was still off between them. Had been ever since he'd said good morning on his way to get his first cup of coffee for the day.

"Okay, let's review a few things." He cringed with the thought of all the ways this afternoon could turn bad. "First, stay within sight of me at all times. No jumping in the pool. No wandering inside or outside without me knowing. Got it?"

She inhaled a deep, loud breath and bit the side of her lip. He could tell her inner steam engine was about to explode. Too bad. This assignment was his, and he planned to follow his usual routine because he hadn't lost a client yet. Didn't plan to start today.

Swiping the sweat from his forehead, he couldn't believe the heat and humidity was still as intense as the first night he got to town. Dressing had been a thought process that started with the chest band holster for concealment, then the gun. And as an afterthought, clothing that might give relief from the weather.

"If I yell 'ground,' you hit it without thinking. Same goes for you. If you see anything suspicious, just yell and I'll react." He calmed his breathing and his mind. "And when I say it's time to go, we go. No questions asked."

As they walked, he reached out and took her hand. She jerked away. He rested his hand against her elbow to guide her and she stepped aside. He held his crooked elbow out for her to hold. She gave it a passing glance, then ignored the gesture.

"What is your problem?" he growled.

"You." She stopped in the middle of the sidewalk as they turned the corner toward Grey's house. "I am not a little girl who needs to be told how to act or walk or...or... Maybe you've forgotten I was a cop for many years, but I sure haven't. Some training stays with you forever, so let's get on with this foray into the public eye."

He took her elbow once again, but she not only jerked it away, she didn't step forward with him this time.

"Stop pretending, Josh. You made it clear last night that

this is nothing more than another assignment to you. I'm nothing more than a far-flung friend, so stop with the nicety-nice gestures." She pushed loose strands of hair behind her ears.

"I'm just trying to—"

"Trying to what? I know the drill for staying alive. Or maybe you're trying to say I'm too young and immature to understand what's expected. That I can't measure up to what you need in a woman." She stepped in front of him and invaded his space. "I heard you loud and clear on that count ten years ago."

Where the hell had this come from?

She moved a step closer and finally made eye contact. Fuming, madder-than-hell eye contact. "I relived the most horrifying day of my life yesterday. Spilled my guts to you. And all you could do was close the door behind me when I went in my bedroom."

Evidently he was about to get an in-your-face takedown from Mackenzie. One he might or might not deserve. He steeled his resolve to remain a professional agent, one OPAQUE had taught him to be in all circumstances.

"No kiss. No hug. Not even a can-I-get-you-anything." She poked him in the chest. "Well, that was the last straw, Joshua Slater."

A couple walking down the street in the direction of Grey's house took a wide berth around them. The man nodded and gave Josh a "hell hath no fury" look of condolence. As the pair walked on past, he held his hand for her to be quiet, which he figured only made things worse.

"This is not the time or place to discuss what happened last night." Josh lowered his hand.

"Don't you mean what didn't happen?"

The quiet that surrounded them wasn't one to be easily broken, but someone had to make the move.

"I'm sorry I wasn't more considerate, Macki. But we did make a pact to be friends." He deserved whatever she decided to fling at him, and something about the way she crossed her arms and tilted her chin up told him she had more to say. "We can talk about this later, because standing out here in the open for this long is not part of the plan."

She closed her eyes and inhaled a long, quiet, peaceful breath. "When you left ten years ago, you said I wasn't old enough for you. To me, that meant I hadn't satisfied you. Sure, I was naive. Didn't know what...or how to...to..." She opened her eyes and scrubbed the sides of her palms beneath her eyes. "Do you know how much that hurt when you left me standing at that door?"

Hell yes, he knew. He'd been the one who had to say the words. Make the break. Walk down the steps of her house. Get in the taxi that Drake had set up to take him to OPAQUE headquarters to begin his new life. Josh had been in so much pain, he'd wished he were dead.

From the pain he saw on her face now, he realized his pain hadn't come close to hers.

"I loved you, Josh. I'd waited my whole life for you. But in the end, I was too naive. Funny, because no one else I ever dated thought I was too young. No one."

He felt the vise-like clench of his teeth, the expansion of his chest with inhales and exhales like a fireplace bellows fanning the flames. He felt the flare of his nostrils like the time he'd been subjected to a slow scrape of a blade against his skin. He'd be the first to admit he sure hadn't been celibate, but not once in all the years he'd been gone had it crossed his mind that Macki had needs, too.

Yeah, this conversation was a slow scrape all right, one he damn sure didn't want to hear. He'd left to save her the pain of hating him. Instead, he'd shattered a part of her that no one deserved to have crushed. Her self-confidence, her belief in herself. What had he done? What the hell had he done?

Maybe leaving hadn't been the kinder road after all.

Control. Right now, he needed to concentrate on one of his focus points of no feeling. If he didn't, he'd lose his edge and fail them both. He swallowed his gall for himself. "We should go in, Macki."

"Not yet. I'm not finished." She didn't move. "Gradually, I realized I didn't need to prove anything to myself. I was already okay. The pain of my parents' death and you leaving had warped my emotions for a while, that's all. So I forced myself to accept that you were nothing more than a hormone-driven boy who took what I had to give. Then tossed me aside to go hide under some rock."

He opened his mouth to disagree, but the look she gave him shouted, "Shut up." He let the moment go.

"You're so self-centered you probably think I had the cutting board made with the scene of our afternoon together to keep you in my thoughts. Well, I hate to shatter your ego, but that was the furthest thing from my mind." She turned and stood beside Josh, facing down the sidewalk toward Lieutenant Grey's house. "I didn't have the board made because I still loved you. I had it made because of the hell I'd walked through and survived. And if you look close enough, you'll see I'm still surviving just fine."

Again, the quiet was thick. He'd just had the beat-down of his life. Hard to get up from that kind of you-meant-nothing punch. His eye twitched. A tic he still couldn't control in dire straits. She'd seen his reaction, because her gaze had softened for a split second before setting in place once again.

He exhaled, blowing the last few minutes out of his mind, then held out his hand palm up. "If we're finished here, you and I need to get back into character for this charade. I need you to take my hand or arm, or at least act like you care about me, because people are always watching. See if you can stop this I-hate-your-guts party long enough to play along."

"Play along? Sure. I'll do everything in my power to keep us both alive." She grasped his hand, digging her nails into his flesh for a split second, then relaxed her grip. "But when this is over, I want you to leave Riverfalls and never

come back. Understand? Never."
　She pasted a smile on her face. He didn't.
　Never was a hell of a long time. So was a woman's fury.

CHAPTER FIFTEEN

Every time Mackenzie walked into Lieutenant Grey's house, she expected her high school friend Peggy to rush over and give her a hug. That comfort of being able to count on someone for friendship forever had died along with Peggy's overdose. It still hurt, hurt bad. Mackenzie had thought that would subside after Grey moved to this new house a few years back, but it hadn't. Her friend might have died a long time ago, but it sometimes felt as if college was only yesterday.

As far back as she could remember, Grey's annual end-of-summer barbeque had always smelled of hot dogs and hamburgers on the grill. Of course, the previous yard had been a lot smaller. This house had a big custom-made river-stone barbeque pit along with a state-of-the-art outdoor kitchen. Misters and overhead bamboo fans completed the entertainment area.

She kept her hand in Josh's as they navigated the crowd, some known, some not-so-known, huddled in groups around the flagstone patio leading to the pool. Josh had insisted there'd be no swimming today, even though cooling off about now would feel good in a lot of ways.

Reconsidering the way she had spilled her emotions on him a few moments ago, she realized standing on a sidewalk in public hadn't been the best place for that to happen. She regretted that misstep, but she damn sure wasn't sorry she'd done it. At least now they were both on the same page as far as the past and present.

"Mackenzie. Mackenzie!" Grey waggled the grilling tongs high in the air, waving her in his direction.

She pulled her hand from Josh's as she neared the man who'd taken on the role of backup dad to Drake after her father had been killed. Flicking his grilling apron that read "Smokin' Hot," she leaned in and gave him a hug. "Looking pretty snazzy there."

"Looking pretty snazzy yourself." Once Peggy had overdosed, he'd never been quite as demonstrative. His friendly hello hugs had stopped. "Bet there'll be quite a few single guys here who'll be telling you the same thing before the night is over."

That was different. Usually he was pushing for her not to rush on with her life. To let Blake's death settle before she got serious again. If only he knew, if they all knew. Nothing had ever been serious between her and her so-called fiancé.

"You remember Josh, don't you?" She took the elbow she had rejected less than fifteen minutes ago and pulled him into the conversation.

He held out his hand. "Thanks for inviting me, Lieutenant Grey."

"Just call me Lieutenant." He handed the tongs to what appeared to be a member of the catering staff, then yanked the apron off over his head. Scowling as if he was about to come in contact with hazardous waste, he took the offered hand in an obligatory handshake. "Besides, I doubt Mackenzie would have agreed to come otherwise. You've got quite a hold over her, why is that?"

"I don't know what you mean." The laughter coming from the pool area contrasted with the tone of the men's conversation. "We're just good friends, aren't we, Macki?"

Maybe she should reach out and knock both their heads together. Instead, she ignored the unnecessary claim staking.

Grey laughed. "Didn't look like friends out there on that

sidewalk. Looked to me like a lover's spat or an all-out argument."

"How did you..." She glanced across the yard in that direction. They would have been blocked from his line of sight by shrubs and trees and a tall privacy fence. Nothing. There was no way he had been able to see her and Josh from this angle.

"Never mind. Now why don't you two go grab a steak." Grey headed to the sliding doors leading into the house. "When you've got a moment, come inside. I want to show you something." He closed the door behind him, then opened it again. "And when you see Cummings, tell him to come in also."

The smell of barbeque lured her in, so she and Josh filled their plates and found a table to the side of the crowd. A lot of the people seemed to stay together in their own small groups, two or three couples sitting around, laughing, playing the game of friendliness. The groups of single men or women caught her eye. Not many here yet, but as the evening wore on, she had no doubt that number would increase as the couples left the get-together. Very few stopped by her table to say hello. Didn't surprise her. She wasn't one of them anymore. Wasn't privy to the cases hanging open in the department. Wasn't laughing at the jokes being bantered between the departments. When had it stopped being fun to come to these barbeques?

Finished with her food, she headed to the bar that had been set up on the lawn and Josh followed, his hand at the small of her back, only this time she sensed it was more of a guidance mode because his eyes were busy surveying everything and everyone in the confines of the yard. He was smooth and had the surveillance down to a noncommittal movement.

"You do realize most of the people here are off-duty police, don't you?" She leaned against the granite high-top bar and pointed to a bottle of white zinfandel for the bartender to pour her a glass of wine.

"I know who they are." He took a fresh-drawn beer that was offered him by the guy manning the kegs.

"Maybe he's been away so long he forgot how to trust the Riverfalls Police Department."

"Cummings, I didn't see you there. Where have you been?" She stiffened as he eased his arm around her shoulders and scrunched her against him.

Josh didn't overreact. Instead, he nodded as if he and the detective were old friends...or at least friends. "Good to see you, Cummings."

"I doubt it."

"I doubt it too. But...this is a party." Josh swiped his fingers across the still-visible mark on his cheekbone from the night in front of the hospital. "I'm sure two men such as ourselves can play nice for at least a few hours."

She felt the 450-degree oven-like weather they were all living in suddenly notch up to broil in this private conversation. "Like I said, where were you? Grey's been looking for you."

"I was over there. Keeping an eye on possible problems." Cummings nodded in the direction of the horseshoe pit, then stepped back and sipped a gold liquid on the rocks from his clear plastic glass. "Looking out for you."

"Seems to be a lot of looking out for Macki going on around here." Josh angled his body partway in front of her. "Any particular reason or is that just par for the course?"

Cummings chuckled and glanced at the patio door that Grey had walked out of a moment before. Cummings nodded in answer to the lieutenant's one-jerk wave that he was needed. "Unlike you, we've been here for Macki all along. And for the record, we take our responsibility to watch out for her welfare very seriously."

If Josh felt the jab of words, he didn't let on.

"Don't forget that, Mr. Slater. I promised Blake to watch out for her." Cummings took a step and turned toward the house, deliberately bicep-knocking the cup of beer from

Josh's hand. Cummings stopped. "And I intend to keep that vow forever."

She rounded her eyes in anticipation of the exchange of blows about to happen right in front of her. "Josh, let's—"

Never taking his eyes from the man in front of him, Josh grabbed a handful of napkins from the bar's countertop, wiped the front of his shirt, and tossed them back on the tile. The guy by the keg brought him a fresh beer.

Josh eased his other hand in hers and tugged. "Didn't Lieutenant Grey say he wanted to show us something inside the house?"

She sighed with relief and closed her fingers around his. "Yes. Yes, he did. I'd already forgotten."

"That's one problem I don't have."

"What is?" She pasted a smile on her face once again.

"I don't forget anything." Josh's usually expressionless face crinkled with a cheek-rounding grin. "Ever."

Cummings still hadn't moved as she and Josh walked around him and headed to the house.

* * *

High-cranked air conditioning. And from what Josh could tell, an expensive money-worth-it dehumidifier greeted them as they stepped through the sliding glass doors. Today that felt like pure paradise.

Macki headed toward the sound of women's laughter and the hum of chitchat as it trickled from the great room, while he lingered near the door pretending to watch people at the pool. Lieutenant Grey walked out of the kitchen with a plate of appetizers and motioned for a few men he'd invited inside, plus Josh and Cummings, to follow him to a room across the hall.

Josh didn't like being out of sight of Macki, but as long as he could hear her voice every so often, he'd feel okay. After all, if someone were going to snatch her, they'd have a lot of good-guy cops to deal with on their way in and out of the house, never mind escaping the compound-type yard that surrounded the place.

"Any of you guys up for a game of eight ball?" Grey cajoled.

"Not my game." Cummings took up residence at a high-top table in the corner.

Josh shook his head. "Mine either."

The sleek and vibrant shuffleboard along the far wall counterbalanced the other end of the room lined with pinball and slot machine. From the leather upholstery to the gun cabinets, sports memorabilia to the wall of ego, the surroundings shouted *If you don't like it, leave.* This was a lawman's room filled with weapons and toys and bravado.

Grey picked out a cue from the wall rack as the other three men in the room nodded their plan to play. First, steaks of every size and type on the main grill outdoors. Open bar stocked with everything from champagne to premium hard liquor to three kinds of beer on tap. And now what appeared to be a custom wide-legged mahogany pool table complete with leather mesh pockets and imbedded badges on the top of the rails.

Riverfalls must be paying its police above-average salaries nowadays. Way above average.

"Nice place." Josh heard a distant giggle from Macki. Sounded like she was having a good time with the women in the other room.

"I like it." Grey's shot only succeeded in moving the balls around the table. "My wife gets to decorate the great room and the changing rooms for the women, and I keep the rest of the place the way I want."

"Really? She must be one heck of a woman to let you have final say on the house."

"Oh, this isn't our home, this is the pool house." Grey chugged the rest of his drink, then walked to the small bar on the bookshelf and poured another shot of bourbon topped with a splash of water from the built-in sink. "Our house is on the other side of that small stand of trees to the right. But this place here is my refuge."

Josh didn't remember the Greys as being wealthy when

he was in high school. In fact, far from it. Peggy had borrowed money from Macki many times, for small things like lunch or a milkshake after school.

"Must be nice."

Leaning toward him as if sharing a joke, Grey chuckled. "Helps when your wife is rolling in money." The man paused and leaned closer. "If you play your cards right with Mackenzie, you could have the same." He winked and elbowed Josh in the side.

He didn't react to the words or the focused jab against his side. The lieutenant had made sure to get his elbow to slide along Josh's ribs and under his arm until it touched the gun tucked in the chest holster. "Doubtful. I'm not much on having a woman take care of me."

Grey's lips tightened into a straight line. "Give it a try sometime. You'll never know what you're missing if you don't take a taste."

"The lieutenant's got a private poker room in the basement." Cummings walked in to join the conversation. "And one hell of a shooting range."

A split-second eye-blink and nostril flare rode Grey's face before he stroked his fingers across his lips, then stacked his cue back in the wall bracket. The men busy at eight ball kept right on playing. Evidently they'd been there enough times to know not to bother him right now.

Josh stacked the info in his mind, then let it go for now as he walked to the wall covered with photos. Some signed by sports figures, some by entertainers. Lots of pictures of Grey along with the men in blue. Some local. Some not. One frame holding pictures in various forms of photography dating back over a hundred years caught his eye, and he leaned in closer to read the names.

"That's a picture of all the Riverfalls police who fell in the line of duty in the 1900s." Cummings pointed to the empty space on the wall next to the time-honored display. "That's where the frame for the 2000s usually hangs."

"Usually?" Josh noticed Grey had left the room. Good

time to share some pretend camaraderie and get some answers.

"Yeah. Had been Blake and Thompson, but it's at the framing place being updated."

"Thompson?"

Cummings jaw worked along with a deep swallow. "He's the one who took my place the day of the explosion. He died alongside Blake."

Like the detective or not, Josh could tell Cummings still held himself responsible for his squad partner's death. Because he hadn't been there? Or because he'd been involved somehow?

Josh felt like he was pulling teeth the way he had to keep asking questions to get even a short answer. "Why's the frame being updated?"

"Because Detective Lynette Lawrence was killed working vice down on D Street a couple weeks back." Cummings glanced at the door, then the pool table, then the wall of pictures. He swallowed once again. "I'm glad Macki wasn't still working that beat."

"Me, too," Grey interjected. "She got out of this field of crime fighting at the right time."

The scent of jasmine floating past Josh's senses caught him off guard as Macki walked up with the lieutenant. Touching his arm, she smiled at him just enough to make it appear they were a couple. He gave her a soft nudge with his arm along with a quirk of the corner of his mouth. Everything fell in place like cream and sugar. They were good as a team...an undercover team, if nothing else.

"What did you want to show me?" She followed Grey as he walked to the wall behind them.

Small individual photographs littered the space with a larger picture centered among them. Josh felt her stop before she did, before she got all the way to the wall, before she tucked her arms against her body straight and tight. Before she trembled.

"What's wrong?" He placed his hand against her back,

rubbing lazy circles.

"The...the picture..." Her voice was barely a whisper.

"What do you think?" Lieutenant Grey beamed as he touched the side of the frame.

Josh glanced at the photograph, then glanced again. What the hell?

Staring back from the frame was a teenage Macki, her parents, and Grey, along with his wife and Peggy, posed in front of the Cessna jet her parents had owned. Six others posed in the picture. He knew them, too.

The pilot and co-pilot stood at one end of the group, the stewardess stood at the other end. And three mechanics knelt in front of the families. The same mechanics who'd kept that plane running for four years—one grinning like there'd be no tomorrow, one bald with an over-sized earring, and one who smiled through the slump of his shoulders and the droop of his eyes.

His dad.

After his mom had died, his dad had always looked tired.

Macki stepped forward to get a better look. She brushed her fingers across the glass, then pressed them to her quivering lips and chin. Inhaling long and deep, she touched the glass again. "This...this was the last time I was on the plane. Right?"

Grey slid his arm around her shoulders. "Yes. That was a few weeks before the crash. The last trip we all went on. Remember? We flew up to New York for a baseball game and a show?"

She laid her head on the lieutenant's shoulder. "Everybody had such a great time." Moments passed before she stepped back, slipping her hand through the crook of Josh's arm. She hung onto him like a petal fluttering in the storm yet determined to hang on for one more day. When he looked closer, the pinch line between her eyebrows caught his attention. That and her eyes...tired, tired eyes just like his dad's had been.

"You okay?" He sure as hell wasn't, but that didn't matter right now.

Seeing only quiet resignation in her face with no sign of the rosy cheeks she'd come with told him the past was closing in on her fast. Time to go. "You ready to leave, Macki?"

She nodded, then turned to Grey. "Sorry, I'm just not feeling well. Thank you for the memory."

"I didn't realize you'd be upset by the photo." He picked up a gift bag from beneath the table under the picture. "I know you don't want this right now, but I had a smaller copy made for you."

Josh couldn't believe how off this whole scenario felt, almost like a setup to see reactions. Whose, though? Macki's? His? Others in the room? Even if he had a problem with Grey and Cummings, he had to admit they'd been there for Macki more than he had. Claimed to care about her. Even if the gesture had been sincere, why keep pushing the fact when Macki was clearly upset?

He needed time to evaluate. Mostly he needed some fresh air—even the kind that soaked you to the core with sweat.

She eased a hug around the lieutenant's neck as she accepted the bag, then focused her attention on the picture gracing the wall. "Do you think any of the crew or mechanics had something to do with bringing the plane down?"

Her question hung in the air. She'd messed up. As far as he knew, no one else on the police force knew the plane had been targeted to crash besides Drake. In fact only a few FBI confidants, Drake, and some highly trusted OPAQUE agents knew the full story.

The room sounded jarringly quiet as Josh watched for reactions to her words. Would they all think she knew something? Or believe she was so upset, she didn't know what she was asking? He hoped the latter.

Grey took her hand in his. "Mackenzie, it was an

accident. One of them missed something, that's all. Mistakes happen. Haven't you ever made a mistake?"

The tiny upturn of her lips accentuated the brightening of her eyes. "Of course I have." She jokingly nudged the lieutenant. "Why, I bet a tough old bird like you has made a few in his life, too."

"Sure enough. Now you go home and get some rest. If you decide you want the crew or mechanics out of the picture, I'll get them photoshopped out." The lieutenant snapped his fingers. "Easy as pie."

The moment Josh saw the upturn of her lips, he knew she'd realized her mistake. That she needed to fix it. She had. Josh was proud of her comeback. Damn proud of the cop she must have been at one time. She hadn't forgotten her training.

He steered her outside the same way they had come in, but the woman who'd given him what-for on the way inside had deflated in less than a minute in that expensive, jacked-up man cave. He didn't like that. Heading to the compound's gate, he noticed quite a few people had already left but the sound level had revved up. The bass beat was pumping loud and the beer flowing free.

From the looks of things, the real party was just getting started.

CHAPTER SIXTEEN

Had they really parked this far away? Mackenzie didn't remember the walk from the truck to the barbeque taking this long, but this return trip seemed like a million miles. Was it the lingering humidity with the fading light of day? Or the tension of the make-believe afternoon? Or was it because she'd bitched for most of the walk to the barbeque?

Didn't matter. She was tired. That was why she'd messed up at the end. Said something about the plane being brought down. "Sorry about—"

Josh squeezed her hand hard, then leaned in as if giving her a peck on the cheek. "Be quiet," he whispered as he brushed his lips across her ear. Then he moved back to his side-by-side position. "No need to be sorry, I never told you I like my steak rare. Well done was an interesting change."

What was he talking about? She turned her questioning gaze on his warning raised-eyebrows look. He swiped his palm across his chin making sure to raise two fingers across his lips then reached out and took the bag from her hands. Nonchalantly he clicked a button on his cell phone and swiped the display over and inside the bag.

Surveillance? He thought the bag was bugged? Well, that was the most paranoid thing she'd heard lately.

Climbing into the passenger-side door he was holding open, she turned to tell him just that, but he pulled her seatbelt out and leaned across to fasten it for her. With the other hand, he centered the phone in the middle of the truck cab, pushed a button, and waited till a green light flashed clear.

After closing the door, he walked the perimeter of the truck, stooping at each tire. They both knew the routine for protection mode. Finally jumping in the driver's-side door, he had the key in the ignition and the engine revving before he even straightened in the seat.

A block away, his shoulders relaxed as he nodded she could talk.

"Do you trust anybody, Josh?"

"Not many. Neither should you." He glanced in the rearview mirror, then the side.

She found herself glancing in hers also. The man was seriously making her as mistrustful as him. Trouble was, she had no idea what to be looking for at this point. Evidently he'd worked so many cases involving Coercion Ten that he knew their MO. Knew what to check for.

"I understand things aren't what they should be. But to think that Lieutenant Grey would give me a gift so he could listen in to our conversation is beyond disbelief." She pulled the bag from the floor bed, laying it on the seat between them.

"He's shadowing his yard and the surrounding streets, so I don't put anything past him. Did you know that?"

"You mean surveillance? I had no idea. This is the first time I've been to his house since a get-together for New Year's."

"Didn't it seem strange that he knew...saw...us arguing?"

"Yeah, but..." Her mind screamed that she'd let her cop instincts relax being among friends, acquaintances, and people of power in the community.

Josh grumped. "Didn't take me long to spot his camouflaged cameras facing the yard. I spotted a couple facing the outside perimeter as we walked back to the truck. "

Her own security system at the hotel involved long-range cameras for the lobby and hallways, including some on crucial spots along the exterior. All legal and aboveboard. From his response, she assumed Josh had some doubts about Grey's. "Is that why you didn't want me to say anything? Afraid they could read our lips?"

He turned down a side street, then left, then right, then another side street heading away from the hotel as he continually checked the rearview mirrors. "There are some high-tech things in the world. I just wanted to be sure we weren't being bugged. By the way, when did the Greys get to be so well-off?"

"After Peggy OD'd, Mrs. Grey spiraled into a depression. Then cancer. In less than two years, she died. Lieutenant Grey took it pretty hard. Nothing like he'd taken his daughter's death though."

If it hadn't been for Uncle Drake, no telling what Grey might have done. But the two men had walked through the pains their families had endured.

She glanced back over her shoulder. "I don't think Mrs. Grey ever fully faced that Peggy was gone. Even left her room the same way it was when she'd left for college."

"Sad."

"Very sad. Anyhow, Grey got remarried about three years ago to a wealthy widow from New York. The rest is history." She'd been surprised at how short a time the lieutenant had known the woman before announcing they were engaged. But who was she to say when someone should find happiness again? "You know...new wife, new house, new outlook on life."

Josh slowed approaching every intersection, then plowed full-speed ahead if the light changed to yellow. Cars behind had to stop for the red lights and oncoming traffic. "Sounds like an easy out on grief, but I guess some men like that."

"What do you mean?"

"Nothing. Just talking." He shrugged.

Talking? She didn't buy that for a moment. Josh never

just talked. Everything he said had a purpose. Did he even know how to communicate on a personal level anymore?

"I still can't believe you checked the gift bag." She pulled out the photograph copy. Thinking back, she remembered what a great time she and her parents had in New York. Her dad and Grey had gone to a couple of meetings, but other than that they'd played the tourist part.

"What are you smiling about?"

She glanced at Josh and smiled ever bigger. "I don't know. All of a sudden I'm happy with the memories this has brought back."

He nodded at the gift bag. "Looks like there's something else in there."

She reached inside and pulled out something wrapped in tissue paper. A note taped on top read *Hope you like it.* Then a smiley face right above the names Grey and Cummings.

"Feels like another picture frame." She felt a surge of excitement as she unwrapped the tissue paper.

Son of a gun. It was Blake. And her. And their kiss. Not one photo, but a collage—two snapped before and two after, cornered the kiss in the middle. "Damn it, damn it, damn it. Will he and Cummings never stop?"

She shoved the picture back in the bag. Out of sight. Out of her hands. Everyone had been on the two of them about being so private. Never a kiss in public. Never a hug. When were they sealing the deal with a marriage ceremony? They had both hated that part of their platonic arrangement. The constant battering for a show of affection.

That day, she and Blake had kissed, trying to get everyone off their backs. She remembered him leaning in to tell her that they might as well get it over with. Then as she'd turned in his arms, he'd whispered, "Let's make this kiss one that will knock their socks off. Might shut them up for good." She'd agreed.

"Let's see the photo." Josh turned back in the direction of the hotel.

She sighed loudly and pulled the frame from the bag, then laid it on the seat between them. "I don't know why they can't leave it be."

Darkness was beginning to take on the day, so he flipped on the dome light and glanced at the picture, then back at the street. His eyes veered back to the photograph as his brow furrowed with deep ridges, eyebrows pinched together and his lips set in a hard, straight line. He didn't and didn't and didn't look away.

"Josh! Watch the road." She jerked the steering wheel to avoid an oncoming bus.

He recovered and eased to a stop at the light. The red orb glowed through the haze of humidity until it changed to green. He floored the pedal, laying rubber as the truck fishtailed through the intersection. Instincts told her to stay quiet. Something in the picture of her and Blake had put a stranglehold on Josh. One he was having a hard time controlling.

She repacked the bag with both pictures and focused on the passing buildings outside the passenger window the rest of the way to the entrance of her private garage. He stared straight ahead as she pushed in her code on the key fob in her purse.

The darkness of the garage glared into full light as the garage door opened outward. The moment the truck cleared the outer point, the doors started closing and followed close behind the bumper. Drake had had them installed years ago. Said they were stronger metal, safer. Now she knew why he'd been so concerned. Each in their own parking spot, her phony taxi, red sports car, and silver SUV welcomed her.

"Well, we're home." She hopped out of the truck, happy to be able to relax without worrying about someone having her centered in their scope.

Josh beeped his door lock. "By the way, I ordered a new surveillance system for the garage."

"I already have a system linked with the hotel security."

Where had this come from?

He shook his head. "Too easy to compromise. All they'd need to do is bypass hotel security and you're a sitting duck. Besides, this one will have a screen inside the elevator, so you can see what's happening before you open the doors downstairs, just like when you go into your penthouse."

"What about pulling inside the garage?"

"Drake's having one tweaked for you to use on your phone from outside."

Nodding in agreement, she had to admit he might be right on that point. There had been times she'd felt uneasy pulling into the garage by herself

"Now, remind me again about the security currently in place." Ever alert, Josh continuously scanned the garage as they made their way to the elevator.

"First, there are systems in place to scramble anyone trying to tap into the entry pass-code." She pointed to a couple of cameras. "Those are linked in to the hotel security, which is monitored at all times by my in-house team. Only four people have ever known the pass-code, and one of them is dead."

"Who?"

"Me, Drake, Ed the chauffeur, and Blake. Oh, and you...guess that's five people." The elevator doors opened and she stepped inside, leaning against the mirrored wall for support. She needed a good long bath full of bubbles and warm water.

He turned toward the interior of the garage, then stepped backward into the elevator car, pushing the Close button as he went. "When's the last time you changed the pass-code?"

She rolled her head and sighed. "There are five pass-codes that get randomly rotated throughout the year. Codes Drake sat up a long time ago. It's automatically set to change every two months."

"Call down and change it when we get to the penthouse."

"Okay." The elevator binged past her office floor on its way to the top. Sighing, she straightened, opening her eyes. "The new code will be 'hot rod buggy.'"

"Hot rod buggy?" The grimace-grin that inched across Josh's face looked like he was genuinely affected by the silliness of the code. "Guess there's more to the old man than I thought if he came up with that." He all-out grinned. "In fact, I wonder what the first part of that means?"

She punched him in the bicep. "You are bad, Joshua."

"That I am, Macki. More than you'll ever know."

Deliberately closing her eyes again, she didn't bother to respond. There was no doubt in her mind that he was bad when he needed to be. She didn't want to know. Didn't need to know...unless he decided to share his past with her. And she sure as hell doubted that would ever happen.

The elevator stopped, and after a quick scan of the bedroom surroundings through the security peephole, she pushed the Open button and followed him as he stepped off the elevator. She nudged past him on the way to the master bath. "I'm going to clean up and put on some jeans for the evening. Call downstairs if you want anything sent up to eat."

"Maybe later." He headed out the bedroom door, then turned back. "What does 'hot rod buggy' mean?"

"When I was three or four, Uncle Drake took me to the park and rented one of those stroller things that look like a car. Of course I wanted to go fast and faster and faster till..." She paused long enough to untie her sandals, then slipped them off and slung them over her shoulders as she held onto the leather straps. "...he stumbled over a molehill and the stroller car rolled end over end a couple of times. Hit a tree."

Damn, that day had been fun. Just her and her crazy uncle.

"Were you hurt?" He chuckled.

"Not much, but you'd have thought I'd been shot the way my mother reacted to the sight of blood on my dress. We told her I fell from the merry-go-round." She lifted her elbow and pointed to a tiny white scar. "Had to have three stitches."

"Why did he pick that as a code?"

"Because neither one of us ever told another soul what happened." She felt the rounding of her cheeks with her smile. "It's always been our secret. He said it would make a great pass-code."

Josh reached in the gift bag and pulled out the photographs. "He's right. The fewer people who know why a code is a code, the better. Every OPAQUE agent out there knows that rule."

She unzipped her shorts and started to push them down, then stopped and glanced at him before she rezipped. Didn't matter. He was staring so intently at the pictures, she doubted he noticed she had made a clothing boo-boo.

"Why all the concern about the garage security?" she asked, leaning against the bathroom doorway. "I doubt anything can get past you."

He lingered in the bedroom a moment longer, meeting her gaze with a half-lidded stare and parted lips. For a moment, he let his gaze drift from her face to her toes and back again. Then he blinked, and the other Josh reappeared. "Want to make sure you'll be safe when I'm gone."

Her stomach reflexed inward with the implication, but she kept her eyes on his. "That sounds ominous. Like you've already planned when you need to leave. What...you got a schedule you need to keep? Got another client who needs protecting?"

"That's my job."

"Job? I'm nothing but a job? Then you shouldn't care if I'm standing stark naked in front of you." She ripped the zipper on her shorts down again and stepped out of them, then whipped her top over her head. She was sure he'd seen more than his share of half-dressed women in his field of work as a protector. What was one more? "I'll show you job."

Clutching the tank top in front of her, she unhooked her bra with one hand and let it drop to the floor. *Let's see where that takes you, Agent Slater. Are you still in control now?*

"Will you let me know when you're leaving this time, Joshua? Or will you just disappear into the night without a moment's notice?"

"I'll tell you goodbye." His breathing had increased, causing the rise and fall of his shoulders to betray him. But his grip on the pictures hadn't lessened.

She walked up to him until the only thing between them was the tank top clutched in front of her breasts. His eyes dilated with the quiver of his jaw, the tilt of his head. She stepped close enough to feel his hardness press against her belly through his pants. Guess control had gone out the window.

He didn't move, but the quiver intensified with the glistening of his eyes. Her own pulsing breaths betrayed her composure also. *Josh...oh, my Josh. Why? What could possibly be so bad that you can't reach out and touch me? So bad it's tearing us apart?*

She eased her fingers into the palm of his free hand and made easy, lazy circles pressing deeper and deeper into his callused skin. As she pressed herself closer against him, she dropped the tank top on the floor beside her.

He grunted, jerking his hand from her hold, then steeled his arm straight down at his side as his expression shot fire in her direction. No sign of passion or anger or need, just a look that drilled right through her and shouted she'd gone too far. Gotten too close.

"Back off, Macki. Don't make this any worse than it is." He scooped the top from the floor and shoved it back in her hands. "And get the hell dressed."

She tugged the top over her head, struggling to find the strength to get her arms through the sleeves. Over...everything was over for them. She'd made a fool of herself, and he'd called her on it.

Slowly, realization ground its way into her head. There was no chance for them to resurrect what they'd once had. Josh and Macki were no longer there. For whatever reason, they were both gone. Over. Done. They had both died that day at the door as he'd said goodbye ten years ago. No more Macki. No more Josh. No more afternoon in the park.

She sat on the side of her bed, knowing he wouldn't follow. He had his pride or creed or whatever the hell he lived by, and she was the line he couldn't cross. She backhand-brushed her cheek, then the bottom of her trembling chin. Wetness... When had the tears started to roll down her face? She didn't want to cry. Didn't feel like crying. In fact, there was nothing left to cry about. Yet the tears kept overflowing her lower eyelids, and she couldn't stop them or the tremble.

Facing the pain, she let it continue to roll out of her body.

"Will you at least give me the respect to tell me what the hell your gut-wrenching problem is before you leave? I think I deserve that much." Lifting her head to face him was one of the hardest things she'd ever do. "Don't you?"

The breath he'd been holding escaped into the air.

"Yes, I'll tell you." His grip on the pictures clutched in his hand white-knuckled, then he walked away. "I'll tell you everything."

CHAPTER SEVENTEEN

Josh slammed into the chair in front of the computer system he'd set up a few days ago and punched in the code for Drake. This had to stop. Had to stop now before he couldn't stop himself from giving in. After all, he was a man. Macki was a woman...a beautiful, enticing woman who stirred his core. And they were living in close proximity. Too close.

Of course, every other protection assignment he'd ever taken had been in close proximity. None of them had made him feel like this.

When Drake assigned the job, Josh knew dealing with her would be a test of his will. He'd put his barriers in place before he hit town. Everything had been fine at first. Gone as planned. He'd compensated for their past. Made maps in his mind of how to avoid any pitfalls they might encounter. Stayed true to the whole "we're just friends" shield. Until today.

Something had changed between them in the past twenty-four hours. Something he couldn't put his finger on. Something he couldn't click back to how he'd felt the first night.

So this had to stop—now!

Drake's image popped onto the screen. "What's going on?"

"A lot." Josh raked his fingers through his hair. "A whole hell of a lot."

"Such as?"

"You need to send another agent. Or at least send her driver Edward back. Let him keep a close-up watch. I'll watch from a distance."

His boss leaned into the camera screen on his end. "Has Coercion Ten made a move? Have things gotten bad this fast?"

"No. I mean... Yes. I mean you need to send another agent to protect her." Josh would rather be any place in the world right now than sitting here trying to explain he couldn't keep his act together.

"I'm not sure what you're asking for, Agent Slater. And for the record, we still haven't heard from Edward or his wife Darla." Drake's eyes squinted with the words. "What's going on? Are you calling for backup?"

"No, sir."

"You're saying you can't handle this assignment, Agent Slater? Is that it?"

Josh didn't know what he was calling for. The woman had him so bamboozled, he couldn't clear his mind long enough to give an update for the day to his boss.

Drake cleared his throat in that listen-to-me manner he controlled his world with. "Now I don't know what just happened on that end between you and my niece." He raised his hand. "I don't want to know. That's a problem for the two of you. But the protector I know you to be needs to step back and take a deep breath. Then tell me what you called for."

Josh didn't wait to be told twice. From past experience, "take a deep breath" meant *You're overthinking the situation. Overreacting. Get back to the basics.* He pushed the Hold button on the keyboard and watched the screen go green as he walked away. Sometimes the old man made sense.

Josh stared out the window, walked to the guest bath, splashed water on his face, then walked back to the window. He could do this. Whatever had changed in the past twenty-four hours wouldn't change back, but he could change with it. Follow his training and make damn sure he didn't get the client hurt in the process.

He sat back down in front of the screen and pushed the Resume button, nodded at Drake's image as it popped into view.

"Which is it, Agent Slater?"

"Neither, sir. I was just calling in with the evening report." Josh rolled the pen between his palms. "Where are we on deeper background checks for Macki's list of visitors?"

They talked about each person once again, but nothing new had risen to the top. Sure, there were things that a husband or wife would be shocked to hear, but nothing to signal the people involved had been blackmailed into spying on anyone. All in all, they were still at square one.

"I handed the listening crystal off to a courier early this morning. Have you got it yet?" Josh hoped it would give a clue on where it had been made.

"Systems is working on it, but they've only had a couple hours." Drake jotted a note. "Tell me about the barbeque. Everything go okay?"

"Lieutenant Grey gave Macki a photo of her parents with the crew and mechanics in front of the plane. Seemed strange to me. Upset her."

"What upset me?" She walked through the doorway and into the room, pulling up the vacant desk chair to look into the screen at her uncle. A loose top, jeans and almost-dry hair completed her attire as she settled in.

"Josh was just telling me about the picture."

"Which one? The one that upset me." She looked at Josh. "Or the one that set you off?"

Josh raised his palm to stop her from going further with her confrontational questions. "I told him about the picture of your parents and you."

"Figures."

Drake cleared his throat. "What does that mean?"

She propped her elbows on the desk, folding her hands in front of her as she leaned toward the screen. "Means Grey and Cummings gave me a photo of Blake and me kissing." She jerked a finger in Josh's direction. "Seemed to upset him greatly."

"I didn't say a word," Josh replied.

"Didn't have to. I could see it in your attitude."

Josh blanked his expression because this was going nowhere fast. They needed to be talking about their next step. For all they knew, Coercion Ten was setting their people in place even as they spoke. Since no one local had fingered Macki, they'd bring in outsiders. Guns for hire.

In fact, this situation was taking way too long to come to a head. Usually Coercion Ten put out the word and moved fast. Why were they dragging their feet on this one? Were they trying to put more leverage in place? If so, who? Drake would have told him if there was anyone else they could use against him.

The rising voices of Drake and Macki brought Josh back to the moment.

"I'd like a different protector," she said nonchalantly. "Josh has done a good job, but I feel some new eyes on the matter might make a difference."

The screen went green.

She tapped the edge of the keyboard. "What's going on?"

"He's taking a break." Josh grinned at her not because he was happy, but because he could imagine the choice words his boss was shouting into thin air at the moment.

"Why?"

"Because you've pushed his last nerve for the day and he's doing his damndest not to lose his temper. Got it?"

"Got it." She fidgeted in her seat. "He used to get up and walk out of the room when I, like you said, pushed his last nerve."

A minute later, Drake's expressionless image reappeared on the screen. "I believe we discussed this the first night, but I'll reiterate the short version. Josh has the most experience with Coercion Ten in these types of threat situations. You're smart enough, Macki, to know how to follow his lead when it comes to staying safe. That's all I'm concerned about—both of you being alive when this is all done. Understand?"

They both nodded but didn't look at each other, and neither picked up the portable screens to see everyone on the conversation.

"But..." she said.

"There will be no change-outs." Drake leaned back to a straight-as-nails position in his chair. "Whatever problem you two have got, work it out. Because it damn well better not interfere with this assignment."

A distant ring of her phone caught everyone's attention and she ran to answer the call.

"I mean it, Josh. I don't care if you two knock heads or beds, but I sure as hell don't want to know about it." Drake poked the screen with his finger. "You're a grown man who can do whatever the hell he wants. And as you may have noticed, my niece has a mind of her own. I thought by now you'd have figured out she's not that sweet little Macki anymore."

"That's the problem, sir. She's damn sure not the Macki I remember from high school." Josh eased back in his chair and blew out a long sigh, rubbing his thumb across his lower lip. "Not even close."

With a loud groan, Drake leaned back too. "Aw, hell!"

The second hand on the desk clock ticked off a few seconds.

"Now I'm concerned about you two becoming a leverage situation." Drake drew out his words. "Watch you don't—"

"I can do my job, if that's what you're wondering."

"And when it's over?"

"Macki deserves better."

"What does that mean?"

"I leave."

Drake slammed his hand on the desk in front of him, the sound vibrating through the speaker. "How many times do I have to tell you you're not responsible for what your father did?"

Josh answered his boss's slammed hand with one of his own. "Not until I've brought the bastards to their knees. And I can't help thinking I'm responsible." He glanced at the open doorway and heard Macki's muffled voice in the distance. "I may not carry the same last name, but the man's blood runs through me. Just because my parents never said 'I do' in front of a judge doesn't mean I'm can't feel like I should right a wrong he did."

The flick on the screen meant Drake had pulled a screen panel loose and was pacing around his office. Josh followed suit. Evidently, the boss had more to say.

"I'm gonna try this from a different direction," Drake mumbled.

"Say what you've got to say and get it over with. She'll be back soon."

"What if, in the distant future, someone rules that OPAQUE overstepped its bounds on some case? That you were the agent in charge and you screwed up." Drake had stopped pacing and was seated back at his desk because his image had popped up on the main screen. Straight as nails again.

Josh mirrored his boss by sitting in the chair. Mulling over the fact that a lot of what he had to do walked a fine line between right and wrong, he still knew everything he did was for the right cause. The outcome justified the means. Of course, some people might not see it that way. "I'll face that when it happens."

"Oh, and did I mention that by then you have a son?"

"I'm not doing this, Drake." Josh knew the drill. The old man would try to break him. But in the past ten years, that had never happened. Never would. No matter the topic.

"Is he responsible for what you did?"

"Not playing."

"In fact, you have two sons, maybe three. Boys with the same blue eyes as you." Drake's tone lowered in timbre. "They walk the same as you. Smile the same. Which one of them is responsible for what you've done?" Drake slammed his hand on the desk again. "Pick one, Josh. If you're so damn right, then pick one to sacrifice his future for what you did. Pick one. Right now. Before you take another breath. Pick one!"

"You need to take your fuckin' head games somewhere else." Josh felt the pounding of his heart, the rush of blood in his ears. He wouldn't do this. He would not lose. Would. Not. Go down that path. "I swear I'll disconnect and walk right out that door if you don't shut up."

Drake hadn't moved. His stone-faced expression hardened more and more with each passing second. "You won't shut me down because a piece of that hardheaded brain of yours just shouted that you might be wrong. You've held onto the hate so long, you've lost touch with the reason you hate. For once in your damn life, you're thinking you might be wrong."

"I said, get out of my head." Josh felt like his skull would explode. Explode any second if the pain didn't finish him first. Pain for a son he hadn't yet fathered.

"Answer the damn question. Is he responsible, Josh? The boy who waits for you by the door every night. The boy who wants to play catch every weekend. Your son whose blood is yours. Is he responsible?"

Josh tried to clear his mind to his focus points. Nothing helped. Instead he kept seeing a boy's face...a boy's smiling face. "Stop it, Drake. Enough."

Drake charged forward at the screen on his end. "Then answer the question, Agent Slater. Answer me. Now! Is your son responsible for what you did on that last mission in South America, Agent Slater? Is he responsible for you scaling that compound wall and taking out—"

"No! Hell no! And I'll kill anybody who says he is." Josh grabbed one of the screen sections and flung it into the picture hanging over the bed. The glass shattered in hundreds of tiny round orbs. He dug his hands into the pellets and flung them against the wall. "No."

Again. "No."

And again. "No." His breaths came in chocking gasps, trying to kill him as he struggled with the words on the tip of his tongue. Struggled and lost. "My son...would not be responsible for what I did that day."

He braced his hands on the desk in front of the monitor, slowed his breathing, his heart rate. Slowly he lowered himself into the chair. Hell, no.

Drake leaned back in his chair, and the corner of his mouth lifted an iota. "Then don't you think it's time you stop being the martyr for something your dad did, Joshua? If your son wouldn't be responsible...why are you?"

From out of nowhere, an image of a smiling little boy again crossed Josh's thoughts. One holding on to his hand. His hand? He looked closer...that was his dad's hand, his dad's scar from getting his hand sliced by an engine blade. The smell of brats and popcorns popped into his mind, and he felt himself smile. They'd gone to the ball game that day...his dad had saved enough money to buy two bleacher seats. And they'd gone to the game. Just him and his dad.

Dropping his head in his hands propped on the desk, he sucked in a deep breath and closed his eyes. When had life gotten this complicated? When? Suddenly nothing seemed black and white anymore. Good and bad mingled. How could that be? He shoved the thought aside and sat back up. Looked his boss in the eye.

"Will you at least think about what I've said?" Drake asked.

Chewing the side of his mouth, Josh glanced around the room. Stared at the broken glass before he turned back to the screen and shot his boss a quick nod. Paused and swallowed deep. Then nodded in earnest. He'd think about it.

"Josh. Josh." Macki screamed from down the hallway.

"Everything's okay in here. A picture fell, that's all." He raked his fingers through his hair and blanked his face. He was in control once again. In control. Even though his insides felt like he'd been ripped to shreds right in front of his own eyes.

Macki barged into the room with panic written on her face. Barely glancing at the mess littering the bed and floor, she raced to stand next to Josh in front of the screen. "That was Detective Cummings on the phone. We need to get to D Street. Fast. A woman's been roughed up, but she won't go to the hospital. Says she can't leave till she relays a message to..."

He watched as the tan on her face lightened a shade.

She sucked in a breath. "...OPAQUE Agent Joshua Slater."

CHAPTER EIGHTEEN

Josh drove out of Macki's private garage, steering in behind the police car waiting to give them an escort down to D Street. On the one hand, he liked the idea of not having to stop at red lights or follow the speed limit, but on the other, he didn't much care for someone knowing his exact route. Least of all the police.

Closing in on the crime scene, he motioned to an officer pointing to a vacant space that he'd pull his truck into the spot. "I can't believe you and Drake talked me into letting you come along."

"You both knew if I didn't, I'd just get in the car and follow," Macki said.

Josh also figured Drake had realized that they needed all hands on deck, including Macki, in this case. This wasn't a usual OPAQUE case. This time the person being protected had training in defense besides being stubborn as hell.

Macki tapped her fingers against each other in a nervous, tented gesture. Her eyes darted from side to side as she sucked in a breath. "Besides, Drake said it wouldn't hurt to have someone familiar with the area take a look around. See if anything looks out of place."

Josh had to admit that leaving her back at the penthouse would have been a hard decision to make. One, she would have been alone. Two, she was the closest they had to a baseline of what should or shouldn't be happening on D Street nowadays.

"Maybe so, but that's all I want you to do. Tell me even the slightest detail that makes you take a second look. No running around saying hello to people." Josh jumped from his truck and spotted Detective Cummings standing next to an ambulance. "Definitely no interaction with Roxy."

Arms crossed tight across his chest, the detective looked like he was none too happy about either one of them being there. Should be interesting, since Josh didn't plan to be shoved around by anybody this time.

Macki joined him at the front of the truck, her breathing jerky right along with her quick looks from side to side. Ever since the phone call had come, she'd been jumpy. Afraid? Maybe. More likely, he figured she was reliving the night she got beat up.

Back at the penthouse, she'd verbally fought him about wearing her pink-fringed vest and hooker outfit. Told him she wouldn't go without it. He'd told her he wouldn't go at all then. Took a bit of doing, but finally she had admitted it was her shield against D Street. She'd never walked into the neighborhood as herself until now. In the end, she'd left the outfit hanging in her closet. He was proud of her. Took a lot of guts to face your fear.

Josh nudged her arm with his. "You okay?"

She nodded, taking a step toward the ambulance. "First we need to talk to the woman so she can get to the hospital."

"I'd feel better if you make the first contact. Ask how she's doing. See if she needs anything." Josh moved to the other side of her, putting her on the ambulance side of the street. "Then introduce her to me. I'll take it from there."

She glanced at Cummings. "What do you plan to tell him about being an OPAQUE agent? I doubt he's ever heard of the organization."

Josh grinned. "He's heard of them. Especially in the town where it originated. As to what I'll say...depends on what he asks." He knuckled the spot on his cheekbone. "One thing for sure, he better ask nice cause I'm in no mood to take any of his bull tonight."

"How can you stop him?"

"I only have to make a couple of phone calls and he'll find himself off the street talking to some agents who carry federal badges. He sure won't push them around."

Cummings walked out to meet them, blocking their path to the EMT van's open doors. They jogged to the side to go around and he stepped in front again.

"Look, you're the one who called me." Macki stood her ground, no fidgets, no nerves. Nothing but in-your-face solid footing anchored her to the moment. "So get out of our way."

The detective turned sideways for them to pass, then closed in behind.

Josh stopped. "Go ahead, Macki. Do what we talked about."

Nodding, she made her way to the ambulance, taking time to talk to the medic before she climbed inside.

"You don't give the orders around here." Cummings growled.

"Neither do you."

"Now play nice, boys." From the periphery, Lieutenant Grey entered the two men's confrontation with his words, then his body. He glanced at his detective. "Evidently, Agent Slater is a member of OPAQUE. One of the best allies a police department can have." He turned toward Josh. "Too bad you didn't notify the Riverfalls Police that you were in town. I'm sure they'd like to show you their appreciation for all OPAQUE does on their behalf."

Josh controlled his urge to tell the lieutenant that trying to get on his good side wouldn't work—he had no good side when it came to business.

Cummings flicked his handcuffs out, toying with them in his hand. "I don't care who he is or who he works for. He's got no authority here. Maybe Mr. Slater would like to take a ride downtown for a little conversation."

"Don't push it." Josh eased his phone out of his pocket,

glancing back at the lieutenant. "Which button should I push first? FBI? DEA? Or maybe the NSA?"

Grey held his hand up and waved it from side to side. "I think you'll agree we don't need anyone else here. And put those damn cuffs away, Detective."

Josh tucked his phone back in his pocket and watched as the lieutenant walked back to the perimeter of the crime scene tape. "Was the lieutenant already here on the case when you talked to the woman? Or did you call him after she asked for me?"

"Not that it's any of your business, but I called him. He left his barbeque and came right over." Cummings stayed cemented to his position.

"Got over here mighty fast, didn't he?"

"Maybe you and Macki got over here a little slow." The detective crossed his arms again, broadened his stance. "For the record, Slater, I've heard of OPAQUE. They're known for catching guys on the take. Doesn't do me one damn bit of good."

Josh rolled his shoulders to nudge the sweat forming beneath his shirt. He watched the clouds for a moment, hoping the distant sound had actually been thunder. Hard to see the lightning in the bright city lights, but he felt a change in the weather tonight. A slight breeze that came and went.

"Did you hear me?" Cummings leaned closer. "I'm a good cop, and most of the police I know are damn good. All you guys do is cause a lot of friction in the department to nab a few bad ones. Why come to Riverfalls to stir up trouble?"

"Do your research and you'll see that the people I hunt down don't play nice. And just for the record back at you, I don't spend my time looking for guys on the take. A buck here, a baseball ticket there. That's for Internal Affairs to handle." Josh shifted his stance. "I search out the ones who are trying to control the good guys by every means possible."

Macki stepped out of the EMT van and motioned him over.

Cummings grabbed Josh's arm. "All I'm saying is—"

Josh shoved his hand aside. "Get your facts, detective. OPAQUE agents are also sent to protect people who are targeted not only by Coercion Ten, but other lowlife sons of bitches." He waved to Macki that he was on his way. "You better hope you're never in a situation where I have to do you 'a damn bit of good,' as you say. You might find yourself in one hell of a bind."

"Cut to the chase, Slater. Why are you here in Riverfalls?" Cummings kept step with him.

Did Josh trust the man or not? Didn't damn well matter at the moment, but he was going to take a chance. One he hoped he didn't live to regret. Or die regretting. He stopped and faced the detective. "You want to know why I'm here?"

Cummings narrowed his eyes. "Hell, yes."

"I was sent to protect Macki." He raised his index finger and whipped it in front of him, pointing to move aside. "And you damn well better stay out of my way." He raked his hand across his cheek. "If you don't, I'll put you on the ground and you won't get up."

"Give it your best shot, Slater."

Josh felt the furrow of his brow and the evil clown grin that had enveloped his face. He'd seen himself in the mirror one time and come up short as he realized the devil inside him. The one that could do what had to be done. Hell, was the guy in front of him crazy or stupid? If it meant Macki's life, he'd take Cummings out in a second and every witness there would swear it had been an accident.

Turning his attention back to her, Josh calmed his body and expression and soon-to-be-heard voice in order to not scare the woman in the ambulance who'd been beaten just to get a message to him. As he neared, he saw the redness on Macki's cheeks as she swiped her hand across her nose. Whatever had happened inside had been hard on her. Biting the side of her lip, she climbed back into the ambulance and he followed.

She gently patted the woman's arm. "This is Agent Slater, Tessa."

Josh nudged Macki aside and took the woman's hand. "I'm sorry you had to go through this, Tessa."

Bruised and battered, the barely twenty-year-old stared at him as if he were the answer to her prayers. "They...they said..." She glanced at Macki, then fear inched across her expression as she gripped his hand tighter. "Only you...I can only tell you...they said they'd be watching..."

Macki inched out the doorway. "I'm gonna go now, Tessa. But you hold on, because you'll heal. May take a while, but you'll heal." She closed the ambulance door behind her.

Tessa motioned him to come closer. The closer he got, the more clearly he remembered the first night he'd hit D Street to wait for Macki. This had been the woman who had wanted to help him with his need. The one who'd looked fresh on the street. The one he'd hoped would stay safe. Once again, hope had slapped him in the face.

He leaned his ear next to her mouth, never letting go of the grip of fear the woman had on his hand. "Take your time. Tell me when you're ready."

"They...they said to tell you to back off or...or"—she glanced at the closed door—"your woman will get this...again. Is that nice lady your woman?"

Without a second thought, he nodded. "Yes, she's the woman they're talking about."

Tessa jerked trying to sit up, grabbed the front of his shirt. "Then stop. Stop whatever you're doing. Nothing is worth this. Nothing..." She leaned back, gasping for her next breath, as the medic opened the back door on the ambulance. "No...no...wait."

Josh motioned the man not to come in, and the door closed again. "Is there more?"

She nodded again and again and again, then glanced to the left, stared off for a moment. He'd wait for her to remember. Waving him forward again, her face eased into concerted effort to get what she had to say right.

"They said if you don't leave town, the three of you will fall...like dominos. One. Two. Three. Within twenty-four hours." She struggled to sit up again, but reached for his hand once again. "You will be first."

"Any idea who the men were?"

She shook her head.

"What did they look like?"

"Black knit ski masks. The alley they pulled me into was so dark, I can't even tell you how tall they are." The woman closed her eyes for a bit. She trembled, then her lashes fluttered open again. "One man had on a gold bracelet. You know...the...the kind made out of big links."

Josh's memory clicked back to the first night once again. The man who'd taken his place with this woman on the street. Josh leaned closer to her. "Anything else you can remember about that man in particular?"

She shook her head. "Not really. Except he...he seemed to be the one in charge."

There was more info being shared in this conversation than the woman knew. Josh needed even more. He hated to push further, but she might hold the only clues. "How do you know?"

"When he said do something, the other two did. And he'd just stand there." Shudders of fear grabbed her body. "The last time I fell on the ground is when he flicked on his cell phone flashlight and crouched down beside me. That's when I saw the gold bracelet."

"You're doing great, Tessa. Now what else? What did you see in that light?"

"Touched my hair. Me. Then he shoved me away with the side of his shoe."

Shoes? Josh squeezed her hand lightly. "Tell me about his shoes."

"Black. Shiny." She trembled again and touched her ribs. "Hard. Really, really hard."

Son of a bitch. Josh zeroed back to the hotter-than-hell night he hit town. The bastard had paraded himself in plain view. Right there on the sidewalk. Right in front of Josh. The man had waited. Waited for Josh to arrive.

Sure, the black horn-rim glasses, button-down shirt, and gaudy toupee had all been a disguise. But the gold link bracelet and black shiny-shiny shoes? Those were things someone might wear without thinking with a disguise. Something they might forget to take off.

Or the man might have worn them to feed his power ego. To say *Come and get me if you can.* Tonight, though, was the gauntlet being thrown down. The direct challenge. Josh had no doubt that he and the man with the gold bracelet would meet face-to-face. Where and when remained the mystery.

One thing was clear as day, though. Local problems and Coercion Ten threats were all wrapped up in one package. Macki's dad, the FBI, Drake, and OPAQUE had been right all these years. Coercion Ten was anchored in this city.

Josh's insides tensed with the newfound realization. The end was near. He could taste victory in his mind. After all these years, his search had brought him right back where he'd started when he was twenty years old. Now all he had to do was stay alive long enough to take them all down. Coercion Ten. Dirty police officers. And the man who bought his dad with a handful of money.

CHAPTER NINETEEN

As she stepped from the ambulance, Mackenzie's heart pounded like a heavy bass drum. Bracing her back against the side of the EMT van, she flattened her palms against the cool smoothness of the metal for support. She grimaced with the intense jab of remembered pain as a ghostly sting shot through her ribs, chin, cheek. Her hand flew to her face before she knew she'd moved.

"No. No." The fear she felt crushed her with victim panic. Gradually, the ragged gasps of breath shaking her body shook her back to the present, and she felt the deepening crease between her brows begin to release. Struggling, she fought her way back to here and now. She was okay...she was okay.

She slid her palm down the side of her cheek, and it came to rest on the pulse of her throat. Her chin followed till it rested on the top of her hand. This was not two years ago in the alley.

Now, Josh was only a step away inside the ambulance. Tonight she was safe.

"Are you okay, Macki?"

Cummings?

She raised her head, clearing the traces of panic from her expression. "Sure. I think the heat's starting to get to me."

"Yeah. We could all do with some cooler weather." The detective jerked his thumb in the direction of the EMT van. "Might calm things down here on the street, too. This kind of weather, the hotter people get, the meaner they are."

The heat and beat of D Street had a life of its own. One that didn't need the weather to make it hotter than hell. She heard the back ambulance door open, then close rapidly as the EMT walked a short distance away again.

"I need to find some kind of breeze." She patted the back of her hand against her forehead for emphasis. She doubted the conversation going on inside the ambulance could be heard where they were standing, but to make sure, she needed to get them a good twenty feet away.

Cummings followed. "Why'd you two leave Lieutenant Grey's barbeque so fast this afternoon? The party was just getting started."

None of his business, as far as she was concerned. "Better question is why you and Lieutenant Grey felt the need to give me a picture of Blake and myself?"

"What picture?"

"You know. The other gift in the bag with the photo of my parents. The collage of me and Blake kissing. As if shocking me with a family photo wasn't enough trauma for the afternoon. You two tossed in another tragedy for good measure." Disgust simmered in her words. "How do you think that made me feel?"

"I didn't give you a gift."

The lowering of his eyebrows and shift in his jaw line hinted that he was confused. Confused or well-versed in a cover she hadn't mastered of his?

"That's not what Grey said." Her stomach churned in agitated response at the memory of pulling the picture from the bag. "He said you and he had a gift for me."

"He said that?"

She nodded, pointing at Grey walking down the other side of the street evidently heading to his parked car, ready to leave. "Maybe we should ask him."

Propping his hands on his waist, Cummings lowered his eyebrows and jutted his jaw to the side. "All I know is Grey asked if I had any pictures of Blake and you, so I shot him that set of pictures from my cloud. I had no idea what he planned to do with them."

"Sure you didn't." Enough was enough. She'd had all she could stand of everyone pushing into her life. "I don't believe you."

"Well, I don't give a damn if you believe me or not, Macki. In fact, I don't care why Grey gave it to you." Cummings leaned closer. "I would like to know how you and this so-called Agent Slater are involved. And don't give me that 'old friend' baloney."

Ah, the conversation had shifted. The man had got to where he'd planned to go with his casual interrogation. Whether he knew it or not, his shoulders had inched back as the set of his mouth straightened into an I'm-serious unbending line. Undercover instincts warned her to be more than careful with her wording.

"We are old friends. Went to high school together. That's all."

"You knew his family?"

"No. I never met them."

"Don't you find that strange?"

She cocked her head a tad to the side, pursed her lips. Where the hell was Cummings going with this? "Josh's mother died when he was young. And his dad worked long hours."

"He told you about his dad?"

"No, my father told me."

"They knew each other?"

"I guess."

"How did they know each other?"

Both her parents had said they knew Josh's dad. That he was a hard worker. Worked long hours so his son could have a better life. They'd both given her their blessing to date Josh. That was all she'd ever needed to know. They'd given her and Josh their blessing. "This conversation is over, Detective Cummings. Move on to a different topic."

The waiting for Josh to exit the ambulance was

beginning to wear on her. What type of message had the thugs who beat Tessa up left for him? And why was it so important for Mackenzie to wait outside?

"Agent Slater said he's here to protect you. Or was it that your friend Josh is here to protect you and he's usually an agent? Which is he, friend or agent?"

That had come out of the blue. Why would Josh tell Cummings anything?

"Nice try, Detective Cummings. Did you learn that slip-in-slip-up questioning on the first day of Detective 101?" She formed her words, giving him a you're-full-of-it look. "Don't try to make something out of nothing. He's in town on business and I have an extra bedroom, that's all."

She needed to up her game. Stop ending her statements with "that's all." She wasn't about to admit Josh was an agent assigned to protect her, not until she got permission from him or Drake to do so. "Besides, I doubt Josh would tell you the time of day."

Cummings grinned. "I'm not the only one with tells, you know. So fess up. Why do you need protecting? From who?"

More no-answer questions. She looked past him and analyzed the street. Most people didn't give a second look at the flashing lights of the ambulance as they clustered outside the clubs or stuffed food into their mouths around the food vendor stands. A few of the girls at the corner of 10th and D kept right on hawking their wares as if any dangerous customers had already made their hit that night.

Roxy pushed the edge of her stretchy neckline strap down over her shoulder as she sipped on a glass of who knew what. She leaned against the high-top table that had been her prop for the past five years. Evidently the evening was slow, otherwise she'd be perched on the bar stool she kept close, her legs crossed in such a way to not only smoothly entice but to bounce with the beat for the tougher crowd.

Sliding her eyes back to the EMT van, Mackenzie

blinked away the haze lingering in the night air. What was taking Josh so long?

"Who sent him?" Cummings invaded her space, staring her straight in the eyes.

"None of your damn business." Mistake—she shouldn't have acknowledged that he'd been sent. Of course the detective and Grey already knew Josh was an OPAQUE agent from Tessa's insistence on getting a message to him. But Mackenzie sure as hell wouldn't let slip the fact it was her uncle who had done the sending. The world, at least for the most part, didn't know Uncle Drake was the head of OPAQUE, and she planned to keep it that way.

The click of the ambulance door caught her attention, and she took a step in that direction.

Cummings blocked her path. "All I'm saying is, what do you really know about Slater?"

"Josh," she answered calmly. "I know him as Josh. A friend."

"Don't pretend to be naive with me. High school was a long time ago. What's he done since then? Where's he been? Who's he shacked up with during all that time? Ever thought of that?" Cummings appeared pleased with his wording.

He should be. The questions had finally hit the bull's-eye with her.

At the sight of Josh exiting the ambulance doorway, she stepped around the detective.

"Hell, Macki. All I'm saying is the guy you knew ten years ago is not the same Josh Slater now." Cummings fell into step with her. "What the hell do you know about him? He could actually be the one you need protection from. Face it, you're not acting like the Macki I knew on the force. The one who made sure she knew everything about everybody involved in a case."

She stayed focused on following Josh as he started across the street. His jaw was set and his walk was straight forward, leaning into anger.

"Where's that tenacity now?" Cummings insisted on staying by her side. "Why are you afraid to ask him the same questions you've asked others a hundred times before?"

She walked faster toward Josh.

Cummings lagged behind. "What are you afraid of, Macki?"

She caught up with Josh, but he reached out his arm, motioning her to keep an arm's distance away. Then he stopped and walked toward the detective. She followed. They were not going to have private conversations while she was in the same arena. Not anymore.

"I don't know why I'm trusting you, Cummings, but I need your help." Josh scanned his eyes over the upper-floor windows of the buildings on D Street. "Tessa says—"

"Who?"

"The girl in the ambulance, the one who said she had to talk to me. She relayed a message from the men who beat her up." Josh glanced at Macki, then back at the detective. "They said I'm going down within twenty-four hours."

She sucked in saliva on her gasp, then devolved into a coughing fit. Wheezing to catch her breath, she forced herself not to reach out to shield him. First of all, she wasn't big enough to be a shield. And second, he would not take kindly to her taking chances. Never mind his damn pride.

Cummings nodded. "What do you need me to do?"

"While I was in the ambulance, I notified OPAQUE on my secure cell network that I need backup protectors sent. But they're spread all over the world, so the timeline I need them here by may not be possible." He reached out and pulled her between him and the detective. "My main concern is Macki."

Nodding, the detective started scanning the street also. "Do you think they'll come after her as soon as they take you out?"

What the hell? She was standing right here and they were point-blank talking about life and death. Hers. Josh's.

And no telling who else. They needed to get off this street. To go hide back in her penthouse. Never come out. Never... She jerked herself back. No, they couldn't do that. This was their opportunity to strike first.

"Doubtful." Josh nudged her to the left a bit, then let her hand go. "They'd wait...but not long. Maybe a day. They'd want to see if they got their point across enough that their ultimatum is met. By then my backup would be here. It's those few hours in between that I have to trust you to handle." He held out his hand, palm up.

Cummings clinched the outstretched hand in his grasp. "You can count on me."

From what she could tell, the men were good with each other for the moment, so she stepped to the side of Josh. Easing her hand inside her purse, she rested it on her gun. The cold metal against her palm always brought her peace and strength. She had a permit to carry concealed, and she wouldn't hesitate to pull and fire in a heartbeat if needed. "What do we do next?"

"Roxy looks lonely." Josh grinned and started across the street. "Think I'll go have a talk."

Macki hurried to match the long strides with two of her own. He was in a hurry. She failed.

"You know what this is about?" Cummings kept pace with her, but far enough away to not be involved.

She nodded.

"Has he got a valid reason?"

"Oh, yeah, he's got a reason." She wouldn't pretend to protect Roxy from the onslaught of questions. The woman had targeted her with that listening device in the crystal. Time to find out why.

Cummings angled across the side street and took up a stance on that street corner. Guess he figured he should hang around since most of the police had already left, but didn't plan to intrude on the "conversation" unless called for. Besides, he had made a pact with Josh to protect her. One she hoped he didn't have to keep.

Roxy straightened to her full height as Josh neared, her eyes darting around for someone she couldn't seem to find. Mackenzie eased up behind him then stepped to the side, backing against the brick wall of the building. They weren't here to play good-cop-bad-cop or let's-see-what-we-can-coax-out with friendly banter, they were here for answers. She crossed her arms over her chest.

"How you doing, Roxy?" Josh braced his elbow on the high-top and leaned in as if talking about the weather.

The woman glanced down the street again, both ways.

"You looking for somebody in particular?" He turned and eyed the same directions. "Guess your friend cut out on you."

"Why don't you take a hike?" Roxy gave her hundred-dollar smile, stretching her neck as she twirled her dangle earring. "You're bad for business."

On the round, stained, cigarette-pitted Formica, Josh tapped out a beat in time with the strip club's gyrating music from down the street. "Shame about Tessa."

Roxy inched around the table to be directly across from Josh, as far away as she could get. "I didn't really know her well."

"Was she new to town?" Mackie questioned.

"No. She's been around a while. Kept to herself mostly. Worked closer to the jewelry store down the street."

"Bigger tricks down there?"

Roxy nodded.

Mackie eased in on the side of the table. "Bet that didn't sit well with some of the women."

"You're damn right. We're all one big happy family down here. And a family watches out for each other." Roxy pulled her stool over and slid on top, crossed her legs so they bounced at the side of Josh.

He looked her invitation up and down. "How about you? Did it make you mad that someone was cutting in on your territory?"

"No. I've got plenty of business." She made sure the next

bounce of her foot slid up the side of his leg.

In a flash, he flicked her shoe off and turned it over to view the label, then turned it for Macki to see. "How much you think those set Roxy back?"

Macki didn't blink, didn't smile, didn't show any emotion. "At least a grand."

"I figured something like that." Josh quirked the side of his mouth. "Well, Roxy...you must be doing something right to be able to afford a thousand-dollar pair of stilettos."

The woman held her leg out, arching her foot and wiggling her toes.

He slid his hand beneath her calf, and slowly slipped the shoe back on her foot. "You'll excuse me for saying, but from what I see, you ain't got the assets to make that on the street anymore. Where you getting the money?"

Jerking her foot away, Roxy shot him a look that would have killed a normal man dead in his tracks. Not Josh. Would take a lot more than that to stop him. Still Mackenzie had a hard time biting back her emotions at the sexy-as-hell way he had touched the woman.

"Who gave you the crystal to plant in Macki's place?" Josh's voice had lowered enough to strike fear with its edge of a snake's hiss. "Whose blood-money did you take to betray a woman who thought you were a friend?"

As he waited for an answer, his eye color changed to a steely, gray-blue shade. He was Agent Slater to the core now—don't get in his way.

"How much did they pay you to bug her place? Fifty? A hundred?" He sneered a grin across his mouth. "Or did you hit the big time? A cool, hard grand? Maybe two?"

Roxy jumped off her stool. "I don't know what you're talking about."

"Yeah, you do." Macki slipped from her stool, leaning forward to invade the woman's space. Her voice had roughened with the thought that the person in front of her hadn't been a friend after all. "The crystal you had Darla bring me. You even told her where it needed to be placed.

Remember, you made sure to say it had healing powers."

Josh eased to the other side of the aging woman. "We wanted to get one for Tessa. She's going to need a lot of help healing and..."

"It helped me so much, I wanted to do the same for her." Mackie cringed at the bile crawling up her throat with each passing word, knowing there was nothing they could do in the end no matter what Roxy said.

"I don't remember where I got it. And nobody paid me to do anything." The woman raised her hand in Cummings's direction, motioned him over as she bit the side of her lip. Smiling, she glanced at Mackenzie. "You're all healed now. Give her yours."

"Can't." Josh slammed his hand on the tabletop, making it reverberate with the strike. "I smashed it wide open. Shattered it into little pieces. Guess what I found?"

Her expression morphed to fear as she flitted her eyes up and down the street once again. Her mouth moved in quiet words.

"Sorry, I didn't quite hear you." Leaning into her personal space, he was tenacious in his words, his tone.

"They...they said it was unbreakable."

"Who said?"

Roxy's breathing intensified as she shook her head. "Nobody. Nobody said anything."

Macki sighed heavy and loud. She wanted off this street—now. A low-grade panic had taken hold again. She pushed it down again. Shoved the fear to the bottom of her core, but she still wanted off this street. Something wasn't right. This couldn't be happening right before her eyes.

Whatever Roxy knew couldn't be worth risking their lives, could it? Sure, the woman wouldn't think twice about making a few bills by placing something. Still hurt like hell to think she'd been betrayed, but nothing could convince her that Roxy was any more than a pawn. A runner, so to speak.

Cummings walked into the group. Flashed his look

around and nodded.

"Detective, you didn't say where Tessa was found?" Josh took a couple steps back, scrutinizing everyone in the circle with the same ease he'd use to watch a documentary on sailing or some such thing.

Cummings pointed to a dark alleyway.

"That's the same one." Mackenzie heard the words clear her mouth before she thought them.

Josh eased his hand in hers. "Who found her, Detective?"

"Roxy heard her scream."

"That's right." The woman stared into Macki's eyes. "Lucky I heard her. Otherwise, no telling what might have happened."

Macki tightened her grip on Josh, otherwise she might knock the woman right off her stilettos. Never...never in her life had she been so sure of anything. She'd been set up. Turned on for a price. Nausea sucked the breath from her lungs. "Luck? Is that what you call it? How dare you...you..."

Cummings glanced between her and Josh. "What's going on here?"

Josh turned to Macki. "Your call. I've seen what I needed to see to get my answer."

Anger shivered through her body, bursting to be released. Thinking of the future, the case that would be made later, she knew she had to watch what she did. What she said. "I was assaulted in that same alley a few years ago. Roxy heard my screams that night, also." She grabbed Josh's hand again. "Lucky coincidence? Or were Tessa and I both set up by Roxy and her friends?"

Flipping to face the accused woman, Cummings yanked out his cuffs. "Let's take a ride downtown, Roxy."

"What for?" She backed up till her back flattened against the wall. "I didn't do anything. Honest I didn't." She stepped toward Macki. "Honey, you know I always treated you like one of my girls on the street. Watched out for you like you were my daughter."

Mackenzie shifted away from the outreached hand.

"I wouldn't hurt you for the world."

Josh waved off Cummings's handcuffs. "We're not filing charges."

"Why the hell not?" The detective glanced at Mackenzie, but she shook her head.

"Roxy's small potatoes." Josh turned his head enough to crinkle his brow at Cummings. A signal to back off for now. "She's nothing but a little fish in the barrel. Probably couldn't stop herself from getting used by some smart guys. Needed the money. You know how it is..." He glanced at the woman fluffing her hair for probably the millionth time while standing in the glare of this street corner. "Sometimes that wad of cash in a person's hand makes them do things they wouldn't do otherwise."

The image struck a wave of forgiveness in Macki for whatever the woman had done. No—no. Everyone made their own choices, there'd be no pity. People had been hurt. People could have died. People had had their trust shattered. She tugged on Josh's hand. "Let's go. It's been a long day."

"Sure." Josh headed toward the truck with her by his side. Suddenly he stopped and snapped his fingers. "Son of a bitch! That's it."

He kept hold of Mackenzie's hand as he took a couple steps back, then pointed at Roxy. "I should have thought of this sooner. You...you didn't do it for the money, did you?"

"Leave me the hell alone."

"They've got something on you. Something big. Really, really big." Josh cocked his head to the side as if listening for the unspoken. "What is it, Roxy? What's so hellfire important that you turned on your friend?"

Roxy slammed her hand on the tabletop and looked straight into Josh's eyes. "You want an answer, it's gonna cost you."

As one, Macki, Josh and Cummings closed in around

the woman, blocking others from her view.

Macki couldn't believe they might be closer to having their answers than even five minutes ago. Sure, Roxy might be a petty criminal, but deals were brokered every day. Roxy's nervous glancing of the street started again, but every so often she'd look back at Josh and make eye contact.

Finally, Roxy walked into Mama's Kitchen. "Detective Cummings, would you mind keeping watch at the front door?"

Josh and the detective exchanged shrugs as Roxy walked inside and sat at the last booth. Macki and Josh followed a short time later, taking seats at the small table a foot away from the woman.

"Mister agent man, can I trust you?" Roxy's voice quivered ever so slightly. The volume barely audible.

"Yes, I give you my word. But you need to give me some good answers." Josh fingered the one-page menu, looking first on one side, then the other, as if deciding on dinner. "Answers I can use. Understand?"

The woman nodded. "First, you've got to do something for me."

The smell of hot pastrami and fresh-baked bread and just-brewed tea brought back memories of slow nights Macki'd spent with the working women. All of them huddled inside the restaurant to get out of the rain or snow. Times someone had a birthday and the others would chip in for a cake or ice cream or one of Mama's Kitchen's specialty desserts.

Those were the times Roxy truly smiled or laughed. But she never let anyone know her birthday or where she came from. Tonight though...Roxy wasn't laughing or smiling. In fact, she looked scared as she fan-folded the paper menu.

"What do you need? Money?" Josh raised his eyes to make contact with hers as he tapped his fingers against the years-old tabletop.

She shook her head.

"A way off the street?" Still he tapped.

She shook her head again.

"Protection?" His fingers slowed with the word. Stopped.

Roxy nodded so quick and so short that Macki would have missed it had she not been watching. The woman flashed two fingers.

"You and who else?" Josh asked.

Roxy scribbled on the edge of her menu, then handed it to him as she stood. For a second, her fingers dug into his arm. "Don't let me down, Agent Slater. And for damn sure don't let the police see this."

CHAPTER TWENTY

The drive back to Mackenzie's personal garage had been quiet. Too quiet.

Once she and Josh had got in the truck, he'd read the note Roxy gave him out loud: "Daughter, almost seventeen, lives out west someplace, born—Chicago, name—Sandy D. Street." Then he'd made a call to Drake. Afterward all he'd said was that OPAQUE would work out the details and get back with him.

Mackenzie couldn't imagine being so cut off from her past that she'd give her child the last name of where she worked. But that's exactly what Roxy had done. Questions whirled through Mackenzie's mind about where the woman had come from and why she was so adamant she keep herself unknown. Questions with no answers, except ones she didn't want to consider right now.

"You know Roxy looked scared out of her wits?" Macki hated to see anyone in that predicament.

"I know." He clenched his jaw. "And if the people she knows are tied to Coercion Ten, then she's got a reason to be."

"How long till you hear back from OPAQUE?"

"Drake's on it. Should be less than twenty-four hours. He'll send someone to handle Roxy's protection once we get the information." Josh turned on the radio as if he didn't want to talk anymore.

From the look on his face, Josh was jamming everything

he'd found out, and not found out, into a neat little cubbyhole in his brain. Maybe processing past cases through his mind to see if any similarity shook out. She hoped it did. Then maybe this case could fall into a neat wrap-up. No one hurt...no one dead.

The music played until he parked in her private garage and turned off the key. So much for any question and answer time.

Mackenzie slid out of the truck to follow Josh to the elevator. Something about Cummings's questions about Josh had hit a nerve. What did she really know about Josh? His family? Back then? Now? She had no doubt that Drake knew what he was doing by sending Josh to protect her. Probably had a file on him and his family, otherwise he wouldn't trust him to be in OPAQUE.

This might not be the best time to ask Josh any questions. Then again, this might be the only chance she got. No matter which way the next twenty-four hours went, he'd be gone. Either he'd go down for the last time or the case would come together...and he'd walk out the door. Then she'd never have her answers. Maybe Cummings was right. What was she afraid of?

"I am so ready for this day to be over." She swiped her hair behind her ear. "Let's talk about something besides Roxy and this case."

He pushed the elevator button for her penthouse. "Like what?"

"I don't know. Tell me about your family."

The long-lingering look he shot her darkened his eyes in a way she'd never seen before. Said more than any words he'd ever speak. She'd opened a wound.

He stepped on the elevator and turned toward the steel doors, staring straight ahead. "What do you want to know?"

"Tell me about your mom. You told me she died, but that was all." She'd never asked anything else for fear she'd hurt him. If that's what she was doing right now, she was sorry. More sorry than he would ever know.

The elevator doors opened in the penthouse and he walked to the kitchen island. Leaning against it with his hip, he crossed his arms over his chest. "When I was ten, she got sick. A few months later she died."

Mackenzie touched his forearm with her fingertips, and he dropped his arms to his side to get away from her touch. "You don't have to be afraid of me, Josh. That wasn't a pass. I'm trying to have a civil conversation with a friend." She backed away, grabbing a glass from the cabinet. "You lost your mother. I lost mine. I thought we might feel better if we shared our memories."

He took the glass from her hand and grabbed another for himself, filling them both with ice and water before setting them on the granite top. "You're right. My mom deserves to have her memory voiced. She had me when she was nineteen, then worked as a secretary in the school system, and picked up odd typing jobs even after her and my dad hooked up again."

Mackie took in the fact that she'd probably had him out of wedlock. Didn't matter. "Did you live in Riverfalls?"

"No, we moved here when my dad was offered a promotion." He downed his glass of water and refilled. "Wasn't long after that that she got to feeling bad, but she wouldn't go to the doctor. Didn't want to spend the money. So..." A hairline crack in his voice betrayed his emotions.

"So by the time she saw the doctor, she was really sick?"

He nodded. "Cancer. The doc tried everything, but it kept spreading. Pain got worse. Treatments got harder on her. When the clinic told her that anything they did would be to prolong her life a month or two, she said no." He sipped his water slower this time. "My dad begged her to keep trying, but she shook her head. She was done."

Macki hated herself at the moment. Why had she opened this wound? Asked him to relive something so painful? She realized knowing about Josh's family wasn't worth the hurt in his voice. And sure as hell wasn't helping him. She'd been wrong to do this. "I'm sure she loved you all very much and wanted to spare you any more suffering."

When she touched her fingers to Josh's arm this time, he didn't pull away.

"Yeah. My dad went outside to the garage and sobbed like hell. I saw him...down on his knees beating his fist into the side of the workbench. He never knew I saw him, but she'd sent me out to keep an eye on him. Make sure he was okay." Josh set the empty glass in the sink. "He didn't shed a tear at the funeral. Stood there stone-faced until they lowered her in the ground. Guess he'd said his goodbye out there in the garage that night."

"I'm sorry about your mom."

Josh walked over and wrapped his arms around Mackenzie, resting his head on top of hers. "I'm sorry about yours, too."

She couldn't breathe, couldn't swallow, couldn't push away. This was heavy. Way too heavy. They needed to move on to something lighter. To something about life. She needed to steer them away from sadness. Find something good out of all this and change the conversation.

Stepping out of his hold, she forced a smile. "Tell me about your dad."

"He died." Josh walked toward the patio door, picking up the gift pictures from this afternoon. "Didn't you say you still needed to do some work when we got back?"

Evidently, he was finished with family sharing, and this time she wouldn't push the matter. She could ask Drake about Josh's father. Find out how her own dad knew him. Surely there couldn't be anything secret or classified about that detail.

"I'm glad you reminded me." She settled in the chair at the desk, popped open her laptop. "I still have some work to get ready for my presentation. You know this is the final meeting before the event at the end of the week."

"This week?"

"Yes." She wouldn't bother to argue about whether she'd attend—at least not now. Who knew what four days might bring. Better to work this scenario one day at a time.

From the corner of her eye, she saw his face develop into a half-snarl-half-grimace expression before he shook his head and sighed. He'd probably reached the same conclusion. Just cool it for now on ultimatums that might not come to pass. Lost in thought, he walked back to the kitchen island and laid the two photographs on the counter, studying them like his life depended on it.

She let him simmer on his own while she quickly tackled the gala particulars. Shouldn't take more than fifteen minutes. Then off to a nice long bath and bed. Food was the furthest thing from her mind.

"Did you love Blake?" Josh's voice slammed through her. Not so much the words as the tone...the suggestion.

Again? They were going to go through this again. Next he'd ask if she loved Cummings. "No. I told you we served each other's purpose to appear connected. That's all."

Josh tapped the glass covering one of the pictures. "That's not what I see in this collage."

"Well, I don't give a damn what you think you see in the pictures. In fact..." She took a couple quick steps to the counter and reached out to take the frame from him. He jerked it back. "Give it to me, Joshua. I've taken all I'm going to take tonight. Maybe you should get a hold on your jealousy."

"Jealous? What the hell are you talking about?"

She reached again. "You're jealous of Blake. Jealous of someone you never met. Who never meant a thing to me. Now give me the picture."

"First of all, I could care less who you've been with." He laid the frame back in front of him and motioned her to his side of the counter. "But I sure as hell care about being lied to. Look at this collage objectively."

Pacify him shouted loud and clear through her brain. Otherwise, she'd never get any rest tonight. "What am I looking for?"

Josh pointed to each of the five small oval-matted

pictures in the frame. "First one, you laughing. Second one, him trying to dodge the camera. Then the kiss in the center one."

She nodded. "Okay, we've been over this before. It was a fake kiss meant to shut everyone up."

He jutted his jaw out as he leaned toward her. "That's one hell of a kiss to be fake, as you call it."

The memory of Blake's lips on hers oozed through her thoughts. She'd hated his arms being around her, touching her like he had a right to. Then his mouth had settled on hers, opened and engulfed hers as he eased one hand up to her hair, cradling the back of her head...his palm against her back, pushing her closer and closer until she'd finally dug her nails into his arm.

She hard-swiped the back of her hand across her lips, nauseated by the taste of remembrance. "Look at my picture as I walked away. Does that look like I loved him?" She jabbed her finger onto the glass. "Look at it... Objectively. And tell me what you see."

Josh stared at the bottom picture of her, the one after the kiss, the one with her hand knuckled across her mouth. "You look like a woman who's been ravaged by a kiss."

"And?"

"And you're disgusted as hell."

"Damn right. Disgusted and struggling to compose myself. I ruined the whole routine by telling him what a lowlife move he made."

"I'm sorry, Macki. For then and now. I should have taken a closer look before I said anything." He eased the picture in her direction. "But look at him. The last picture. The one after the kiss. What do you see?"

She stared for a few moments. Nothing jumped out at her except Blake's expression looked different than any she'd ever seen on his face . Buzzed? Sick? Thrilled? Worried? "I don't know what I see."

"Well, I do. I see a man who felt something he hadn't counted on feeling." Josh tapped the glass. "At that exact moment, he realized something had changed in his life. Something between you and him had changed."

Her insides stilled to nothingness. "He felt the kiss?"

"He felt the kiss." Josh nodded. "He felt you. Felt the chemistry. And it scared the hell out of him."

"But I felt nothing...just sick. And a little afraid. Even took to locking my bedroom door." She shook her head. "In fact, I was relieved when he stayed more to himself here at home after that. Seemed like he went out of his way to not be around when I was."

Josh stacked the picture of her family on top of the kiss one and pushed them to her. "Did he give you any reason for keeping his distance?"

"Said he was busy, that's all."

"Did he mention the kiss?"

"No. We never talked about it. He died two weeks later in that explosion."

She lifted her family's photograph and smiled. The picture was beginning to grow on her. She'd need to send Grey a thank-you note.

Gliding her fingers across the faces, she remembered that everyone had agreed on two things when they'd landed—they were all tired as heck, but it had been a fantastic trip to remember. They'd all been happy to gather in front of the plane for the camera op. Even the mechanics had been included that day. Why not? They kept the plane running in tip-top shape.

"Hey, look at this." She pointed to the mechanic on the end, the one kneeling in front of her dad. "This man's got your eyes. Your look. I mean... He stares at the camera the same way you stare at things most of the time."

Josh glanced down briefly before he started to walk away.

She touched his arm and he stopped. "I'm not saying anything bad. Everybody's got a doppelganger somewhere in the world. But you two sure as heck carry the same characteristics." She brushed her fingers over the glass.

"Now you know what you'll look like in another twenty years."

He narrowed his eyes as if she'd called him a name. "Of course I look like him, Macki. That's my dad."

"What did you say?"

She couldn't have heard right. The man in the photograph couldn't be his dad. She'd never heard the last name Slater ever mentioned except in conjunction with Josh. Besides, she knew everybody who worked around the small airport where they had hangered the plane. She'd grown up around them. Talked the mechanics into giving her rides on the Gator tractors. Got them to teach her the ins and outs of what kept a plane in the air. She knew them all.

There'd been no one named Slater.

Without acknowledging that she'd spoken, he started down the hall to the guest room. "I need to check in with Drake and a couple of back-ups before I hit the shower. I probably won't see you till morning. You need anything?"

"No." The whisper of her voice betrayed her struggle to act as if nothing had been said.

A clue had been tossed into the wind. She could finally get an answer to a lot of her questions. Why hadn't she noticed the similarities years ago when she'd first met Josh? Maybe he'd needed to grow into the man he was, with hard-packed muscles and eyes that said they'd seen what the world had to offer. Seen the tough, unkind—even brutal and unforgiving—world.

No need to ask Josh anything else, because he'd only clam up. But she'd get her answers on her own.

"Good night, Macki."

"Good night, Josh." She watched him disappear into the guest room and shut the door. The click of the lock seemed loud tonight. Or maybe this was the first time he'd locked the door. Why? *What are you hiding? What?*

She rebooted her laptop as she sat down. Within a couple of minutes, she'd found the airport's web site, then its history, and a gallery of planes from throughout past years. Scanning the shots for ones with mechanics in them, she clicked through each photo. One by one by one. She thought she remembered the man's name, but wanted to make sure. There he was working on the landing gear of a plane...name—Garrett Rogers.

Why would Josh and his dad have different last names? Because his parents never married? Didn't matter to her. But it did matter that something about this had taken Josh prisoner in a solitary life all these years.

Her heart was pounding as she typed the name into the search line. She was close to answers...maybe the answer to why Josh had left so suddenly ten years ago. A few clicks and she might know why and when Drake had taken Josh under his wing.

The obituary. She'd find the obit and work backward. Her mind and fingers raced as she clicked on the *Riverfalls Dispatch* newspaper website. That newspaper had pretty much folded last year, but the archives should still be available. The sound of the guest room shower distracted her for a split second. There wasn't much time.

Search Garrett Rogers...searching...searching...

A short one-paragraph obit popped on her screen. She glanced at the date. Her palms felt sticky and damp as she pressed them together against her mouth. The day after her parents' plane crash? Couldn't be. Why wouldn't Josh have said something at the funeral? Why was he at her parents' funeral when his own dad lay in a mortuary across town?

She scanned the few sentences. Decorated veteran. Died of natural causes. Preceded in death by his wife...no name. Survivors...one son...no name. That was it? No mention of where he'd worked. No names for his wife or son. No mention of which area of the city he lived in or his religion. She clicked again, tried another search.

Something was strange about this. The info was too vague. Too short. Too neat and clean. Her cop instincts flashed—almost as if someone was hiding something.

Why? What had happened? She searched again, this time on ambulance runs for that day.

She trailed her finger down the list. Garrett Rogers...Garrett Rogers...Garrett Ro—

The water in the shower kicked off. There wasn't long. Where was the report from the EMTs? Where? For the first time since she'd left the police department, she took a chance and clicked into files she should no longer have access to. Surely they had denied her access by now.

After a couple of redirects, she was allowed access. That didn't make sense, but she didn't stop to analyze, just clicked to where she needed to be. Then there it was...a photocopy that had been scanned into the system. Strange to say the least.

Garrett Rogers. DOA. Found by Captain Drake Lawrence of the Riverfalls Police Department. Apparent...then a smudged-out word that had started with su...accidental overdose. Next of kin...one son—Captain Drake Lawrence will handle notification.

CHAPTER TWENTY-ONE

Josh stood quietly watching Macki from the hallway leading to his bedroom. She was doing exactly what he would have done if the tables had been reversed. Finally, the pinch of her brows together, combined with the wilt of the corners of her mouth, told him she'd reached the end of her search. The day after his father's death, Drake had insisted there be a short obit put in the newspaper. He'd said Josh's father deserved at least that for all the good he'd done during the war.

In hindsight, that had worked out well. Made a good place to begin Josh's confession. "Did you find what you were looking for?"

Her fingers tapped a few keys, then she lowered the lid on the laptop. "What do you mean?"

"Don't play games with me. We're both too tired for that." He picked up the picture from the counter. He'd thought that day years ago had been the worst day of his life. Now it paled in comparison. "Before I left the room, I deliberately dropped you a clue to my father. You're smart. You looked."

"You set me up to look for information?" Her tone was accusatory, but not angry. More of a blank slate waiting to be written on.

He shrugged as he settled on one end of the sofa. "I figure we're done with secrets. Time we lay everything on the table. Agreed?"

She moved to the other end of the sofa. "Agreed."

Placing the photograph on the cushion between them, he pointed to his father kneeling in front of her dad. "When my mother died, there were a lot of unpaid bills. A lot of people think only in terms of medical expenses with cancer. Figure insurance will pay most of the bills. But a lot of incidental expenses stack up."

He couldn't do this sitting down, so he got to his feet and started a slow pacing back and forth in front of the closed curtains covering the wall of windows. Somehow, he had to make her see that he needed to share the responsibility of the pain his dad had caused. The only way to do that was to present this like a business meeting.

"Even though my dad could have ignored the bills, he worked two, sometimes three jobs at a time to keep life the way it had been before she got sick. Of course I was too young to understand that he had refinanced the house, taken out loans on everything he owned, just to pay off bills he could have walked away from." He raked his fingers through his hair. "You see, my mom and dad never got married. Oh, he wanted to, begged her to, but she said no. She didn't want to ever think she'd tied him down."

Sucking in a deep breath of air to stop the quiver trying to inch into his voice, he couldn't believe how out of his element he felt right now. This should be easy, but for some reason it wasn't. He'd thought saying the horrible thing his dad had done would be easy. That making sure only the bad came out on Garrett Rogers would be a piece of cake. But it wasn't. For some damn reason it wasn't. He had to get this over with—now.

"Long story short—my dad is the person who tampered with the plane. Made sure it went down. Then he took his own life the next day." Josh lowered himself into one of the soft, comfy chairs across from her.

Bracing his elbows on the tops of his knees, he rested his head facedown in his hands. He'd got it out. Now he waited for her to scream or yell or pound him with her fists.

Instead, the room stayed as quiet as solitary confinement.

Raising his head to see if she was still there, he couldn't believe the look of compassion on her face. A slight tremble at the corners of her mouth as she batted her eyelids. Tiny teardrops on her cheeks. She wiped them away and walked over to him. Kneeling in front of him, she took his hands in her own.

"I'm sorry, Josh. Sorry you've carried this alone all these years."

"Sorry? You're sorry for me?" He jerked his hands away and stood. He would not take pity. Hers or anybody else's. "Don't you understand, Macki? My dad killed your parents as sure as if he'd pulled the trigger."

"I understand. But you're not responsible for what he did." Rocking back on her toes, she turned and slid into the chair Josh had left. "If that's what you think, then you're wrong. Dead wrong."

"You sound like Drake. All these years he's tried to let me off the hook. Get me to let go of the past. But I won't let you or anybody else change my mind." He heard the growl in his voice. "Wrong or right, I feel the guilt my dad laid on my family. Don't you see? I feel responsible for ruining your life."

He slammed the French doors to the balcony open and walked outside, letting the heat pour through the open doorway into the penthouse. Wind-whipped moisture hit him in the face and he turned aside. Rain? Stinging pellets of water pecked at his skin as thunder ricocheted through the clouds, lightning sparked off to the right. Wouldn't last long, but at least it would wash some of the suffocating heat away. Macki stepped up behind him, and he tensed. Shoved any thought of accepting her forgiveness into the pit of his anger.

"Look, it's raining." Macki's hand lightly brushed across his shoulder, then she walked up to the rail and lifted her head. Closing her eyes, she opened her mouth and stretched her neck upward, her cheeks rounding into small apple globes as she smiled and brushed her palms across her face. "It's finally raining..."

Was she crying, or was it the rain flowing down her face? He couldn't tell. Either way, she kept smiling. What could there possibly be to smile about? He'd just spilled his guts. Thrown enough hell at her to crush a person. Yet she was still smiling. Just like the first time he'd ever seen her there on the ground after he'd run into her catching the football.

God, she was resilient. He'd never known how resilient until now. Drake had been right. Macki wasn't devastated.

"There's something I need to say." She swept her hair back and tucked it, wet and shiny, behind her ears before turning to face him. "I want to thank you."

Shaking his head, he stepped back from her, held his hands up in front of himself, palms facing outward. He might not be able to stop her words, but he could stop her touch.

"Hear me out, Josh. Sure, on a cop level I've still got a lot of questions, but on a personal level...I thank you." Focusing on the lights of the city, she licked her lips, appearing to savor the taste of the rain. "You see, for years I've wondered what I did wrong to push you away. Even after my brain said it wasn't my fault, part of me still wondered." A tiny, husky giggle escaped her mouth. "Turns out I didn't do anything wrong. I thank you for giving me that peace."

"That's not why I told you." He couldn't believe what he was hearing. The woman who should be damning him to hell was thanking him. He lowered his hands because he had no defense against what was happening. Was this another form of torture the gods had sent to cut him to the quick? "I don't want your thanks...for anything. I don't deserve—"

"I'm not finished." She raised her own hands, sliding her fingers back and forth in the air. "Ever since you and Drake told me about the real reason the plane crashed, I've been wracking my brain, trying to figure out who could have done such a thing. Knowing Coercion Ten had been behind it wasn't enough for me. I needed a person to put with the crime."

"So now you know it was my dad and that makes you feel better?" Josh shook his head to loosen the rain pouring down his face. "That doesn't make sense."

"Don't you see, that's not the point." She patted her chest. "I've been going crazy trying to figure out if it was a friend of mine or of my parents. Maybe one of the staff here at the hotel. Someone on the police force. Or someone like Roxy who pretended to be my friend when they weren't."

She turned and sighed. "The past few days have been horrible. Then in one statement, you put it all to rest. You gave me the answer I needed. Otherwise, I'd have kept searching for an answer. Maybe forever."

He understood the unending search. For him, he would never be whole until he discovered the person behind Coercion Ten. The one who somehow knew his dad needed every dime he could make to keep the two of them going. Someone who knew a big enough offer could turn even a good man bad. Yes, Josh understood the unending search, so for not putting her through such agonizing pursuits, he could feel some relief.

"Macki, can't you see that when all this happened we were too young to see the gray of things? Back then, there was only black and white, good and bad. I had to leave. Surely you don't believe you would have reacted the same at that time as you have now."

"Oh, I'm not saying that at all. In fact, if this had all come out back then, I don't know what I would have done." She shook her head. "I imagine I would have pushed you out the door. Screamed and yelled and...I can't begin to imagine what I would have called you. What I would have said."

"You'd have said 'like father like son,' just the way you

did the other night when you were trying to figure out who had done such a thing." Right now, he almost wished she'd shout that in his face, but she wouldn't. By her peaceful expression, he could see she wasn't lying about how she felt.

She reached out and touched his arm. "That was anger talking. Anger and confusion. I'm sorry for everything I said the other night. I'd never want someone's family to suffer. Never."

The rain pummeled harder, and she once again lifted her face to greet the storm. "Nothing can bring back my parents. Nothing can change what your father did. But you and I aren't the same Macki and Josh we were back then. We've grown in so many ways. Done a lot of things in our life that we're proud of. Probably a few we aren't so proud of, too."

She swiped her palms down through her hair. "All I'm saying is you're a man and I'm a woman who deserve to get past the past. For me, the closure came tonight. For you... Well, you have to find your own closure, Josh. I can't find it for you. I can only hope that someday you give up your personal battle."

He wrapped his arm around her shoulders as they both got drenched in the escalating downpour. That much he could give her. That much he could give himself. Hope would have to lie in her corner, not his.

"Come on. We need to go inside." He pointed at the approaching lightning. Back in the penthouse, they each grabbed a towel from the kitchen to dry off, only he focused on wiping her face instead of his own. "You should go change."

"Not yet. How come Drake was the one to find your dad?"

"What?"

"The ambulance report said Captain Drake Lawrence found your dad."

"There is no such report."

"Yes, there is. I just saw it."

Josh flipped open her laptop. "Show me. Where did you see that? Nothing has ever been on the Internet, or anyplace else, for that matter. Nothing except the small obit Drake made me put in the paper."

"I read that first. Seemed vague. Then I took a chance and tried to get into some password-protected police and EMT files. My password should have been deactivated three years ago when I quit the force, but it let me in." She keyed in a duplicate search from before, then the password.

Denied popped on the screen. She entered the password again.

Denied.

He nudged her out of the chair and typed in code letters that should take him deep into the machine's history. Nothing showed up. He clicked the specialized search key on his phone and held it against her laptop. No history showed for the past hour. Whatever had been there was gone.

Coercion Ten had succeeded in getting the info to her. Had set him up. Had brought emotions into play. They were closing in for the kill—Drake, Macki, and himself.

Sparks of adrenalin shot through Josh's blood. Coercion Ten had started their mind game part of planting what they wanted you to focus on. Counting on the fact that you would believe anything after enough proof. Distract you enough to make you miss a clue.

"Tell me what the form looked like." On his cell, he connected his secure text to Drake, ready to key in all the gleaned information he could get from whatever she told him about the file.

"The form looked strange, for one thing. Not like any report I'd seen before."

"What did it say?"

She gently shook her head, focusing to remember. "It had your dad's name. DOA." She glanced up at him, then looked back down as she concentrated. "Said Captain

Drake Lawrence found him and that he'd notify Garrett Rogers's son." She looked up again. "Did he? Is that how you first learned what happened?"

"Yes. Drake handled everything that day."

"And you trust him?" Whipping her hand in front of her mouth, she blushed. "Where the hell did that come from?"

"Of course I trust him. Otherwise I wouldn't be here." He shook his head as he keyed more info into the protected OPAQUE line. "Drake will get a kick out of being doubted by his own niece."

"Don't tell him."

"Too late. Besides, you reacted the same way an OPAQUE agent would react."

The phone binged with a return message.

Josh felt a legit grin fill his face for the first time in a long, long while as he read the damn-it-to-hell reply from her uncle. "Ends up Drake's not amused. But he said you might make a good agent one day."

Josh didn't like the raised eyebrows or the sudden light in her eyes. "Don't get any ideas, Macki. Now, what else did the form say?"

"Something about it being an accidental overdose, but that's where it was strange. A different word that started with an *su* had been smudged out and the accidental part written in."

"No telling how long ago Coercion Ten planted that info for you to find."

"Why didn't OPAQUE find it?"

"In all likelihood, it's encrypted with your password as the trigger to open. OPAQUE would have never searched with that key because they didn't have it." He finished his message to Drake and ended the feed. "My best bet is that once you logged off the site, everything you saw automatically erased. Disappeared into thin air with no tracks left behind."

He smiled. "At least no tracks they think we can find."

She rubbed the dishtowel across her dripping hair once

again. "Can you find it?"

"Tech experts at the office are probably already tapping their computer keys to find a trail. Question is how long will it take. Could be all night. Could be a week. Maybe longer."

He wouldn't tell her that sometimes it was only in hindsight that codes could be completely deciphered. For some reason, he doubted that would happen this time. Whoever had set this up locally had wanted her to find that information, but they would give it time to simmer before they made their next move. Time was all OPAQUE needed. One more second of time, again and again and again.

"Well, I'm going to take a bath and crawl into bed. It's been an exhausting day and I can't think about this anymore tonight." She tossed the towel on the counter, then headed to her bedroom.

"Everything we talked about earlier, you need—"

She paused. "I've already said what I had to say. But I will repeat it one more time so you understand once and for all. Then never again." She glanced back with the determination of a woman in charge of her destiny. "Never. Got that?"

Amazed at the difference the day had made in her confident attitude, he nodded in agreement.

"In my mind, you are not responsible for the past. I've already let it go on a personal level. I don't think any less of you than I did this morning. And I don't think any more of you for carrying the load all these years." Stepping into her bedroom, she slowly grazed her palm down the side of the door. "You seem to be the only one hung up on your martyr-responsibility theory. That's a shame, Josh. One hell of a shame."

Watching the door, he noticed that once again she had left it ajar. How could that be? How could she have listened to what he had to say and still offer him the world? Didn't make sense. He couldn't have been wrong all these years, could he?

Hell, as much as Drake, and the other men Josh trusted in OPAQUE, had tried to convince him otherwise, he'd never faltered in the pride he took in carrying the past's responsibility. Like a badge of honor.

But had it been a badge? Or a shield? A shield he'd held in front of him for years to keep from facing the gray in life and moving on. Damn, a thirty-minute conversation with Macki had not only put a mile-wide crack in his thinking, a world of weight had lifted off his back. He wasn't sure how he felt about that. One thing for sure, she was right when she said this had been an exhausting day. A hell of an exhausting day.

A soft whisper of music floated through the open doorway to her room just like every other night, then the damn vanilla and jasmine enveloped his senses...just like every other night.

This time the ache in his core grabbed with a vengeance. Tightened and twisted and threatened to take him to his knees. His need pulled him to live for the future, while only a tiny echo tugged him to the past.

His conscience shouted, *Close the damn door, Josh. Walk over and close her bedroom door before it's too late.*

"Aw, hell." He hurled his towel against the cabinet. It was already too late. Jerking his head back to stare at the ceiling, he realized he might never understand why he'd put himself through hell the past ten years. But he knew for damn certain that out on that balcony in the rain half an hour ago, the past stopped dictating his life.

Breathing in the sweet scents coming from Macki's bath, he palmed his jaw line back and forth, then grinned. He needed a shave.

CHAPTER TWENTY-TWO

The oversized tub had taken forever to fill, but Mackenzie had to admit it was worth the time as she watched the bubbles grow larger and larger. She finally settled back in the tub, positioning herself on the molded contours of the bottom until the foam tickled her chin. Resting her head back against the soft pillow inset, she sighed and let the warmth and scent of the bubbly water soothe her from a day she'd never forget.

For once in a long time she felt free, felt like she could breathe without any constraints. About time...because she was ready to move forward and meet the rest of her life. Sighing, she realized the other thing she felt was alone—more alone than ever before. Tonight she'd let all possibility of the past fly out the window when she released the young, carefree Josh and Macki of ten years ago.

Now they were a man and a woman...older, wiser, more experienced...who to all intents and purposes appeared to be worlds apart. Each with their own base to start the future. She smiled deep inside at the unknown filling that vacant view. Somewhere, sometime there would be a man who filled her with a glow to last a lifetime. She could wait for him, knowing she was okay the way she was for the time being. One thing for certain, she'd know him the moment she saw him...someday.

Clink-bing...clink-bing...

She jerked her head toward the French doors leading to

her bathroom, zeroing in on the sound. Two crystal wine glasses clinked together upside down in the fingers of one strong hand. Another hand gripped a bottle of wine. Her focus expanded and...

Lord help her, there he was. Agent. Joshua. Slater.

Not the boy she knew ten years ago or the agent she'd met on D Street a few days back, not even the man who'd held her in the rain on the balcony an hour ago. The guy filling her doorway was shirtless, tanned, and tempting. And the expression on his face made her blush to her toes.

She'd never had a man look at her like she was a luxury car with cockpit design, leather seats, and a 625 horsepower engine—bright, shiny, and waiting to be driven.

Damn it to hell and son of a gun, she wasn't sure she was up to this.

His muscles were tight and hard across his chest and biceps, and something told her the view from the back would show the same for his shoulders. His jeans hugged low on his sides with just enough view to make a woman's mouth water. Just enough covered to make her dream.

Fiddling her fingers below the waterline, part of her wanted to follow their lead and squish completely beneath the bubbles to escape the heat in his dusky blue eyes. Part of her yelled, *Hide, be shy, what do you know about satisfying a man like this?* Another part yelled, *Bring it on! What are you afraid of?* She stilled her fingers and listened to the "bring it on" voice crackling in her core.

A grin quirked the side of his mouth as his bare feet expertly evaded the fluffy rugs and stepped across the cool granite, coming to a stop next to the tub. He was everything she'd wanted all these years— No, what she'd envisioned had been a pale comparison of what stood before her now. Because this Josh was hot—holy-as-hell hot.

"You feel you can just walk into my bath?" Her voice sounded sultry even to herself. Soft, sassy, and sultry? She needed to be careful. Not assume too much.

He bit his bottom lip and raised his eyebrows. "Well, you haven't told me to leave, so I figure we're okay." His gaze slid across her and the tub. "Awful lot of bubbles in that thing."

"What can I say...I like bubbles." Her fingers paddled to make more.

He barely cocked his head to the side. "They smell nice, I'll give you that. But you look like a head floating on a sea of foam."

She bent her knee, then straightened her leg high in the air with her foot arched and pointed to the ceiling. Lazing her ankle in a slow circle, she couldn't believe how wicked she felt. "You never know what's lurking beneath the bubbles."

Slowly, she lowered her leg back beneath the bubbles.

"Well, that was something. Got any more tricks?"

She backed up in the tub, stopping where the bubbles continued to cover her breasts as she slid her arms on the edge of the rims. "That's it for now."

"So there's hope for later?"

She swished her palm across the top of the bubbles, pelting him with the spray.

Glancing at the bubbly mess mingling with the dark hair on his chest and twining pathways downward, he smirked as if everything was going as planned. He held up the bottle of wine. "I thought you might want something to drink. Says it's a Riesling that goes with about anything. Doesn't say anything about bubbles, but why not?"

Balancing the two wine glasses in his hand, he poured them each a glass and set them on the rim of the tub. He held his hand in the air to stop any comments, then headed to the doorway. Returning quickly, he balanced two small plates on his palms, setting one within her reach and taking one with him.

A whiff of aftershave caught her senses. "That looks like an awfully close shave there."

"Glad you noticed." He raked his fingers through his

wet, tousled hair, then crouched beside her, setting his plate on the tile.

Bracing against the side of the tub, he eased his gun from the back of his jeans and laid it on the floor beside him as he sat down. Something about the ease with which he did it seemed as natural to him as breathing.

He leaned back against the towel cabinet and closed his eyes, sighing long and easy as if he were a man home from a long day at work. "This is nice."

The minutes ticked by as they each sipped their wine. She nibbled on the cheese and peaches on her plate. He gulped down the cheese and salami on his. Maybe this was what life was all about. Just enjoying the foods and scents and feelings of being completely at peace. She could do this forever.

"You ever been to the pyramids?" His relaxed tone belied the intensity in his eyes as they opened, watching for her reaction with their scrutiny.

"No."

"Asia?"

She shook her head. "Nope."

He cleared his throat. "South America?"

"I'm more of the European side. England? France?"

This time he shook his head.

"How about Holland or Sweden? I went there last year."

"No. Can't say as I have."

He poured them a refill of the wine that went with anything, but something in his expression had dimmed during the question and answer.

She couldn't read Agent Slater like she could Josh, but there were still a few tells. Right now he was testing the waters, so to speak, but which waters she wasn't sure. "Why all the travel questions? What are you searching for?"

Blowing out a cheek-puffing breath, he intertwined his fingers and stretched his arms out in a hands-backward movement. Then he braced his hands on the floor as he glanced at her, at the gun next to him, and then at the doorway. For a second, she thought he was getting up. She let him be until he leaned back against the cabinet again, till he seemed comfortable with whatever was going on in his brain. This time when he looked at her, she didn't turn away or make a joke or smile—only waited for more questions.

Downing the last of his wine, he rimmed his fingers around the edge of the crystal. "What did you do last Christmas Eve?"

Christmas? That should be a safe subject. "Uncle Drake and I shared dinner with the staff here at the hotel. Helped serve dinner at a couple of the local food pantries on Christmas Day, then flew to Hawaii for a week of vacation." She felt as if that wasn't a good enough answer for him. "Why? What did you do?"

"Drake assigned me and Granger, another agent I work with sometimes, to a special case the day before." Josh shook his head. "About noon on Christmas Eve, I burrowed in through a makeshift tunnel to rescue a five-year-old girl who'd been kidnapped by a man and woman. They'd planned to make a hell of a lot of money off her family."

She felt the crease in her brow. "I thought OPAQUE was all about saving people who've been targeted by Coercion Ten as leverage."

"We take on other cases too. Some with people who need out-of-the-norm protection for whatever reason. And sometimes we're referred, so to speak, by law enforcement. This family needed help in...uh, creative...retrieval."

"Sounds like you saved a little girl. Got her home for Christmas with her family. That's wonderful." She couldn't imagine how worried those parents must have been. "I hope the kidnappers got what was coming to them."

"Yeah. They got exactly what was coming to them." His breathing intensified, along with the clinch of his jaw, his look focused on a distant thought through suddenly steely, gray-blue eyes. "From the looks of the place, they had no intention of ever releasing her."

Neither spoke for the next couple of minutes. The

expression on Josh's face told her everything she needed to know.

He twirled the goblet stem between his palms. "She was a cute little girl with big brown eyes. Once I took care of business in that room, she wrapped her arms around my neck in an air-sucking grip. Wouldn't let go till her dad opened the door back at the estate and she jumped in his arms." He paused, swallowed hard. "I never saw a man so happy in all my life."

Mackenzie had no words to compare with that memory.

"Before I left, he handed me and Granger each a bottle of...well, let's just say those were the oldest bottles of scotch I'll ever see in my life."

"Bet you spent the night with a bottle of scotch and a pretty lady?" She teased him with raised eyebrows, for some reason hoping that had been exactly the release for him that night.

"Nope. Granger had to leave for another assignment, so I had him drop me off by a park with a bunch of homeless men staking out their spot around the fire can. Me and that ragtag group opened that century-old bottle of scotch and passed it around. We toasted every damn thing we could till there wasn't a drop left."

She couldn't change the difference in their holidays, but she wasn't the one who had to get past that. "If you hang around here till Christmas, we can make some new memories."

"Hang around? Make new memories? Hell, Macki, by then I'll be on another rocket-to-hell assignment where some other low-level rodent of society gets what they're due." Harsh...his tone had been harsh and matter-of-fact. Josh jumped to his feet, grabbed his gun, and started for the door. "We're done here."

"What's wrong? Where are you going?" She felt him slipping back inside himself. "Come back and explain to me what the hell you're getting at with all these questions."

True, she couldn't save him from himself, but surely

there was some rope, some lifeline, she could toss him. Something like the round life-buoy that people threw to swimmers floundering in the water. A buoy that all the person had to do was reach out and grab.

He jerked his jeans up high on his hips and walked back to the side of the tub. "Don't you see, Macki? We have nothing in common. Nothing at all."

"What does that mean to you?"

"Means we can't do this. Because if we have nothing in common, then this is only about sex, and I won't do that to you. You deserve better."

"And I won't accept just sex either. We can't change the past." She touched his fingertips with her own, then tugged the side of his pants leg, inching the jeans lower on his hips. "Only the future. Think about it, Josh, and sit back down. Please."

He narrowed his eyes, but he sat back down on the floor, once again placing his gun on the floor beside him.

In that moment, she'd never felt so cherished in all her life. She wasn't alone, she just needed to give him time to realize they were about more than sex. Although right now that sounded damn good to her.

"What's your favorite kind of cookie?" She downed the remainder of her drink.

He leaned back, staring at the ceiling. "That's silly."

"What's your favorite kind of cookie?"

"Big, plump oatmeal cookies loaded with raisins and walnuts. Satisfied?"

Oatmeal? Did it have to be oatmeal? Every time she tried to eat one, she gagged on the consistency. And raisins? Raisins were not on her fruit list.

"Oh my gosh. Me too!" She rounded her eyes in a show of excitement, trying to remember how people who loved oatmeal cookies ate them. "Sometimes I heat them up in the microwave for breakfast."

"Me, too." He grinned. "And there's nothing like two of them with marshmallow cream for a middle."

"Oh, so, so good." She was going to need to do penance after these fibs. "See, we do have something in common after all. Right?" She popped the last bite of cheese in her mouth. "Cheese. Riesling. Oatmeal cookies."

His laughter filled her with its sound. "Okay, Macki. I'll give you that one. We do have something in common. Not much, but it's a start."

He edged closer and closer to where she leaned against the back of the tub. With each movement, she felt him change back to the man he'd been when he walked into her bathroom. When he was close enough, she brushed her hand across his, leaning her head and parting her lips to wait for what she saw in his expression.

As if reading her need, he lowered his mouth to hers, tangling his fingers in her hair till she released to his hold. His tongue had its way with hers as she clutched at his shoulders, his face, any part of him she could hold onto for even a second. Afraid that if she let him pull away, she'd never taste him again. And he tasted so damn good all she could do was wallow in the pure pleasure.

He grasped her hands in his and pushed back just a bit. "Slow down, Macki. I'm not going anywhere."

"You almost walked out a while ago." She listened to her breathing as it slowed. Had she been so desperate for his touch she'd lost control and become the drowning person who needed the buoy herself?

"Yeah, well I didn't, did I?" He lowered his forehead to hers.

"No, you didn't."

He grazed his eyes lower. "Now that's interesting."

"What?"

"Evidently, bubbles disappear after a while."

She glanced down, slapping her hands across her breasts. He laughed for a moment as he nibbled his way down her neck to her collarbone to her shoulder tip and the waterline. Then gently nudging her hands aside, he made one long pass of his hand down and up the middle of her body. She straightened in the tub, arching to his touch as he cupped her breast, teasing his thumb across the tip.

When his hands left her body, she ached for the warmth and seduction to return. She wasn't finished. She wanted more. Suddenly she heard the click of the drain being released and the rush of water down and out of the tub. Unable to keep her gaze away, she watched him as his hand caressed the arch of her foot, teased with an upward stroke of her ankle, across the back of her calf, her knee. When she bent her knee in tickle-reflex, he kissed the top as if kissing her lips.

"I saw a picture of you in your sailboat once. Your hair all tangled in the wind and your long legs stretched out on the rail. Every time I've been on a boat, that image has been somewhere in the back of my mind." He quickly paddled the water, returning a burst of small bubbles, then tapped a dollop of the foam on her nose.

She brushed the bubbles from her face. "See, that's something else we have in common. We both like sailing."

"I didn't say I liked to sail." He winked and lifted her leg up in the air the way she had before. Teased along the back of her calf, her knee, her thigh.

Heaven help her, she wanted him more than life itself. Wanted to wrap her legs around him as he leaned into her. Wanted to tuck her legs between his as they snuggled together afterward.

"I liked the legs...your legs." He lowered her leg, trailing his palm down and upward once again, slow and easy with just the right pressure to push her to the edge. "Your long, silky legs."

At some point along the way, she closed her eyes, tempted only by the feel of his hand on her flesh. Slowly, oh so slowly, his fingers caressed the inner part of her thigh till they brushed lightly against her parting and over her mound, pausing as if feeling the pulse of the moment.

His own breathing, loud and labored, called attention to his own arousal. His own need and want. She clinched her fingers in his hair, trying to steer him, but he eased them away and continued his tracing path upward from her breast to her shoulder to her mouth once again.

This time, he allowed her need to come at him with the same power he'd given her until his groan mingled with whispers of passion and he pushed away. Still in his jeans, he walked to the shower and stepped inside the oversized, two-person glass enclosure, turning on the water and angling the shower heads in the walls and ceiling before stepping out again.

He reached into his jean pocket, pulled out a handful of foil packets, and laid them on the edge of the tub. Then he unbuttoned, unzipped, and pushed the jeans to the floor. Lord help her, there he was again...Agent...Josh Slater in all his manhood. Hot and sexy and hers for the taking.

Crossing back to the tub, he held out his hand. "Come on, Macki. Time to rinse off."

She took his hand and as she rose to her feet, her other hand teased up his thigh, his side, his chest. Leaning toward him, she brushed her fingers down to feel his strength, but he nudged her aside.

"Woman, I don't have much control left right now. And I plan for this to be all about you."

"I think this is about us." She looped her arms around his neck, trailing her kisses across his chest, tasting the salt of his skin with her tongue. "Besides...don't you think those thick fluffy rugs on the floor need to be initiated?" She scraped her nails lightly down his side. "Now."

He scooped her out of the tub, and her legs folded around him as he turned and went down to his knees on the hard granite. Laying her gently back on the rug, he braced his elbows beside her as he kissed her lips. Slow and to the point, he pulsed his hard length against her core.

Once... Twice...

She palmed his face in her hand. "Oh, how I missed you, Josh."

"I missed you too, Macki. Really. Really. Missed you."
...Three times.

CHAPTER TWENTY-THREE

Josh opened his eyes to make sure he hadn't dreamed the past hours. The ones involving him and Macki, bubbles and wine, a rug, a bed and— Hell, he felt good. Felt the way a man should feel who just spent the night making love to the woman he loved.

He shifted closer to her warmth and slid his fingers over her breast. She sighed. Then, stretching like a lazy cat who had laid in the sun too long, she wiggled herself into the mold of his body. God, he was one lucky man. Waking up beside her was all he ever wanted for the rest of his life. Just not everything he wanted this morning.

"You gonna sleep all day?" He smoothed his hand down the curve of her hip as she slid up enough to kiss his lips.

She smiled at his touch. "What are you doing in my bed, Agent Slater?"

"Couldn't quite seem to crawl out of the covers. Some woman kept pulling me back all night."

"Really? She must have been one crazy broad."

"Oh, she was crazy, all right."

She giggled as he popped his head under the covers. The muffled sound of his cell phone ringtone made him stop and shove back the covers as he rolled out of bed. He grabbed his gun from the nightstand, then ran to the master bath where he'd left his phone the night before. Life had rushed back in a flash.

He grappled with sliding into his jeans as he accepted

the call. "Hello."

"Hey, it's Granger."

"Yeah. Where are you?"

"I'm here at Hotel MacKenzie. Evidently only one elevator goes all the way to the penthouse floor, and it's down for service."

"I took that one out of commission for security reasons." Josh tucked his gun in the waistband of his jeans as he headed back to the bedroom. Where the hell were his shoes?

Macki leaned over the side of the mattress and put her head next to Josh's as he knelt down. Her breath against his ear stymied what little control he had at the moment.

"What are you looking for?" she whispered.

He held the phone away from his mouth and answered quietly. "Shoes."

"You didn't have them on last night." She shook her head as she brushed her fingers across his shoulders. "Are you coming back to bed any time soon?"

He laughed, then tweaked her nose before leaning over and kissing her soundly. "Afraid not. Duty calls."

She turned over and cuddled back into her pillow.

"Hello? Hello?" Granger's voice brought Josh back to reality. "Anybody there?"

"Yeah, I'm here." Josh started down the hall. "Come up the stairs. I'll meet you at the fire door entry."

"Already did. All fifteen damn flights of stairs. Me and the two heavier-than-hell bags I'm holding." Granger grunted loudly and to the point. "Now forget about the damn shoes and open the stairwell door."

Josh ended the call on the way to the outer hallway. Once there, he opened the stairwell's steel fire door, and grabbed one of the bags from Granger. One look at the smug expression on the man's face said his team member had heard everything.

Granger nodded as he took in Josh's appearance. "No shirt. No shoes. Bet you got service, though."

"Stop before you say another word." The guys had always joked around, but Macki wasn't a joke. As of last night, she was off-limits to every other man out there. "'Cause I swear I'll put you on the floor."

"What? Since when can't I have a little fun with my agent buddy?" Granger set the bag he'd carried inside over by the kitchen counter, then slapped Josh on the back. "Nobody ever said paybacks weren't hell. Where's your sense of humor this morning? You look like you've had a busy night."

"Yeah, so do you."

"I bet you had more fun though."

"I said, don't go there."

A tried and true shrug of his shoulders meant Granger had already left the topic. Team members knew each other's ins, outs, shrugs, smiles, growls, everything that meant anything. Little nuances sometimes transferred information. Sometimes saved their lives. And sometimes just said leave me the hell alone. Or I'm already gone.

He and Granger had been part of a team for a long time. They'd watched others fall. Winced when the replacements showed up. Swore they'd keep their distance and not make friends with the new additions. But they had. And they would. That was how a team succeeded.

Josh walked to his room, returning with shoes on his feet and a shirt in his hand. "And don't think for one minute I believe you climbed all fifteen flights of steps. You may be dense as concrete, but you still know how to take the elevator to the fourteenth floor, come through the unlocked stairwell door, and walk up one level."

Granger laughed, but didn't claim either statement as true.

For the next couple of minutes, Josh filled the coffeemaker with water and coffee grounds, then waited for it to brew. He needed caffeine. Good super strong coffee and caffeine. Granger looked like he'd spent a long ragged night of travel to reach Riverfalls this early. That's what

OPAQUE agents did when one of their own needed help. Or when the job they were on split into more than one trail.

"I haven't heard anything from Drake yet, so we've got a little time." He nodded toward the hallway to the guest rooms as he walked to the balcony door. "Second room on the left will be yours if you want to clean up."

"We've got a problem." Granger opened the refrigerator just like he lived there, then pulled out a jug of orange juice. After flipping open a couple of cabinet doors, he found a glass and poured it full. Chugged it down and refilled. Chugged again.

Nothing to update explained why Josh's boss hadn't called back.

The bedroom door opened and Macki stepped into the room. Wrapped in a barely closed sheet, she rubbed her fingers across her eyes as she glanced in Josh's direction. "Do you want me to make breakfast for us?"

Granger set his glass on the counter and grinned. "Well that's mighty nice of you, ma'am. 'Cause I for one am famished."

She jerked her head up and to the right in one quick move. Her hands seized the sheet in a vise grip, clutching the material against her body. "Who...when...uhhh."

"This is Agent Granger. He's the man your uncle sent to protect Roxy." Josh walked over and put his arm across Macki's shoulder. "And this is Mackenzie Baudin. The boss's niece.""Ma'am." Granger nodded, then shot Josh one of his *What the hell do you think you're doing* looks.

"Agent Granger. I'm glad you got here so fast." Macki inched out of Josh's hold. "I think I'll get dressed now."

Raising his eyebrows, Josh narrowed his focus on Granger, daring the man to say anything out of line. Granger simply stared down at the counter and poured himself another glass of orange juice.

"Since we've got a lot of work to do, why don't I call down and order up breakfast?" Josh moved toward the house phone.

"Sounds good to me." Granger glanced around the open space of the living room and kitchen, no doubt taking in the security systems Josh had already installed.

"Me, too. Make mine blueberry waffles and bacon. Remind them to call when they start up the last flight of stairs, so we can let them in." She glanced at the empty juice container on the counter. "Have them send up a couple jugs of orange juice also."

Josh was proud of her. She'd handled herself as if nothing out of the ordinary had just taken place. She hadn't been embarrassed or thrown off for even a second.

"Thank you, ma'am." Professional Granger was on the job now. This was also what OPAQUE agents did. They were polite, courteous, and unseeing of personal occurrences.

"Call me Macki." She disappeared into the bedroom and closed the door behind her.

Josh walked back over to the balcony windows and stared into the jumble of buildings jutting into the skyline. Some tall. Some short. Some old. Some shiny and new. Riverfalls had everything a large-size city should have. This was the first time since he'd arrived back in town that he'd taken time see it for the place he called his hometown.

"She the one?" Granger's question, the tone, was as a friend. One who'd listened to Josh's story for years.

Josh felt the corner of his mouth quirk in a half smile. "Yeah. She's the one."

"Well, believe it or not, I'm glad you worked things out. Everybody deserves..." Granger rolled his hand into a fist and rubbed his thumb across his knuckles. Josh recognized the move as one his teammate used to fight the memory of his own loss. Then as if a switch had been thrown, Granger spread his fingers and grinned as he walked over to the bag in the corner. "Everybody deserves breakfast. Make that phone call and let's get down to business."

He opened the case and pulled out his laptop. "'Cause like I said. We've got a problem."

* * *

Macki had showered and dressed in record time, finishing just as breakfast arrived from downstairs. Seated or standing around the kitchen island, she, Josh, and Granger ate as they tried to piece Roxy's puzzle together. And there were a lot of missing pieces.

"No daughter?" Macki felt the pinch between her eyebrows. "That doesn't make sense. You said OPAQUE tracked down the birth certificate. So of course Roxy has a daughter. I mean, why would she make something like that up?"

Granger pushed his plate away. "I'm just saying the trail from the hospital is cold. And if OPAQUE can't find it, then there's no trail to be found."

"Adoption? Death?"

"Both of which would have a paper trail. There is none."

She thought for moment. There had to be another lead. "What about the money Roxy used to send the girl? I went to the bank with her one day. I actually saw her wire the money to another account."

To the point and straight, Granger held his index finger up. "There's the rub. She sends money at least every other month. Always has. It goes to an account in Arizona. The first of each month, there's an automatic withdrawal that gets sent to a bank in California."

Macki braced her elbow on the counter and rested her forehead on her fingertips. "Ooooooooh, Roxy. What's going on?"

The agent swigged down a gulp of coffee. Pointed again. "Wait. There's more. Every three months, the account in California gets swept, leaving only enough to not incur bank charges. And that money goes to an off-shore account in the Cayman Islands."

"Let me guess. That account is owned by some dummy corporation." Mackie had helped the FBI take down just such a group when she was a cop. Following the trail was hard, occasionally impossible without months of investigation. Right now they didn't have much time.

"You got it." Granger finished his coffee

Josh walked his plate to the sink and leaned back against the counter. Instead of tossing questions into the conversation, he seemed to just be listening. And thinking. She could almost see the wheels turning.

"Get Roxy on the speaker phone." Josh still hadn't moved.

Macki dialed the woman's number.

"Hey, you've got foxy Roxy. What can I do for you?" Same tone. Same words. Same purr-like-a-kitten breaths.

"This is Mackenzie Baudin. I've got you on speaker phone."

A long pause, then even longer. "Who's listening?"

Josh motioned for the phone to be put on the counter. "Do you recognize my voice?"

"Yes."

"Well there's me, Macki, and one of my associates who's come to town to help you. But we need your help locating your daughter. From what we've found so far, she's not showing up."

"Then I...I..."

Granger pointed at himself meaning he'd ask some questions. "Roxy, you don't know me yet, but I'm trying to put everything into place for you and your daughter...Sandy...Sandy D. Street. Right?"

"Yes."

"The birth certificate I got from Chicago didn't list a father. Now, if you could give me that name it would be a big help. Maybe she's using that last name." The agent held his hands up as if to stop any fuss back from her. Acted just as if she could see him. "I promise I won't contact him. You've got my word."

"No. I can't give you that name. I...I..."

Macki motioned the others to be quiet. Roxy never stuttered. "What's wrong, Roxy?"

The woman's breathing became jerky, almost as if she

was near tears. "I need to go. I can't keep talking to you."

"Just two more questions, I promise." Granger's tone was calm and friendly. "Okay?"

"Hurry up before somebody traces this call."

"Hang up, Roxy. We'll call right back." Josh ended the call. They waited thirty seconds, then Macki redialed.

The phone rang and rang and rang. All the while, Macki visualized D Street. The women. Roxy. Life. Death. Fear. Lots of fear. First of all, Roxy must have been getting a bad vibe from whoever had her wrapped around their finger. Otherwise, she'd have never agreed to give Josh any information last night. And right now, Roxy had to be scared out of her wits.

Phoning again and again, all Macki could do was pray Roxy would answer sooner or later. Granger walked to the window, then back and forth, back and forth.

Josh motioned once again for Macki to lay the phone on the counter. "If Roxy's going to talk to us, it will be on her terms. So all we can do is wait."

"What if—"

The phone rang and Roxy showed on the caller ID. Macki clicked the call to speaker as Granger walked back to the counter. Nobody said a word.

"Talk fast, Mister Agentman."

Granger grabbed his pen and paper. "What number do you call when you talk to Sandy?"

"I've never talked to my daughter."

"What do you mean you've never—"

A pitiful noise came through the phone as Roxy sucked in a breath. "I never...even got to...hold her. I...I..."

Macki shook her head to let the men know she didn't know what to say. Had no information on this count. She opened her mouth to ask for an explanation, but Josh motioned everyone to be quiet. To wait for Roxy.

The woman blew out a sigh. "I'd been powerful sick with that pregnancy. Almost died. So the doctors knocked me out for a few days when she was born. By the time I came to, the adoption I'd agreed to beforehand had already happened and she was gone." Roxy cleared her throat. "I never even got to see my beautiful daughter."

"So who told you to send her money?"

"Nobody. I just do."

"Who set up the account for you?"

"Her father."

"And how do you know she needs protection?"

"Her father told me. Told me I...I... Listen, I've got to go. I can't talk to you any longer."

Macki knew time was of the essence if there was a trace, but the question had to be asked again. "Who's the father, Roxy?"

"No."

"Tell me who the father is so I can find Sandy for you?" Granger used a firm but understanding tone this time. "You know she's in danger. And you love her. I know you love her, Roxy. I know you want to hold her in your arms. So help me find her before it's too late." He paused. "Who's the father?"

Roxy's breathing echoed through the phone in loud puffs. "No. No. It's better living the way I've been living than to chance her life any more."

Josh leaned forward over the phone. "Why? Why can't you tell us who the father is?"

"It'll all be there when I give you your information. I promise you that. Now find my daughter." Click. The line went dead.

CHAPTER TWENTY-FOUR

Search. Search. Search. That's all Josh had done for the past couple of hours since he, Granger, and Macki had spoken with Roxy. They hadn't got much from her except she was scared. And the father was the key to everything. Maybe even to Coercion Ten.

OPAQUE had picked through every lead they could find. Roxy's daughter had simply vanished from the hospital. No adoption papers. No tax record exemptions. No social security card for a child named Sandy D. Street born on that date, or any date close to that. Thinking the new parents might have changed her name entirely, the group checked by birth date, city, hospital with just the first name. Nothing.

By mid-afternoon the three of them had to admit they were getting nowhere fast. They dialed up Drake on the secure line to Miami's OPAQUE office. The five-o'clock shadow on the boss's cheeks said he'd had a long night and day also. Josh, Macki, and Granger took up spots around the guest bedroom in Macki's penthouse, each with their own screen panel for the conversation. They might be hundreds of miles away from Drake, but the system made it as if they were all in the same room.

"So what do you want me to do?" Granger asked.

Drake shook his head. "I want you out on D Street. See what you can find. Make contact with Roxy and let her know we're trying. Maybe she'll say something of value."

Macki's phone chirped with a text message. "What the?" She keyed a response.

"What's that about?" Josh kept his seat in the oversized corner chair.

"The Planning and Zoning Committee of the city council has called a special emergency meeting at five thirty today. They want everyone to attend."

"Isn't that kind of short notice?"

She rounded her eyes and nodded emphatically. "That's just what I told them. I also told them I'm tied up. I'll send someone in my place." Her phone chirped again. She shook her head after reading the message. "Now they say the mayor insists everyone be there. Guess I'll have to go."

Josh leaned forward, resting his elbows on his knees. "Does this strike anyone else as strange?"

Granger nodded.

"Happens sometimes." Macki shrugged. "Besides, everyone got the message."

"How do you know?" Josh walked over to stand beside her.

"See the To line? That's everybody's name that's on Planning and Zoning."

He walked around the room as if analyzing the bedspread, the lamps, the chest of drawers. "I've got a bad feeling about this. Somebody already got into your text messaging before I arrived. And after that whole thing with the laptop and police access last night..." He plopped back in the corner chair. "Hell, maybe I'm just being paranoid."

Granger took up the room-pacing. "Go with your gut, man. It's never failed you."

"I agree." Drake braced his elbows on the desk in front of him, clasping his fingers as he stared over the monitor. "Macki, text one of the members directly. Make that two. Ask if they got that message."

She keyed in the text and sent it off. One councilman answered in about twenty seconds. The other's response chimed in a few seconds later. "Looks like they got the same message."

Nobody seemed ready to commit to yes or no on her going. Then everyone began talking at once. Most times, OPAQUE agents worked on their own, and right now that was exactly what seemed to take place.

Drake finally got the group's attention. "So here's the plan. I'm heading to Chicago to talk to my contacts face-to-face. Depending on what I find out, I'll head on down to Riverfalls or wherever the info takes me."

Josh glanced in his partner's direction. "I'll be point on Macki while she's at the committee meeting. And I don't plan to let her out of my sight."

"I'll back you up until the meeting is finished," Granger said. "After that I'll head to D Street."

"Sir, have we got any other backup in the area that we can trust?"

"Yeah, I sent someone I'd planned to meet in Chicago in your direction. But listen up. He's not really there." The boss paused. "Under no circumstances is he there. Got it?"

"Got it." The three said in unison.

"Good. Sounds like everything's covered for the moment." On his end, Drake was already on his feet, turning to leave.

Josh saw the moment concern inched across Macki's face. Not fear. Not anger. Not confusion. But an odd expression he'd never seen on her.

"Before we go, I've got something to say." Macki laid down the security screen she was holding and turned in his direction. "I don't know if Josh got a chance to relay the warning Tessa gave him from Coercion Ten last night. The one that targeted me, Drake, and Josh. Well..."

"He told me," Drake said.

She brushed her palms against her jeans as she nervously fidgeted. Biting her lower lip, Josh could swear he saw her chin tremble. This wasn't like her. She was always strong. Always on her game, from what he'd seen the past few days. What had her so upset now?

Drake sat back down, listening to his niece. Evidently he'd picked up on her demeanor also. "What's on your mind, Macki?"

Raising her head till her gaze met Josh's, she bit her lip even tighter. "Well, did he tell you that they specifically said Josh would be the first to go down?"

"No, he left that part out."

Josh shook his head at her. "That wasn't an important detail. I can take care of myself."

"Well, it's important to me." She didn't move from her spot. "You're important to me."

"Macki..." His chest burned with her words. He'd waited a lifetime to hear those words from her. Now that she'd said them, he was shaken to his soul with how much they meant to him. He'd never realized how much he needed her in order to feel whole.

"I never said you can't take care of yourself." She fidgeted again. "And yes, you've been a protector a long time. No doubt you've handled a million situations a hell of a lot more dangerous than this."

He wasn't so sure on that count, because Coercion Ten should be feeling threatened themselves right about now. And when a group like that got cornered, all bets were off. Rules and long-range plans went to hell. Same for OPAQUE.

"But this time, it's different." She reached out and touched his arm. "Because I love you, Joshua Slater. And if last night was any indication—"

He folded her into his arms and kissed the top of her head. Love. That had been the look he'd never seen. The reason she was nervous. God, this woman was his life. "Shhhhh. I love you, too. But we don't need to talk about last night in front of everybody and the world, you know?"

"I know. But you better not go and get yourself killed." She pulled away enough to shoot a glance at Granger and then Drake. "And you two better not let it happen either."

Shaking his head, Granger laid down his security panel

and walked out of the guest room, mumbling something about threats and women and never going to happen to him.

Over the top of Macki's head, Josh watched Drake's image on the computer. The man looked like he might explode. "I've waited a long time for you two to get your act together. But now is not a good time."

"Sorry about the timing, sir."

"Damn it to hell, Josh. This is nothing but one big cluster..." Drake held his breath, turning red behind the stubble of his unshaved beard. "Complication."

Josh knew the boss had a different word in mind. One he wouldn't use in front of his niece. Didn't matter. Josh had already figured the same thing out for himself. Still and all, he loved Macki and that wasn't going to change.

Trouble was if Coercion Ten found out, they'd have all the leverage they'd ever need against him. Except he'd seen what happened when victims held out against the group. Leverage could be emotionally, physically, and psychologically painful. A long, slow death. He'd never let that happen. He'd never let them take her out of his sight.

If he couldn't protect Macki, then the two of them would go down together.

CHAPTER TWENTY-FIVE

An hour later and on the way to city hall, Mackenzie and the agents still didn't feel any better about the hastily called Planning and Zoning meeting. Maybe Josh had been right. Maybe the whole Coercion Ten situation had them all paranoid.

Sure, these types of things could happen, since she sat on the committee. And from what she could tell, the other members had all received the same notice. Yet when paperwork she needed to look over prior to the meeting had arrived by email, she hadn't seen anything that couldn't have waited. Besides which, she'd never heard of the company requesting a special waiver for vacant property on the outskirts of Riverfalls.

Josh turned down the one-way street that ran in front of city hall and ended his call with OPAQUE headquarters. "From the info they tracked down on this company, they're legit. And they're looking to expand to the Midwest. Evidently got some deep pockets for jobs."

"All right, then. Looks like we're a go." She glanced at the surroundings, the same way she noticed Josh had been doing ever since they pulled out of her private garage. "I know you said Granger would be your backup, but where is he?"

"He's already in the area. Right about now, I'm sure he's got eyes on us."

She breathed a little easier knowing her protector and his

backup were in communication. Before they'd left the penthouse, she'd noticed Josh had double checked his weapons. Then he'd taped a microphone to his chest. Granger had done the same. They each seemed to have a little different routine, but ended with the same results. She'd even checked the gun she carried in her bag.

"You got us, Granger?" Josh pushed his finger against the ear bud for the listening device he'd put on a few blocks back. Angling into one of the pull-in spots designated for committee members, he grinned as he came to a stop. "Yeah, well, you just keep your eyes on the street."

Josh pulled an extra Glock from the glove box and tucked it under his seat. Once he arranged everything just so, he glanced in her direction, locking eyes with her for a second before going back to his surveillance scan. She figured his gut feeling must be working overtime. She knew for sure hers was.

"You seem to be the first one here." Josh tapped the side of the steering wheel. "The two of us will wait in the truck till more of the committee members arrive."

Glancing at her watch, she didn't understand why no one else was there. In fact, everything seemed a little too quiet for late afternoon. Of course, the courthouse at the beginning of the next block appeared to be full-on packed, with every parking spot taken and people rushing in and out of the building.

"Josh, are we sitting ducks?" For some reason, she hadn't been able to keep herself from asking.

"Not yet. You got anything on your end, Granger?" Josh shook his head in reaction to the reply, then reached out and touched her hand. "We're good so far. I'm sure there's a rational explanation for this meeting."

"Sure." She rolled her eyes. "That would explain why I'm sitting with one OPAQUE agent in my car. Another hidden somewhere on the street. My gun loaded and easy to reach in my purse. And I'm holed up in a bulletproof truck." She raised her hands and rounded her eyes. "Seems rational as hell to me."

Shaking his head, he laughed out loud. Then she felt a smile spread across her face. Evidently, they'd both needed that release of tension. At least she sure had.

A car pulled in on her side and she nodded to the representative from the second district as he got out. Walking toward city hall, he turned to wait for someone else who'd also just parked a few spots down.

"Are either of them on the committee?" Josh asked.

"No, but maybe the mayor requested they come. Oh...look..." She pointed down the sidewalk toward the courthouse. "That's the mayor coming this way. And Lieutenant Grey's not far behind him." She glanced back at Josh. "Must have been a court case they had to attend."

Confident that everything was okay, she reached for the door handle and slid outside. The moment her feet hit the ground, she realized she'd screwed up. She should have waited for Josh's okay to leave the truck, and the look he shot her said, *Don't forget next time.*

"Sorry." She'd never realized how hard being the one in protection could be. "Okay if I go talk to the mayor and head inside for the meeting?"

"We're on the move, Granger." Already out, he nodded and headed around the rear of the truck as she took a few steps in the direction of the pedestrian plaza in front of city hall.

She looked back and noticed Josh had stopped. She stopped. Watched. Quickly, she keyed in on the fact that he kept glancing from one end of the street to the other. Traffic had thinned. Probably stopped at the corner signal. She'd noticed crews were working on the overhead light signal a couple blocks away when she and Josh had driven down the street.

"Macki, stay where you are."

"What's wrong?"

"The side streets are barricaded. They weren't when we pulled in." He moved his hand to the gun tucked in his back waistband. "And up ahead there are barricades turning traffic to the right." He tapped his ear bud. "Are you getting this, Granger?"

A black cargo van started down the street, followed by a white SUV. Suddenly, a red car swerved from behind the two vehicles, taking the lane closest to Josh. The car increased its speed. Zeroed in on him.

"Down, Macki. Down." He slid across the trunk of the car next to them, pulling his Glock as he landed on his feet.

She dropped and rolled for protection by one of the cars. Lieutenant Grey pulled the mayor out of the line of fire and into city hall. Grabbing her gun from her bag, she glanced over the hood and aimed.

The car veered closer and closer. Rear window lowered. Gunfire erupted. Targeting no one but Josh. He returned fire, then jumped into the road and aimed for the windshield. A spray of bullets from the black van drove him back.

Suddenly the van stopped. Three men jumped out of the rear door. Just as fast, Granger and another man appeared at a dead run on the far side of the street, firing at will toward the van. And at a distance, she saw Cummings headed their direction, weapon drawn.

"Gas. I smell gas." She glanced in the direction of the car next to Josh's truck. Bullet holes riddled the rear side, and the gas tank was spewing liquid.

"Get out of there." Josh yelled as he reloaded and shot, bringing one man down.

She backpedaled to get away. Taking aim, she hit one of the men in the leg.

Josh jumped back in front of the oncoming car. Fired and fired again. The windshield shattered a second before the red car crashed into the rear side of his truck. A fireball ripped upward and outward. Metal and glass splintered the dust as the air reverberated with the boom of the explosion. And in an instant, smoke and fire and heat clouded the scene.

The men on the street dragged their wounded into the van a second before it and the white SUV raced off down the street. Their tires squealed as they turned right at the intersection and disappeared into the city. Considering the interstate was a block away, she knew they were long past a quick police pursuit.

"Josh! Josh!" Macki turned and ran toward the explosion as a secondary explosion echoed across the emptiness.

An arm wrapped around her and she fought, kicked, yanked backward at his hair as the man took her to the ground.

"Stay down, Macki." Granger's voice drilled into her mind as he protected her with his body. A couple of feet in front of her in a heat-fueled haze, she saw Cummings crouched with his gun arm straight in front of him, circling the perimeter of an unseen circle around her. They'd made sure she survived.

Where was Josh? Why wasn't he the one beside her? "Josh?"

She'd seen him jump onto the hood. Then the crash. The fireball. Then nothing. Nothing. The last few seconds played back over and over in her mind. Slowly her insides grasped the outcome. She'd lost him. He'd gone up in the explosion.

Her mind moved in slow motion. Screaming to go back...go back to yesterday...go back to this morning...go back to when they laughed less than five minutes ago. "Noooooooooo."

Like a deflating balloon, the fight went out of her, and she eased her struggle. No matter what OPAQUE ever did to Coercion Ten, it would never be enough to ease her pain. Because nothing would change what had just happened. Nothing would bring him back. "Josh..."

* * *

Josh opened his eyes. Was he dead? Hell no, but he sure couldn't breathe. All he remembered was that he'd fired at the oncoming red car. The windshield had shattered, and he'd fired at the driver again and again. After rolling onto the hood, he'd jumped to the top and catapulted himself off the back as the car careened into the sedan parked next to his truck. Then one damn big explosion.

He'd landed flat on his back. Hard. Evidently hard enough to knock the air out of him. Cough...try to cough. No matter how many times he'd been in this position, having the wind knocked out still hurt to blue blazes. But he knew this pain. Knew the drill. Knew not to panic.

He stretched his arms over his head, sucking in air through his nose. Then laid them back down to his side. He needed to breathe. Move. Get to Macki. Make sure she was okay. He tried blowing air out, then moved his arms overhead again. Finally, his diaphragm kicked back into action and he gulped in one long, deep breath.

Bracing up on one elbow, he focused through a break in whatever he seemed to be penned behind. For all intents and purposes, the street looked like a war zone. The gunfire had ceased, replaced with shrills of approaching sirens. The two men in the car had bit the dust, but what about the SUV and black van? Had they got away empty-handed? Or had they grabbed Macki before they made their escape?

"Hey. Anybody there? Get me out." He banged against what appeared to be pieces of scaffolding and wood. There had been window washing equipment set up across the street. The men had been taking a break near the curb. Surely he hadn't been thrown that far. Then again, maybe the stand had tumbled with the explosion.

He tried to lift the steel with his shoulder. Didn't budge. He had to get out. What if no one knew he was there? Digging and muffled voices came from above. He scraped and shoved his hand through enough of the rubble till he felt the fresh air of outside.

Someone grabbed hold. "Hang on. We'll get you out."

Within seconds, he saw the faces of three men as they lifted the mess off of him.

"Thanks. Thanks a lot, guys." He crawled out of the

debris and tried to stand. His side hurt with the pain that said he'd fallen hard against metal, but at least he could move.

Another man reached out and pulled him to his feet. "You okay, buddy?"

Josh recognized him. CIA. Trenton...Reese Trenton. Where had he come from? "Why...why are you—"

"I'm not here," Trenton muttered under his breath as he pointed him toward city hall, then turned back to the other men. "Yeah, he's okay. Just a little wobbly. Let's see if anyone else is in this pile of rubble."

Josh heard the group begin to dig again, but he'd got the message that he should ignore Trenton. That he should go forward...across the street. He shook his head to clear the ringing in his ears as the sun's glare bounced off shards of glass littering the area. He stumbled, then ran toward the last place he'd seen Macki.

He detoured onto the sidewalk, pushing through a gathering crowd of spectators and reporters. Damn, how long had actually passed? Someone tapped him on the shoulder and pointed him at a man appearing to shout at him.

"Cummings?" Hell, why wouldn't the damn ringing in his ears stop? He pounded his palms against his ears as he walked forward. There, that was better, or at least he told himself it was. At least he could hear again. "Cummings."

"You look like you've been run over by a Mack truck." Cummings tucked his gun in his holster as police cruisers and cops populated the area. "Looks like the paramedic may need to take a look at you."

He caught a glance of his dirt-and soot-covered reflection in a car window. Clothing ripped and torn with blood on his hand, his arm. He raked his hand through his hair and felt the singe of hairs. But he'd survive. That's all that counted as far as his own body.

Instinctively his gaze searched the surroundings for the only thing he cared about at the moment. "Where's Macki?

Is she hurt?"

"She's okay." Cummings nodded across the sidewalk toward the steps to city hall.

Josh jogged over to the group on the steps.

"You're alive." Granger grabbed him in a bear hug for a second before he stepped away. "We thought you were dead man."

"Close, but no cigar. Hey, I just saw Trenton."

"We'll talk about it later. He's not here."

Suddenly Josh caught sight of Macki. She looked like she was in shock. "What's wrong with her?"

"Don't worry, she's not hurt." Granger slapped him on the back. "But let's just say that expression on your woman's face is one I don't ever want to see again. Like I said, we all thought you'd met your Maker."

Josh climbed the few steps to her. But the closer he got, the more perplexed she looked. As if her feet were planted in concrete, she didn't move. And she stared at him as if he were some kind of mirage. She tilted her head, her expression questioning.

"Hey, Macki." Cupping his hands on her shoulders, he felt her tremble the moment she realized he was real.

"Hey, Josh."

He pulled her against him. Partly for her. Partly for him. Her jerky sobs began small, then increasingly vibrated as she looped her arms around him and gripped. Tighter and tighter.

All he could do was hold on just as tight as he kissed the top of her head. "I'm okay. You hear me? I may look like hell, but it'll all wash off. I'll be good as new."

She stepped back, giving him an up-and-down once-over glance. Slowly, she gave him a weak smile as she battled back the tears. "You look..." She shook her head and smiled bigger. "You never looked so damn good to me in all your life, Joshua Slater."

CHAPTER TWENTY-SIX

Police questions. FBI questions. Questions in his own mind. There'd been too many damn people in Josh's personal space the past couple hours. Wrapping up the scene in front of city hall had been intense, to say the least.

Riverfalls Police hadn't been happy about the FBI sticking its nose into their local business. The Feds had listened to their complaints, then pulled Josh and Granger aside for some private questions. They'd answered questions they felt fell in their jurisdiction. The others they referred to Drake.

Josh's truck had been so close to the explosion, the police had long ago towed it to the impound lot. But not before he'd stripped the truck of anything pertaining to OPAQUE or him personally. The police hadn't been happy about that either.

The tote filled with OPAQUE gadgets from the truck had gone with Granger when he'd headed over to D Street. Securing more information on Roxy and her daughter had taken the backseat for a brief period, what with the attack by three vehicles and masked shooters. Now Granger needed to return to the reason he was in town. Dig deeper on the Roxy issue. Josh had an inkling that her information would rank among the most important at this point.

Finally things had calmed down, and it seemed that everyone had what they needed for the moment. Josh figured he and Macki needed to head home. Only one problem. No ride.

"Don't think there won't be any follow-up questions from me." Lieutenant Grey had the look and tone of a man who felt empowered. "And Macki, I'm surprised you're tangled up with the likes of OPAQUE and Agent Slater."

"Why would you be surprised? Runs in my family." She stood straight with the attitude of someone not about to be put down ever again.

Josh was proud of her resilience, but part of him also wanted her to stay quiet on this subject. He twined his fingers between hers and squeezed lightly. Until he figured out who to trust around Riverfalls, he wasn't too sure he wanted people knowing who, what, when, and how Macki and OPAQUE fit together.

"What's that supposed to mean?" Grey's tone had hardened.

"Did you forget? Law enforcement runs in my family genes." She double-squeezed Josh's hand in return. "What did you think I meant, Lieutenant Grey?"

Grey's phone vibrated with an incoming call, and he walked away.

"Hey, you two want a ride home?" Cummings pulled his nondescript police car up beside them at the curb.

"Sounds great." Josh nodded to the man who had helped protect Macki. He'd picked right when he'd trusted the detective enough to confide in him.

She slid into the back and Josh followed, then he reached beneath his shirt and yanked off the tape and microphone he'd worn for the past few hours. Wouldn't do him any good now that he and Granger were so far apart.

Crossing town toward the hotel, the three of them kicked a few ideas around about how the barricades and light signals had been tampered with to give a clear path prior to the attack. Sure, Macki was the focal point of Coercion Ten's overall plan. But this afternoon, Josh had been the target.

Cummings's police scanner's static changed tone to

incoming: "D Street, possible kidnapping, female, mid-forties, tall, thin, red hair. Goes by the name Roxy."

"On my way soon as I drop off at Hotel MacKenzie." Cummings sped up for the next couple of blocks.

Josh exchanged a quick glance with the detective, then phoned Granger. "You got anything on the Roxy abduction?"

"Not yet. Happened a couple minutes before I hit the street. Snatched her right there in front of everybody." Granger's voice mingled with sirens arriving on the scene. "Seemed a little too coincidental if you ask me. Almost like my timeline had been leaked."

"This whole situation is boiling up on itself." Josh felt the heat rising, and this time the temperature had nothing to with it. "You need anything?"

"I'm on it. Don't worry, I'll stay in the D Street area tonight. See what I can find out. Hey, wait a second." Granger paused for longer than a few seconds.

"What's going on?" Josh asked.

"Never mind. I thought I saw that white SUV, but it wasn't the same model. Listen, I gotta go. I'll contact Drake with intel as soon as I have any."

"Call me if you get in trouble." Josh glanced at the detective. "By the way, Cummings is headed down there as soon as he drops us off."

"Sounds good. See you tomorrow." The call ended.

Josh knew raids and follow-up skirmishes were sometimes all targeted to one day. If they got through today, then maybe OPAQUE would end up with a couple of leads to narrow in on the leadership of Coercion Ten. He didn't like not being out on the street tracking the clues, but his job was to protect Macki. That and nothing else.

Josh shoved the phone in his pocket and compared what had happened today with information he'd gleaned since he'd arrived in town. How many Coercion Ten people were in the area? Had they gotten wind that Roxy might be ready to turn on them? Or had her usefulness to them just ended?

"I want to go to D Street," Macki said. "Maybe I can help."

"No. Absolutely not." Keeping her locked up wouldn't solve anything, but he sure wasn't letting her anywhere near that area tonight. Top priority now was getting her inside the penthouse for the evening.

Cummings pulled up to the front of Hotel MacKenzie, then glanced in Josh's direction. "You all staying in for the rest of the night?"

"You can count on it." Josh nodded in return. "And tomorrow the only thing on Macki's agenda is the gala board meeting."

"Which has been on the calendar for months." Macki unbuckled her seat belt.

Josh got out of the car and extended his hand through the driver's side window to Cummings. "Thanks for watching out for Macki this afternoon."

"Sure thing." The detective shook hands. "Any time you need me."

"Stay safe out there." Josh tapped the top of the car, then walked around the back and onto the sidewalk as the hotel valet opened the rear door for Macki.

She leaned toward the front seat. "Cummings?"

"Yes, Macki."

"Thank you...for everything." She reached out and touched his shoulder. "You're a good cop. And a good man."

"Yeah, well." He swiped his hand toward the open door. "Get out of here, you two. You've got better things to do than shower me with accolades. Besides, I need to get to D Street."

As soon as they both exited the car, the detective popped the police siren on and sped away.

Josh shot Macki a look, then glanced down at himself. Dirty, disheveled, and drained. They looked like the last people who would be walking through the lobby of Hotel MacKenzie, one of the fanciest places in town. The full-time residents who lived on the upper floors in condos would at least know who she was. But out-of-towners would think they were vagrants.

So be it. He didn't care what anybody thought. They'd both fought a good fight today. And lived to tell about it. Couldn't get better than that.

Josh did a nod-bow and swept his hand toward the entrance. "After you, my lady."

"The way we look should make front-page news tomorrow." She walked into the lobby as if she were dressed to the nines.

"Hell, we're already going to be front page news."

Her soft, throaty laugh flashed to his core. All the aches and pains he'd been feeling during the ride over disappeared. His manhood said *You may be sore and exhausted, but you ain't done yet*. Security started toward them, but she gave her signal that everything was okay. But for once, Josh motioned the man over.

"Anybody new on your team tonight?" Josh surveyed the lobby. Nothing looked out of place from what he could tell, but then he didn't walk this lobby every day.

"No, sir. Everyone on duty for the next forty-eight hours are our usual staff."

"Good. Make sure it stays that way for the next week."

Macki chatted with some passing guests while others steered a wide birth. "Bring in extra staff if you think the hotel needs it. And..."

After motioning to the head of security to stay with her even if they'd finished discussing business, Josh walked over to the MacKenzie Library Bar just off the lobby. She was still within his sight. And she'd stay that way until OPAQUE had brought down Coercion Ten's target that had been pinned on her.

He braced his hand on the granite bar top and pointed at the wine rack. "Give me the best you've got. And a bottle of Jameson 12 Year Old Irish Whiskey." His Macki deserved the best. "Put them on the penthouse bill."

The bartender handed the items over without a second thought. Josh grasped the necks of the two bottles between the fingers of his left hand as he walked back across the lobby. It had been a long day. Tonight needed to be better.

Macki looked in Josh's direction, glanced at the liquor, and smiled. Then she winked. He bit the side of his lower lip and winked in return. A whole lot better.

Pausing by the huge vase gracing the center of the main lobby table, he wrapped his hand around a bunch of the flowers and yanked. Before he even finished shaking off the water, he saw a bellhop running to clean up the floor. As if on cue, security backed away as he neared Macki.

"Your flowers, my lady." Josh presented her the bouquet.

She took them while brushing his cheek with a kiss. "Why, thank you, my knight in shining armor."

She curtsied and with a secret of their own, they laughed. Laughed and kissed all the way to the fourteenth floor on the elevator. The one flight of stairs took mere seconds, then Macki entered her pass-code to unlock the stairwell doorway. They easily entered the fifteenth floor and her penthouse.

She pulled a vase from the cabinet and filled it with water, arranging the flowers as she put them in. "Why don't you go clean up? I'll make us each an Irish coffee."

He couldn't stop watching her. The way she gauged the length of the flower stems. The way she placed each one just so in the water. The way she looked as she tickled a flower beneath her nose ever so often, closing her eyes and breathing in the scent. She was so beautiful. Inside and out. How had he been able to stay away all those years?

He'd spend the rest of his life making that lost time up to her. That was, if she'd have him. Josh pushed a strand of hair out of her face, then cupped the back of her head and lowered his mouth to hers. She opened her lips for the sweep of his tongue.

She tasted like sweetness and spice. Like sin and sex.

A week ago, he'd been a lonely man. Now the woman he loved stood in his arms, offering everything she had. He didn't deserve her, but he damn well planned to stay.

He trailed his fingers down her neck, her arms, her sides, stopping at her waist. Gently he slipped his hands beneath her top, wrapping them around her as he made lazy circles. Then pressed his palms against the heat of her skin. She felt like the warmth of a campfire after a long night on guard.

Pulling her closer, he groaned with need. "I love you, Mackenzie Baudin."

"Mmmmmm, twice in one day you've said that." As if they'd been together for years, she easily undid the buttons down the front of his shirt. "You know, I could get used to that...twice a day thing."

He yanked his shirt from his pants and tossed it to the side. "Oh, there's lots of things I can do twice a day, honey. Sometimes more than twice."

"I bet you can." She eased her top over her head. Slipped out of her shoes. Out of her skirt. And his eyes zeroed in on the edge of the lacy low-cut bra and even lacier thong.

His mouth dried and his length throbbed to be free from behind the zipper in his pants. This was a lead-in to disaster 'cause he was still dirty from everything that had happened today. And she'd already pushed his hard and ready button. He needed to slow down, but his body didn't agree. "Macki, Macki, Macki. Give me a chance to clean up."

"We could always conserve water and clean up together." She eased the palm of her hand across his chest. "You know, we never made it to the shower last night."

Shower? There'd barely been time to come up for air once they'd started making love. And right now what she was doing felt so good he couldn't help but grin. "I didn't know you were so concerned with saving the environment."

He moved his hand in the direction of the lace, but she lightly pushed him back. Okay, he'd keep his hands off for the moment. "Oh, so we're gonna play that game?"

She shrugged. Then, trailing her fingers across his body,

she walked around to his back. He flinched as her hand grazed across the one area on his shoulder that hurt like hell and back again.

"You've got a nasty bruise. All black and blue." The playful tone of a moment ago turned to one of concern as she stepped toward the refrigerator. "You should have told me your back was hurt. I'll get some ice for that."

Reaching out, he grabbed her arm. How could he tell her that when she was close his pain disappeared? Replaced instead with a feeling of contentment and peace and something he couldn't even wrap his mind around.

He was always the one in charge. The one who set the pace. But right now all he could think about was letting her take the lead. "No, Macki. Don't stop what you started."

The small upturn at the corners of her mouth said she understood.

"Here, I'll make it all better," she whispered as her lips touched the bruised spot on his shoulder, and he barely flinched. Her throaty sighs caught his attention as she placed soft, tiny kisses down his spine. Damn right she'd made everything better. Right now he thought he'd die.

Suddenly, her lacy bra fell to the floor beside him. A moment later, she moved against his back, skin on skin, heat on heat. Her breaths brushed against his skin, then he heard the loudness of his own breathing as he exhaled.

She stepped back in his arms and kissed him deeply while her fingers played peek-a-boo with the edge of his jeans. Teasing with their touch, her fingers slid inside the waistband. Then she popped the button undone.

His willpower shattered. Hell, they might not make it out of the living room.

Without making eye contact, he twined his fingers with hers and led her toward the master bathroom without ever looking back. Just outside the shower, he toed off his shoes and shucked the rest of his clothes.

Together, he and Macki stepped face-to-face into the glass and ceramic shower, letting spray from the overhead showerheads wash the grime down the drain. He glanced into Macki's eyes, then trailed his eyes downward as he scrubbed his palm across his beard. Right now, a shave was definitely not an option. Stepping closer, she caressed his chest as soapy lather spilled from her hands down his front.

Evidently she didn't care if he shaved either. Good.

He looped his fingers around the sides of her thong, now wet and clinging with shower water. "Here, let me help you out of this."

A second later, the material ripped.

CHAPTER TWENTY-SEVEN

Another sunrise. Another day. Another morning of Josh loving the feel of Macki tucked against his side. The tickle of her hair against his chest stoked his emotions and he turned to pull her even closer, sucked in a breath as her lips brushed against his chest. A second later, smiling, she opened her eyes.

The feel of her leg as she eased it across his, along with her kisses against his shoulder, was all a man could ask for to wake up happy every single day for the rest of his life. Suddenly, she pulled the covers and rolled away from him. He followed till they ended up rolling off the mattress onto the stack of pillows beside the bed.

Suddenly she glanced at the clock, then shimmed out of his hold. "Oh my gosh. The gala meeting is in less than an hour."

He grabbed his jeans from the bathroom floor and his gun from the bedside table where he'd laid it when they came to bed, then bolted toward the bedroom door. He didn't dare look back for fear they'd never make the meeting. Besides, he could shower in the guest room bath and get dressed there. Plus, he needed to check in with OPAQUE. "Can you be ready in thirty minutes?"

"Sure."

"We'll take your SUV."

Hell, he hadn't slept this late in decades. Any chance he had at taking side streets to the meeting had flown out the window. This was exactly why he'd steered clear of her for years. In his line of work, last night might have cost them precious seconds. Might have compromised her safety.

For what?

The entire time he showered, shaved, and dressed, he kept asking himself the same question. For what? Everything came back to one answer, and he didn't much like that answer. Last night wasn't about sex for either of them. Wasn't about love, either. It was about something deeper. A word he didn't want to think, much less ever say.

Marriage...

He shook his head at the reflection in the mirror. "You're a fool, Agent Slater. One damn fool."

Having a life with the one you loved meant putting them in danger every single day. Unless they went into hiding. He braced his hands on each side of the sink, hanging his head in thought. Maybe he could take her with him...together they could both disappear...have a life...raise a family and—

No. He knew better. Knew that someday there'd be a tiny slip in their story, something so simple they'd forget it linked them to his past, but someone would hear. Someone would know. And they'd give up the info for the price of a high on the street.

A taste of fear and reality gelled inside him—once an agent always an agent. His past—jobs, adversaries, enemies—would forever be just a step away. His insides fought him with need, but was need worth the danger to her? What if they had children and he couldn't protect them? What if... What if... What if... The battle raged inside him until he made peace with the ultimate answer—he loved her. Which meant he'd stay forever if she let him.

"Josh. I'm ready." She poked her head in his door. "Are you ready to go?"

Protector mode kicked in deep and hard. He'd never forget last night or the night before. Or hundreds of more nights to come. But when the gun hit his hip, he was a protector. Protector of the most precious commodity in the world to him.

Clenching his jaw, he sucked up his emotions and reset the clip in his gun. "Yes, Macki. I'm ready to go."

* * *

In Mackenzie's elevator on the way to the garage, she couldn't help but place her palm lightly against Josh's back. He tensed, nudging her away by the flex of his muscles.

She knew his rules for the elevator included that she stand behind him and be on guard for whatever might be waiting on the other side of the door opening. And she'd follow his rules, but that didn't mean she had to shut out her feelings entirely. She never wanted to lose what the two of them had found last night.

Of course from the moment Josh had grabbed his gun off the nightstand this morning to now, she'd known he was back in protector mode. No more sexy winks. No more tender nibbles and kisses. No more lovemaking that had erased everything from their past.

In the light of day, she quickly realized that he was only hers till he strapped on his gun. Then he was all agent. They were back to real life and needed to be vigilant at all times. Especially now that Coercion Ten had issued an ultimatum.

The threat to her, Josh, and Drake had always been in play. But for the organization to send a message through Tessa, the woman down on D Street, had been another step in the game. To declare that within twenty-four hours Josh would be the first to go down had put a new spin on the situation. But Coercion Ten's plan had failed. He'd beat the odds at city hall yesterday. Now, the clock was ticking till the organization tried again.

"Are you sorry, Macki?" Josh hadn't turned around, he'd only asked a simple question. "Do you wish I'd never walked into your bath that night?"

With the ease and flatness of his tone, she knew he'd built a wall around himself with only the barest of cracks for her answer to penetrate. If she said it had all been a mistake, he'd close that crack on her words, barely letting himself feel the sting. If she said she'd do it all again, he'd feel the warmth. Question was...what would he do then?

Would he feel vulnerable and run? Or would he fold her love around him like a sheath that no one else would ever know made him feel whole? Would he let her be the only comfort he ever felt in life? The only person he let close enough to feel his love...feel his pain. To know his Achilles' heel.

She'd discovered Agent...Josh Slater was a complex man. Very complex. But definitely the man she loved. The man she wanted to wake up next to each morning for the rest of her life. Reaching toward his back again, she hoped her touch would convey more than the few words about to come out. "Sorry? Never. Don't you know how much I love you? How—"

The elevator doors slid open. Pitch-black darkness greeted them. Where were the lights? Josh reached for his gun, punching the Close Door button. From the shadows, the clicking of a Taser gun ripped the air a split second before the probes shot into Josh's body. He dropped to the floor with a groan, a grunt. Another set hit him from a different direction, .

She heard herself scream. The combined ominous sounds echoed through the open elevator doors into the concrete dungeon of her garage.

Someone reached around the elevator door and yanked her out as another man shoved door holders in the bottom of the opening to keep the doors apart. As if on cue, the bright lights of the garage popped on, blinding her for a second.

The Tasers stopped their muffled clicking, and Josh's body eased. In an instant, she realized the gun he'd been holding was feet away across the floor. With a look of defiance on his face, he reached for his other gun before his body fully recovered. Courage was no match for the two men holding the Tasers. One of them popped another jolt on Josh.

Macki fought at the man gripping her middle, kicked, clawed, scratched. Then she focused on Josh's recovering body as the two men took his two guns and dragged him from the elevator. Cuffing him to the specially made metal grille of her SUV, one of the men withdrew his Taser's prongs from Josh, The other left his in.

She heard the slam of a car door from behind her, then saw the look of recognition travel Josh's expression.

"You son of a bitch." He struggled to free himself, his fists tightening to fight mode as he jerked the cuffs against the shiny grille again and again and again.

She twisted, trying to see around the man who held her.
"Stop it, Mackenzie."
The voice? Grey? Couldn't be...Lieutenant Grey?
Again, she lashed out at the thug holding her.

"Stop it right now, unless you want to see Agent Slater continue to squirm." Lieutenant Grey's voice slithered loud and clear along her spine as he twisted a handful of her hair and yanked. Her head jerked backward with his grip.

Gasping to catch her breath, she stilled in her captor's arms. None of this made sense. Why would the lieutenant be here? "Okay. Okay. Just leave him alone. Please leave him alone."

"Good girl. You learn fast." Grey loosened his hold and motioned to the captor to release his grip around her waist. But he kept the hold on her wrist as the other thug yanked his Taser prongs from Josh's body.

"How did you get in here?" She needed to distract the lieutenant. Give Josh time to recover from the jolts.

"You might want to see about a new hotel security system. The one you've got is real easy to override. Especially if you know the code." His sinister laugh shivered her thoughts. How could he possibly know the pass-code?

Pushing at the hand around her wrist, she fought to gain

a footing on her next move. Josh had been right about her security, but there hadn't been time to install the new one. "Why are you doing this? Josh is one of the good guys. "

"Good guy? Guess that depends which side you're on." Grey laughed again as he walked over and plowed his fist into Josh's jaw. "Welcome to my world, OPAQUE!"

Blood trickled from the corner of Josh's eyebrow and cheek. "Don't you see, Macki? He's the link to Coercion Ten. In fact, I'd say he was a prominent player in the group's formation. Or at least in the death of your parents."

Grey hit Josh with a one-two punch to his ribs.

She gasped, then scratched her nails down the neck of the man holding her wrist. He dropped his hold and she charged across the room at Grey, knocking him away from Josh. Grey turned, grabbing the drive-stun Taser from the other man.

On emotional overload, she couldn't stop herself from pelting Grey with her fists. "All these years, you pretended to be my friend. To watch out for me. You...you"—she hit harder and harder—"were nothing but a two-bit hoodlum. A traitor to my dad. My family."

Grey grabbed one of her wrists with his free hand and held tight. Kicking with all her strength, she felt the tightening of his grip. If he tightened too much, she knew she might pass out, but she was determined to take him down. She took a step back, then lunged forward, aiming her knee at Grey's groin, but he sidestepped her move and punched the Taser against her skin.

"Noooooo!" Josh yelled, jerking the handcuffs against the metal holding him.

Dragging Macki with him, Grey turned and took a few steps back to Josh. Jabbed the Taser against Josh and pulled the trigger for one quick instant. His face twisted in pain as he groaned, deep and loud, bracing himself against the hood to keep from going down.

"Josh!" She struggled to pull Grey's aim away, but she didn't have the strength.

The lieutenant released the trigger and held the Taser up for her to see. "I told you before, Macki. Stop fighting me. Or he'll get it again." He pointed the stun gun at Josh.

"No...no...I'll be good." Jerky breaths poured from her mouth as tears she had no control over poured down her cheeks. She felt helpless to protect Josh, but she had to. Had to stop this before Grey killed him. What could she do?

Deep inside, she felt herself weaken. Was this what it felt like to be a target? How Drake would feel if the organization held her as leverage against him? How could anyone who saw the person they loved in pain not feel the agony—not fight to save them?

Grey released his hold, and she raced to Josh's side.

"Are you okay?" She palmed the side of his face, his lips, his forehead. "Tell me you're okay. Please."

Jerking himself away from her touch, he shot her a look of caution. "Move away. Now." "No. I can't. I'll do anything to stop your pain. Anything—"

"Macki, don't say that." Through gritted teeth and warning eyes, he pleaded with her. "Think what I told you about these people. Think what you're doing."

"Think what I'm doing? Josh, I'm saving your life. I'm..." She flung her hand in front of her mouth. What had she done?

Realization hit her hard and fast—Josh was her leverage.

Her words, her action had verified everything Coercion Ten needed to know about her weakness. The look in Josh's eyes, the set of his jaw, the tenseness in his body told her all she needed to know, too. She'd screwed up.

Josh turned his stone-wall expression toward Grey. "Got what you wanted?"

The lieutenant simply grinned and nodded his head.

"Let her go. You must have cared about her the same way you cared about your own daughter at one time. Otherwise, why would you have saved her from the plane crash?"

"Shut up." Grey glanced at his watch.

"What do you mean, he saved me?" She tried to clear her mind and focus on everything Josh did or said. Without a doubt, each point would have a reason. She didn't plan to mess up again.

Josh leaned back as if he had all the time in the world. "Follow the clues. Where did the baseball tickets come from that day? The ones that kept you from going on the plane with your mom and dad?"

"Lieutenant Grey said he got them from a pal who had to go out of town."

"And when did Peggy tell you her dad said you could stay over that night?"

Grey pulled his revolver and pointed it at Josh. "Shut up about my daughter."

The hate bubbling inside her numbed her to the core. Facing the hard fact, Macki stepped in front of Grey, in front of the aimed pistol. "You set up the crash of the plane, yet fixed it so I would live? Why? Why would you save me?"

He lowered the gun an inch. "Yeah, I saved you. And what did it get me? Nothing!"

Suddenly last night seemed a lifetime away to Macki. The plane crash from ten years ago felt like yesterday.

"Nothing?" She pushed a sarcastic breath through her nose. "You seem to have done okay. In fact, I'm wondering about that house you've got. How did you say you met your current wife?"

Grey leaned into her space and grinned like the devil was peering from his soul. "I met her on a family trip to New York a few weeks before the crash. We hit it off real well." He sneered with venom. "I was glad when Peggy's mom got cancer. But don't think for a minute I didn't make sure she got only the best treatments available...in New York. Made it convenient to have a little companionship close by."

"That's sick...so, so sick." Macki wasn't sure how much

more dirt she could stand to hear, but her cop instincts kicked in and said to keep digging. Except she didn't know where to go from this point. She looked at Josh and raised her eyebrows, hoping he'd pick up that she was spent.

Josh nodded, then laughed out loud. "So Coercion Ten gave you a new wife, a new house, and money by the boatload? Must have soothed your conscience for killing your so-called friend."

"You forget, I didn't fix the plane." Grey pushed her aside and aimed the gun at Josh once again, glancing briefly at her. "Did he tell you it was his dad who took care of that for us? Or did he forget to mention that little part?"

"He told me," she said in Josh's defense.

Grey seemed agitated by the fact of honesty. He lowered his gun to his side and started pacing around the garage. Kept glancing at his watch again and again. The thugs he'd brought with him, his muscle, seemed perfectly content to stay where they were. Ready to let everything play out. Why not? They'd be paid no matter how long the job took.

She noticed Josh followed Grey's movements as if mapping the new world, as if gauging his timing, planning his next words. Something inside her warned Josh's play could be the turning point in this altercation. But without any backup, how could anything help them?

Josh inched himself into a sideways position against the SUV's fender. What was he doing? He looked smaller now. Kind of like a cop positioning himself into a crouch to be a smaller target.

Target? He'd made himself a smaller target because of what he had planned.

"I admit I didn't know Peggy well..." He motioned Macki to step away from him. "But I can't believe she had a part in Macki's parents' death. Guess you never know what someone will do for money."

Grey stopped. Turned. Charged back across the garage. "I told you to shut your mouth about my daughter. Otherwise I'll shut it for you."

Macki picked up the thread of confrontation from Josh. "I agree. I thought Peggy was my friend. Now I find out she helped kill my family."

"You...all because of you. That's why she's dead." Grey stalked toward Macki, and a look of vengeance walked with him. "I should have let you die along with your parents. In fact, I should finish you off right now."

"Mr. Grey, that wouldn't be wise." The thug who had previously held her called from across the garage, the thug's tone more of an order than a reminder. The man had unholstered his own gun and hung it loosely at his side. "Not wise at all."

She and Josh exchanged glances. Something new had been added to the mix. What?

Grey turned to his challenger. "I'm not a fool. I've still got kids and grandkids out there, so chill. I was only putting the fear of the Almighty into her."

Laughing again, Josh yanked the handcuffs against the fender. "Now that's something I didn't expect. The thugs have control over the so-called leader of the group."

She watched the tension simmer in Grey's eyes. If Josh pushed too much, no one might be able to stop the result.

"Did Peggy know what happened?" Josh took his jab, quick, strong and to the point. His tone sarcastic and mean and accusing. "Is that why she turned to drugs? Couldn't live with the knowledge her old man had killed her best friend's parents?"

Grey turned and fired. The bullet ricocheted off the concrete wall behind the SUV as he charged across the room, headed for Josh. Macki tried to pull Grey away, but he shoved her aside, and she stumbled, hitting the concrete floor with a thud.

Standing over her, he glowered. "You want to know why Peggy died? Because I had remorse...I was the one who couldn't live with what I'd done. I tried to get out, Coercion Ten said once you're in, you're in. I told them they could still count on me, just not in the hard-core objectives." He trailed his palm tight down his face, and his voice cracked. "They said I should think about it overnight."

Grey's breathing pulsed with tension, even his head seemed to quiver from his anger.

"The college police called the next day. Said they found Peggy dead in her room. An OD. No signs of foul play. Case closed." His voice cracked deeper this time. "Coercion Ten had killed her. No warning move. Just straight and to the point."

Macki felt herself sway back and forth, felt the puff of her breath in and out through her lips. All these years she'd worried because she hadn't seen the signs of her friend's addiction. Instead, Peggy had been a mark to bring Grey into line. Macki felt sick. Sick and mad as hell.

Suddenly the lieutenant ran over by her. His hot breath blew against the side of her face. "Do you know what it feels like to bury your daughter, knowing you were responsible for her death?"

She shook her head because he actually wanted an answer. And for some reason, she felt she owed him at least that.

"Sir, don't make me shoot you." Her previous captor stood behind Grey, his gun at the ready. "You know your orders said alive."

The click-clack of the garage door opening and the sudden influx of natural daylight flooded the cold of the garage. A black limo pulled inside, angled into a parking spot, then backed out of the space, turning to face the closing garage door.

Was this some type of OPAQUE backup? A way to get inside? But how would they know to come? "Josh?"

"Macki, come here." Josh's tone sounded urgent. As if it didn't matter what she had to do, she had to get to him. "Now. Right now."

Back-stepping away from Grey, she flattened her expression into one of fear...waved her hands in front of her pretending to be scared to death, which wasn't far from true. A foot away, she turned and ran to Josh, knowing that there'd be only a few seconds for whatever he needed to tell her about.

"I'm sorry." Whispering, she brushed her cheek against his, hoping to catch his instructions easier. "I shouldn't have shown my emotions. Shouldn't have let them see what you mean to me."

"That's okay, Macki." Josh tilted his head, laying his lips alongside her ear as if giving reassurance. "Extra key fob. My pocket. Remember. Get it. When I tell you. Stomp it to hell."

Remembering what he'd told her about the emergency way to call for backup—OPAQUE, FBI, local police—she paused only a moment before she inched her fingers to the edge of his jeans pocket. She dug inside...touched the plastic with her fingertips...almost had it...almost...her fingers closed around their one chance at survival.

Grey yanked her back and shoved her toward her previous captor. "Keep her under control. And you..." He pointed at Josh. "You stay quiet if you know what's good for you."

She quick-nodded to let Josh know she had the fob, was ready to move on his command.

Josh looked back at the limo, and she followed his line of sight. Hadn't taken her long to figure out this was not backup. She racked her brain trying to think of anyone else who might have the pass-code to the garage.

The front passenger door opened and a muscle-bound man dressed in black stepped out from the driver's door. He scanned the garage in a circle and back again before opening the rear door. Evidently they were about to meet the man in charge of this Coercion Ten operation.

Slowly a tall, lean, muscular man with broad shoulders and hair cropped so close he appeared bald emerged. He kept his back to the group, but there was something familiar about his stance. Something distant in her memories.

He turned. Removed his sunglasses. Stepped forward into the glow of light. "Hello, Macki. Long time no see."

"Blake? Blake Ransom?" She took a step back. "You're supposed to be dead."

CHAPTER TWENTY-EIGHT

Josh couldn't believe how fast pieces had just fallen into place. Too fast.

Even in the shadows, he'd noticed the man was dressed in a black muscle shirt and black pants. Then he'd stepped forward into the light. Shiny-shiny black shoes and a gold link bracelet completed the look. He'd been the man on D Street. He'd been there all along.

Then Macki had called the man Blake. This changed everything.

He and OPAQUE had run Blake Ransom through the security system. He had never showed up on any blip of a negative background search. Everything had pointed to him being an upstanding citizen. An officer killed in the line of duty. That meant he had to be high up in Coercion Ten to have that level of a covered trail.

"This can't be happening. Lieutenant Grey saw what was left of your body. He said...oh my gosh..." As she back-stepped away from Blake, Macki's arms and hands quivered with the moment. She glanced at Grey. "A lie? You lied to me. Set me up for years and lied to me. Why, Blake? What would make me so valuable all this time?"

"Let's say I needed to keep an eye on you. I had my suspicions your uncle wasn't finished with OPAQUE. We always knew killing your dad wouldn't stop someone else in the family from taking up the cause." The man smirked.

Josh watched Macki's expression change with the words.

Her eyes narrowed, mouth firmed in an almost lipless line. He saw the moment the reality of the past and present sank into her mind.

She straightened her stance and took a step in Blake's direction. "You bastard. You wormed your way into my place. Let me befriend you. And all along you'd killed my parents?"

"Not me personally. Has to be something special for me to get my hands dirty." Blake smirked. "Too bad you and your uncle didn't take the hint I gave you in that alley."

Her expression paled, lips parted. "In the alley...when I was attacked...when..."

Blake laughed. "Like I said, it takes something special for me to take care of business. But in your case, I came back personally to handle that message."

Boiling with a shot of rage from that confession, Josh yanked the grille with his handcuffs till he heard the break of a holding bracket. "You're a dead man, Blake Ransom. A dead man."

"The OPAQUE agent speaks." Blake stepped in his direction. "Slater, isn't it? Joshua Slater. I've heard you're good. Hope you don't mind if I take some credit for how you turned out. In fact, my organization could use a man like you if you're in the mood to change sides."

"Thanks for the offer, but I'm fine where I'm at." He held out his handcuffed wrists. "Although I figured a man with your kind of power would want to meet me on equal terms. Not chain me up so I couldn't fight back."

"Do you think I'm a fool?" Blake didn't take the bait. Instead he took up a position halfway between the limo and the open elevator doorway. "Macki, come here."

"No."

"I said, come here."

Grey grabbed her by the arm and slung her across the room toward the man. The fob fell from her hand as she stumbled, bumping her head against a car fender. She yelled in exaggerated pain as she scrambled to run and hide between the cars. Good. That had jerked their attention from the tiny sound of the plastic hitting the concrete floor to her.

Blake bolted across the garage and seized Grey by the front of his shirt, practically lifting him off his feet. "Don't you ever touch her again. Do you understand?"

Lieutenant Grey gave a slow nod, then turned toward the limo as the muscled man helped Roxy from the back of the car. "Why's she here? We didn't need her for this."

"Thought she might be a piece of leverage against someone here." Blake smoothed the front of Grey's shirt as he let him go. "Say someone like you."

Josh processed what having Roxy in the mix might mean in the current situation. Best case scenario, might provide answers. Worst case—might get her killed.

"Me? I couldn't care less about her." Grey looked at Roxy like she was an annoying mosquito to be smashed. "She's nothing but a prostitute."

"One you used."

"Maybe you should get your facts right. I've used Roxy for Coercion Ten's benefit all these years." Grey patted his pants, scoffing at the group. "Kept her right here in my hip pocket."

Blake chuckled. "Oh that's right. The baby."

"How do you think I got to where I am today?" Grey sneered at the man. "You might do well to learn some of my moves. Otherwise you may end up being my messenger boy your entire career."

Josh noticed Blake's expression flattened, head slightly tilted with the flare of his nostrils. Evidently the man wasn't used to being talked down to. Josh didn't know for sure who Blake was, but he for damn sure wasn't a messenger boy.

Blake moved closer to where his driver still gripped Roxy's wrist. "So how's that daughter the lieutenant knocked you up with doing nowadays?"

Roxy glanced between Grey and the man beside her.

She looked confused, frantic, unsure of what to answer. "She's fine. I've done everything Lieutenant Grey has asked, so she's fine." Again she waggled her glance between the two men. "Right? She's okay...right?"

A quick look at Macki's compassionate expression told Josh her heart was breaking. Didn't matter that Roxy had put Macki in harm's way many times. She still cared about the woman. Josh knew sympathy could get you in trouble quick in this scenario.

"Of course she is. Your daughter is just as well as the day she was born." Blake patted Roxy's shoulder, nodding for the guard to release his hold.

"Shut up." Grey angrily shouted. "If you know what's good for you, you'll stop where you are, Blake."

"Oh, that's right. Lieutenant Grey never told you how sick your child was when she was born, did he? How she struggled to breathe." Blake's tone was emotionless. Bland with a touch of cruel. "How she died within minutes of being born."

Watching Grey was like watching a boring television rerun. Josh saw no hint of guilt or compassion or even caring. All he saw was a man cold as ice on the inside. Had he always been that way? Or had trying to keep his family alive all these years turned him into what Coercion Ten needed most—nothing but a machine?

Roxy struggled to stay on her feet. She braced her hand against the closest wall as tears streamed down her face.

"Roxy..." Macki started toward her.

The woman held up her hand. "No. Stay back."

Slowly, Roxy calmed her emotions, running her fingers up her cheeks as she walked across the garage. Her red hair sparkled like fire in the glow of the halogen lights. Endurance and her three-inch heels held her up, clicking on the concrete with each step she took. Unheeded, the tears continued to spill down her cheeks.

Josh figured years of living life on the street had given Roxy strength. Strength to last a lifetime. But right now life had reached out and stomped her down. Had broken her heart. And she was furious. A dangerous emotion for staying alive in this situation.

She stopped in front of Grey. "All these years...you let me believe I had a daughter? That...that I protected her by doing all those horrible things you asked?" She gulped in a breath of air. "All these years..."

"You should have never got pregnant in the first place." Grey shrugged his shoulders. "But since you did, I just used it to my advantage. You got paid. You got your fancy apartment and anything else you asked for."

She slapped his face with the vengeance of a mama bear whose den has been disturbed.

He slapped her in return, knocking her to the floor.

Dazed, she crawled to the side and leaned against a pillar, trying to get up.

"Roxy. Stay where you are." Josh yanked the handcuffs against the fender again as he pleaded with the woman. "Stay down."

She stared at him as if she'd forgotten anyone else was in the garage. Slowly, she eased back to the floor in defeat.

"Don't think I forgot about you, Agent Slater. But there's a lot going on here today. So give me a minute and I'll be right back to you and Macki." Blake walked past him and on toward Grey.

Josh continued his relentless quest of working his hands back and forth along the fender. Surely somewhere he could find a screw to loosen, a weld to break. Even a piece of loose metal that he might be able to use to pick the handcuff's lock. So far nothing, but he kept searching.

Blake stopped in front of Grey, rolling his fingers as if getting ready to play the piano. "Just for the record, I'm not your messenger boy."

Shooting Macki a look that said *stay out of this one*, Josh watched the scene unfold. He'd been in enough ego-against-ego situations to know Blake and Grey were even on that count. Trouble for Grey was that Blake outgunned him, not only in size but also in power and mean. If the lieutenant was smart, he'd stay quiet. And back down. Josh doubted the man was that smart.

Blake rolled his fingers again. Tapped his index finger against the lieutenant's chest. "Not now. Not ever. Is that understood?"

Grey landed a blow to Blake's face, one to his ribs, then another and another. In between hits, Grey yelled his threats. "I'm in charge. You don't tell me what to do."

Blake just stood there until finally one of the thugs grabbed Grey from behind. The man pulled Grey across the garage and away from the man currently in charge. Once there, the thug kept Grey in his hold.

Now Blake's expression changed from bland to enraged. Livid, he wiped his hand down the side of his face. Looked at the blood on his palm. A growl of a noise accompanied the flare of his nostrils as he pulled his gun. Letting his arm hang at his side with the heavy weight of metal clasped tight in his grip, he walked across the room toward Grey.

Josh felt the fury in the room crescendo. The situation had deteriorated fast. Hot and fast. He kept his voice low, hoping it would be nothing more than a background sound in the turmoil. "Now, Macki."

She stepped from between the cars and stomped on the fob where it had fallen, grinding her foot into the plastic. No one took notice of her small movement as they focused on the melee unfolding in the corner.

Josh began his five-minute countdown. That should be all they needed before backup arrived. If it took more than that, then systems hadn't clicked and chances for survival were dismal. That's what he'd been taught. That's what he knew for a fact.

Five minutes...just five minutes. Right now, that seemed insurmountable with the rapidly collapsing scenario.

Blake confronted Grey. Pounded his fist to the man's middle. "You still don't get it, do you?" He punched again. "I'm the one who's been giving the orders in this region for the past nine years. First you botched the job with Slater's dad and I had to finish what you started. Then you tried to get out of the organization."

Grey slumped to the floor as the thug let go.

"Did you think they would let you be in charge of orders after that? Besides, my dad figured I was ready to take over this region." Blake released the clip in his gun, then reset it. "You were nothing but the face for the local Coercion Ten recruits. The one we figured would take the fall if we were ever found out."

Dad? Who was Blake's dad? Was that the top man? OPAQUE had worked on the assumption that each region had a leader and that major decisions were made by a vote.

Josh needed more. But first he had to keep himself and Macki alive. He was trapped, and she had nowhere to run. Not only did the hulking limo driver block her access to raise the garage door, the other two thugs stood between her and the side exit door. Where was backup?

Blake turned, walking back toward the center of the garage.

As Grey struggled to his feet, his crazy-manic expression portrayed a man out of control. Someone who had lost all sense of himself, his surroundings, and his situation. As if he were a wounded warrior fighting his last fight, Grey's battle yell echoed off the concrete walls as he charged Blake from behind.

Quick and easy, Blake turned. Raised his gun. Fired.

CHAPTER TWENTY-NINE

Josh watched Grey's body jerk with the impact from Blake's shot.

The lieutenant's body crumpled to the floor. Didn't move. One bullet had ended all chances of evidence or information dating back to before Macki's parents were killed in the plane crash.

Once the reverberating sounds ceased, the garage became stone silent except for the evenly paced footsteps of Blake as he took center stage once again. "Before I was interrupted by all the drama, I said come here, Macki. And I meant it. Come. Here."

She didn't flinch. "No."

Blake released the clip in his gun and reloaded. "Now."

"No."

He chambered a round and flicked his gun arm straight up, pointing at Josh. "Now. One...two..."

"Okay...okay." She moved to the man's side.

Josh cringed, not for himself, but for Macki. If Blake got her in the limo, no telling how long it would take him to find her. Long? Too long? Never? He yanked the handcuffs against the grille harder and harder, on and on. Sooner or later, he'd rip the damn thing apart.

Blake lowered the gun and laughed. "Looks like Agent Slater's not much help to you right now. In fact, he's not much use to me anymore, either. Might as well—"

Macki stepped in front of the gun and he backhanded

her, landing her against the limo. He raised the gun in her direction, but Roxy jumped on his back, clawing at his face. He grabbed her hand and hurled her to the ground. Turned and shot twice. Roxy slid to the floor, clutching her arm against her ribs as blood spewed from her side.

"Leave me. Save yourself," Roxy shouted as Macki rushed toward her.

From the far side of the garage, the exit door burst open as Edward the chauffeur, Cummings, and more uniformed police bolted inside. Gunfire echoed throughout the concrete garage as bullets pinged off windshields and cars, followed by moans as they found their targets. Something big and powerful rammed the garage door. It crashed inward a moment before the FBI and SWAT teams rushed through. Rapid-fire shots from both the good and the bad reverberated through the air, embedded or ricocheted off the walls, spewing bits and pieces of concrete through the air.

Macki made a break toward Josh, but Blake grabbed her arm and held. Shielding himself with her body, he dragged her to the elevator. Two of his muscled thugs followed them inside, kicking the door-stops loose a second before the elevator doors closed behind them.

Numbers on the overhead floor-level dial showed the elevator went all the way to the penthouse. Stopped. Stayed.

Suddenly the garage quieted from the gunshots. All that remained was the continuous clang of Josh yanking and yanking the cuffs against the SUV grille. One captor and the driver lay dead on the floor along with Grey's body as the FBI and other law enforcement snaked their way inside and around the vehicles.

Edward and Cummings rounded the side panel of the SUV as a man with the SWAT team headed to take care of Roxy.

"Good to see you two." Josh held up the handcuffs. "Now get these off me. I've got to get up there."

Cummings unlocked the cuffs as Edward shouted he'd work at getting the freight elevator to come down from the top floor. Only Macki had the passkey, but he'd work on jerry-rigging the controls.

"I can't wait." Josh ran to Macki's elevator and rammed the button, hoping the door would at least open. No such luck. Desperate, he edged his fingers in, trying to get them open.

"How are you planning to get up there?" Cummings joined him, and together they pried the doors apart, then shoved the door-holders back in place.

Josh pointed at the cables as he checked his guns he'd retrieved. "That and climbing the metal studs in the side walls. There'll be enough room to snake up behind the car. Drop in from the top."

"I'm coming too."

He still wasn't sure he trusted the man completely, but Josh figured he had to give Cummings the benefit of the doubt. After all, he and Edward had charged in, risked their lives to save him and Macki. "Okay. But you go out at the door to her office. Take the steps the rest of the way. Passcode to penthouse floor is *home*."

"Good idea. At least one of us should make it through."

A couple of the SWAT guys tossed their gloves at the two men a moment before Josh jumped for the cables, Cummings close behind him. Quietly, hand over hand, the men charged upward.

Josh felt the change in the cable when Cummings jumped out at Macki's office floor. A few more seconds and Josh squeezed behind the elevator car and onto the top, then dropped inside. The metal doors were open, and he was greeted by one of the thugs who motioned him to drop the weapons. He had figured the guns would be taken, but at least they were in the arena.

Josh walked through the bedroom doorway into the living area with one thing in mind. Keep himself and Macki alive until OPAQUE backup crashed into the setting. The sight of Macki standing behind the kitchen island with a thug's pistol pointed at her was almost more than he could take. But take it he did. For the moment, he needed to be smart. Stall for enough time that the others could catch up.

"Come in, Agent Slater." Blake lounged in the chair by the balcony window like he was directing a movie. "Welcome to our little party."

"You okay, Macki?"

She nodded. "Yeah. He hasn't hurt me."

Blake chuckled. "Now, you know I wouldn't do anything like that."

"Maybe not you personally." She glanced at the thug standing beside her, then at the one who'd positioned himself near the front door.

"You can't believe you're going to make it out of this building." Josh positioned himself in the line of fire between Blake and Macki, readying himself for whatever happened inside the room or whatever charged through the door.

"Of course I will. I've got the prime hostage of Riverfalls right here in my hands." Blake rose to his feet, then pushed open the doors to the balcony and looked outside. "I mean, can you imagine the outcry there'd be if something happened to the charitable goddess Mackenzie Baudin?"

Josh followed the same line of sight. Then he heard the approaching noise. The thump-thump-thump of helicopter rotors. Louder and louder, closer and closer. OPAQUE? SWAT? He doubted both right now because the look of pleasure on Blake's face said his ride had arrived.

Blake turned and pulled his gun, motioning the thug by the door toward the other thug and Macki. "Help him get her ready."

Get her ready? Ready for what?

Panic shot across her face as one of the men pulled out a lift-harness from his pocket.

"You can't do that to her." Josh took a step toward the

balcony door.

Blake aimed his gun point-blank at Josh's chest. "Like I told your old man right before I pulled the chair out from under him, I can do whatever the hell I want."

Josh flinched with a new kind of anger. "You? You killed him?"

"Sure as hell did."

"Why? He'd done what you wanted."

"The hell he did." Blake sneered in disgust. "A couple days before the crash, Coercion Ten sent a couple guys around. Told your old man they wanted to play a trick on one of their college buddies from the past. He told us to get the hell of out of his airport before he called the police. Can you believe that? His airport? Ha—I showed him."

The sound of Macki's scuffle with the men in the background had quieted, so Josh assumed they'd belted her into the harness. He could not under any circumstance—any at all—let them take her. Yeah, he might actually go down today like the threat had said, but not without one hell of a fight. And not without an answer to the question beating in his mind.

"Are you saying my dad didn't help you? He wasn't the one who took down the plane?" Josh needed that answer. Needed it bad.

"Hell no, he didn't help. But I showed him who was in charge. I had some Coercion Ten guys drug his food the day before the crash. He couldn't make it to work because he was sick as a dog." Blake glanced up at the loud thump-thump-thump. The curtains at the side of the window blew inward as the rotors whipped up the air outside.

"Why did you kill my dad? Put the money in his bank account?"

"Are you that big of a fool?" Blake motioned for the men to bring Macki to the window.

From the sounds going on behind Josh, she was putting up one hell of a fight.

He got ready to die, but he wanted to die knowing the

answer. "Because you needed a fall guy? Someone who could provide a quick closure to the case?"

"The money was just an afterthought." Keeping the gun trained on Josh, Blake chambered a round as an evil grinned across his face. "Your old man got himself killed because once he heard about the crash, he called the police department. Asked to speak to the man in charge of the case. Told the officer everything that had happened."

"That would have been Grey...Lieutenant Grey?"

"Yeah. Grey sent me to take care of the situation." A haunted shadow seemed to glide across Blake's expression. "Funny thing is, I don't think your old man feared me one bit...kind of like you. You're dangerous because you're not afraid of me. Not afraid to die for your cause."

True, Josh had no fear for himself. For Macki, was another story. A swinging ladder dropped down from the chopper hovering above. He had no doubt the attached rope and harness hook was for her.

Josh lowered his head and charged the middle of Blake's body. Knocked him onto the balcony. Fighting for his and Macki's lives, he slammed and pummeled the killer with his own form of pain. He ripped out the knife he had hidden inside his pants leg, slashing it across the man's side. Blake came back with an iron rod of his own.

Inside the penthouse, cursing and gunfire and the growling yells of charging OPAQUE agents gave Josh strength. Backup had arrived. If he went down, OPAQUE would protect Macki.

Blake brought the rod down on Josh's arm, kicking him in the chest as he did, then jumped onto the balcony ledge. Josh pulled his second knife from the strap on his thigh and struggled to his feet.

"Want to know the last thing your dad said? He hoped his son wouldn't be the one to find him." Blake reached out for the swinging ladder and wrapped his arm around the bottom step as it swung away from the building. "That's when I kicked the chair out from under him."

Josh flung the knife hard and straight and true to the bull's-eye of Blake's chest. The man screamed in agony as he lost his grip and plummeted to the street below.

Macki rushed to Josh's side as Drake, Cummings, and Granger stood in the doorway.

"Did you hear what Blake said?" Josh prayed someone else had heard the confession.

Drake gave him a thumbs-up. "We heard everything. I knew you came from good stock."

"Are you okay?" Macki trailed her fingers down Josh's arm as they walked into the penthouse from the balcony.

Josh's breathing had calmed, but inside he was still on adrenalin rush. He knew this wasn't the end of OPAQUE's search for Coercion Ten, but this was the end for his own personal search for redemption. The end of his current assignment. "I'm fine. How about you?"

She smiled and kissed his lips lightly. "If you're okay, I'm okay."

Drake handed him some ice for his jaw and gave her a piece of plexiglass.

The sting of cold against his eye brought Josh back to the situation at hand. He count-checked the people in the room. Had they lost anyone? "Where's Edward?"

"He took off the minute we had things under control. Said he and Darla were going to disappear off the radar for a good while. Maybe start a new life. Probably a good idea." Drake did a slow nod of his head.

"We were damn lucky Edward had sneaked back into town once he got his wife to safety," Granger added. "If he hadn't been holed up in that apartment across from the hotel, this could have had a whole different outcome."

"What do you mean?"

Cummings leaned into the conversation. "Edward's the one who called me even before your alarm call came in for help. Said he'd been watching out the window and thought the limo pulling into Macki's garage was out of line."

"I'll miss them. But I'm glad they'll be safe in their other life," Macki said.

Josh hugged her against his side. He'd never tell her "safe" was only a relative term for anyone who'd ever been an OPAQUE agent. Safe was second-to-second in his world. Now her world.

"But just so you know." Macki huffed out a statement in her sigh. "I don't ever want to leave this life, I'd rather be—"

Placing his fingers across her lips, Josh leaned in and caressed her cheek. "I promise we will never disappear into another life. What you see is what you get."

"And what I see is all I ever want." Smiling, she stretched upward and gave him a kiss that shot to his core. "Your hand, it's bleeding."

Josh quirked the side of his mouth. "No big deal. You're all I need to stop the pain."

Drake bent to help Granger pick up the pieces of the cutting board strewn across the floor.

"What the hell happened to that thing?" Josh asked.

Granger plopped the pieces on the granite counter top. "You'd have been proud. She smashed the one guy in the back of the head with the plexiglass cutting board twice. The second time she hit him, it shattered."

Josh laughed. "The board or the guy's head?"

"Both." Macki dropped the piece she was holding on top of the pile as Josh tilted her chin upward.

"That's okay, honey. I'll get you another cutting board." He brushed his lips against her. "Fact is, I'll get you anything you ever want."

CHAPTER THIRTY

Josh couldn't believe he'd married the sexiest woman alive a little over three hours ago. To wed her and bed her was all he'd wanted, but here they were, still at the reception. He'd shed his tie the moment they'd left the church. But Macki still had on that damn head-to-toe chaste-and-pure white wedding dress. Of course, for the past month, they'd already thrown the chaste and pure out the door.

"You look mighty handsome, Mr. Slater." Macki eased her arms around his neck. "And just so you know, I love you more than all the shoes in my closet. Now and forever."

Her fingers played peek-a-boo with his shirt collar, then the buttons on his shirt, then his belt as she teased her lips against his ear. The woman had him coming and going. Truth was, he enjoyed every ounce of her attention. Plus, he had plans of his own for later.

"I love you, too. Now and forever." Leaning in, he nuzzled her neck. He'd never get enough of hearing those words pass between them, but he was thinking way past words at the moment. "How much longer do we have to stay?"

He wondered how she'd react when she found out he'd locked off the entire hot tub room back at the hotel so they could have an evening all to themselves. Going further, he'd ordered her favorite flowers and music and candles to fill the place. All he had to do now was make one tiny phone call as they started back to the hotel. Catering would not only light the candles, they'd have a wedding-night dinner wheeled into the room and waiting for them, along with chilled champagne and beer.

Stepping back, she took on a serious expression. "Just a little longer. No more than an hour...I promise."

"I'm gonna hold you to that. In fact, I plan to hold you till we're old and gray and..." Hell, he planned to hold her till his dying day, but this wasn't the time to use that word.

He grabbed her close, letting his own hands play a game with the satin of her gown's bodice. She squealed on an intake of breath when he touched a sensitive spot, then blushed as half the room turned to see where the noise had come from. When he raised his hands in an I-didn't-do-anything ruse, the people in the room applauded and lifted their glasses.

"Go see your friends. I'll be here when you come back." He was one lucky man and he knew it.

She squeezed his hand as she trailed away. "I won't be long."

Even as she mingled among friends, he kept an eye out for her. Would he be that way forever? Probably so. Not hovering, but protecting her from things that might be outside her realm of protecting herself. Judging from the broken pieces of the cutting board, there wasn't a lot she couldn't protect herself from, but the world held a lot of dangers that couldn't be quelled with a knock on the back of the head.

Josh raised his glass in acknowledgment to Granger standing across the room. He'd agreed to hang around to help wrap up the case and be the best man at the wedding. Now he was playing the lonely guy to a group of women hanging onto his every word. Before the night was over, Granger would zero in on one, spend a few days seeing the sites of Riverfalls, and then move on to his next assignment. Everybody in the agency knew his dating MO almost down to the second.

Cummings had been invited, but had declined. Said he wanted time to sort out what he'd missed in his time as Blake's partner. Josh figured the man needed to figure out what to do with the rest of his life, since he'd quit the force the day after the shoot-out. Still didn't know Cummings's first name. Or was it the last?

Glancing at Macki in her beautiful white wedding gown, all smiles and beauty and hope, Josh was glad he'd found where he was supposed to be. Right here, or wherever the future took them, with the woman he loved. Drake had asked him to be second-in-command of OPAQUE, putting him in charge on the domestic front.

After some soul searching, Josh had agreed. Of course, he'd talked to Macki first, and she'd convinced him they'd make a great husband-and-wife team for the agency. He'd agreed on one condition...once the children started coming, they'd discuss the subject again. She'd agreed.

"A penny for your thoughts?" Drake looked the dapper part of I'm-here-to-give-the-bride-away. And he had. The tough head of the agency had walked down that aisle, kissed his niece on the cheek, and placed her hand in Josh's.

"They're not worth your money."

No one would ever hear Josh's deepest thoughts except Macki. But there was something he needed to say to the man standing beside him.

"While we've got some time alone, I want to thank you, Drake. You've always been there when I needed some sense drilled into me." He held out his hand. "I couldn't have done it without you all these years."

"You ever need anything, I'm still here." Drake took the hand in his. "You and Macki are gonna be fine. Since you two are out of my hair, maybe I can have a life of my own."

Josh doubted that. The man was too work-focused to think about a personal life. What woman in her right mind would want a man who never laughed, spent half his time undercover, and watched people like his life depended on it? Hell, he'd just described every OPAQUE agent in the world. Himself included.

"I wish we'd been able to find out who Blake's dad is. Who's really in charge of Coercion Ten," Josh said.

"Don't worry. We will." Drake grinned. "At least now we know there's a man in charge. And tracking backward from Blake may be just the lead we need."

"By the way, you never finished our conversation about Reese Trenton."

"I don't recall us talking about him." Drake looked him straight in the eye, then grinned. "Nice try, though."

Josh narrowed his thoughts. Sure, he'd tried to play the boss and failed, but that didn't negate the fact that Drake was keeping secrets just like he always did. "That's fine. But if you don't trust me enough to share what's going on with the CIA and OPAQUE, then maybe I made a mistake taking your offer."

The festive atmosphere playing in the background did nothing to alleviate the silent tension bouncing between the two men.

"Believe me, I do trust you." Drake swallowed hard as he glanced around the room. "You know it's hard to give up bits of security that I've guarded with my life for so long."

Josh nodded. His boss had relinquished his own personal life to take care of others. It had to be hard to let people in when he'd built the walls surrounding him so high. "I understand."

"I'll get better at sharing. I promise. You didn't make a mistake." Drake's tone implied he meant what he said. "Regarding Trenton...OPAQUE could use a man with his experience."

"So he's coming on board?"

"Not yet. But at least he's considering this time I asked. Which is more than he's ever done before."

All thought of business left Josh's mind as the smell of vanilla and jasmine drifted up behind him. He lifted his arm to pull Macki into his side, and her hair tickled his hand.

She'd finally taken off the veil and let her hair down.

He tangled his fingers through the ends, then pulled her even tighter against his side. "I like that better."

"I figured you would." She laid her head against his chest. "I'm tired."

"Ready to go?"

Punching him lightly in the chest, she winked and fluttered her eyelashes. "Don't you wish. What are you two talking about? Did you get Roxy relocated, Uncle Drake?"

"She's in Florida along with Tessa. Seems Roxy felt making sure the young woman got a new start would take the place of the daughter she thought she'd had all these years. They're staying with one of the office staff for now. We'll give them a new life later." Drake nodded in an absentminded way. "From there it's up to them."

Macki kissed her uncle's cheek. "Thanks. By the way, did Josh tell you we stopped by the cemetery after we left the chapel?"

Josh nodded. He'd had his dad's body moved to lie next to his mother after the truth came out. Yesterday, the cemetery had called to let him know the new stone was in place.

"We wanted both sets of parents to see how happy we are today." She smiled with an air of contentment. "Even sprinkled some of the wedding flowers around."

"Well, you are the best-looking couple I've ever seen. Your parents would all be proud. Guess my work is done. And that's my cue to leave." Drake breathed out a long sigh, leaned in for a hug from Macki, a handshake from Josh. "See you two in Florida when you get back from Europe."

Drake pushed past them, taking a cookie from the tray on the side table. He turned back as he reached the doorway leading out of the hall. "About time you had some good desserts at these shindigs, Macki. But I thought oatmeal cookies made you sick."

Waving, her uncle disappeared out the door.

What the hell did that mean? Oatmeal cookies made her sick?

Josh couldn't believe what he'd heard. "Macki..."

She glanced around the room—here, there, anyplace but at him.

"You lied to me?" He cocked his head, raising his eyebrows. She'd toyed with him that night in the bath. Said what she needed to say to entice him to stay. "So that marshmallow between the oatmeal cookies was all made up so you could have your way with me?"

After smoothing the front of her wedding gown, she took an oatmeal cookie from the tray and nibbled a bite. "I don't know what you mean..." She tried to swallow. "I like..." Coughed... "Marshmallow and..." She devolved into a coughing fit that brought tears to her eyes. Finally, she shoved the cookie in his hand.

He held out a glass of champagne to her, then brushed a crumb from the neckline of her gown. He'd married himself a little minx. One he needed to stay one step ahead of...most of the time. "You are so bad, Mackenzie Slater. Bad, bad, bad."

She moistened her lips. "Not nearly as bad as you, Agent Slater. Not nearly as bad."

If he was lucky, she'd never know how bad he could be. Maybe he'd never know either. Watching her walk away to join some guests, he laid the cookie on the discard tray.

Hell, truth be known—he didn't like oatmeal cookies either.

THE END

ACKNOWLEDGEMENTS

Once again, it's exciting to know I've written another book that will, hopefully, entertain readers. I've learned that writing is not a career to be tackled alone, so please stay with me as I pause to thank a number of people. People who have lightened and brightened my writing load, not to mention my world as a whole.

First, to my wonderful family (who this book is dedicated to) for all their encouragement, motivation, love and laughter. You can't imagine how much some of your words and actions have made me smile, giving me that moment of belief that I can do this thing called writing. I appreciate everything each of you do for me and every time you make me laugh. Always remember how much I love all of you!

Second, what would I have done without Kim Killion and Jennifer Jakes of The Killion Group Inc./Hot Damn Designs to guide me through my first self-publishing process? They've been there to help me with everything from my book cover, logo and photos, to formatting, uploading and timelines. Not only are they multi-talented ladies, they are fantastic to work with. Thanks, thanks, thanks.

Also, thanks to Amanda Sumner (Careful Copyediting) and Bev Katz Rosenbaum (BKR Editing Services) for going the extra mile working with my time constraints. You both deserve stars. I'll try to plan ahead better in the future.

And in my writing world, thank you to my critique partners Linda Gilman, Michelle Sharp, and Suzie T. Roos, who are always there for a quick read, brainstorming and fun writing retreats. Plus, Jeannie Lin, my go-to person on writing advice and how to keep my joy in writing; Megan Kelly, who keeps the MORWA CORE group on track for critiques; and the beta readers who've given me feedback on characters and plot.

In closing, I'd like to thank all my readers for buying my books. I hope you liked Slater's Leverage and will come back to visit my writing often. My heroes and heroines want you to read their stories, and I want to keep writing them.

Smiles to all,
Claudia Shelton

ABOUT THE AUTHOR

Award-winning author Claudia Shelton could write her name before the first day of school, but now she writes romantic suspense and contemporary romance, all with sexy alpha heroes and women strong enough to love them.

In addition, she presents workshops on everything from character development to networking to the ins-and-outs of being a new author. Claudia's debut novel, Risk of a Lifetime, released to 5-star reviews, reached Amazon's Best Sellers Romance Series Top 100 and was named one of eBooks Galore top reads for 2014. She is also a two-time Daphne Du Maurier (Unpublished) finalist for excellence in mystery. She truly believes in "paying it forward" and enjoys speaking to all types of groups.

On a personal note, Claudia considers herself a water person and always enjoys a cool drink by the pool, lake or ocean. Of course a hot cocoa in the falling snow is nice, too.

You can learn more at:
Website: http://www.claudiawriting.com/
Facebook:
https://www.facebook.com/ClaudiaSheltonWriter
Twitter: @ClaudiaShelton1

Made in the USA
Charleston, SC
08 November 2015